R. Stuyg

An Englishman born in Cyprus, Richard House currently resides in Chicago and works with the artists' collaborative Haha. His fiction has been published in *Whitewalls*, BOMB *Men on Men 4*, *Discontents*, and the *Voice Literary Supplement*. *Bruiser* is his first novel.

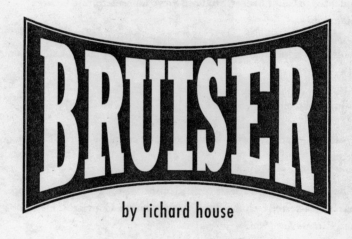

BRUISER

by richard house

SERPENT'S TAIL

HIGH RISK BOOKS

NEW YORK / LONDON

Acknowledgments

Foremost, thanks to Jeff Black, Joyce Fernandes, Travis Garth, Laura Harrison, John Pakosta, Amy Scholder, and Ira Silverberg. I am also indebted to Carol Becker, Hudson, Steve Lafreniere, and George Stambolian.

This book is for my colleagues, John Ploof, Wendy Jacob, Laurie Palmer.

First published in 1997 by Serpent's Tail,
4 Blackstock Mews, London N4, and
180 Varick Street, 10th floor, New York, NY 10014

Cover design by Rex Ray, San Francisco
Set in Janson and Futura Condensed by Intype London Ltd
Printed in Great Britain by Mackays of Chatham

1

A light gray Ford with a dusty black hardtop is stopped in the street before an intersection. Both the driver's and the passenger's doors are wide open. A large man, heavy-set, thick hands, thick neck like a boxer, crouches in front of the car. At his feet lies a small dog. The dog is dead. A scuffed and ripped white plastic bag is tied like a bib about the animal's neck. Black blood coagulates at its nose and runs in the folds of the plastic, and its eye, fully dilated, stares absently at the car that struck it.

Across the street a man sits watching in the doorway of an apartment building, propping the door open with his chair. A newspaper rests unopened on his lap. He leans backward so that the chair is tilted and his head is in shadow. Standing in darkness, in the lobby behind him, a boy buttons his shirt, watching his reflection in the door. Behind the boy is a staircase. As he smoothes his shirt into his trousers he turns toward the doorway, sunlight striking his face and shoulders as he peers indifferently into the street.

Newspaper saturated with rings of petrol covers the dog. The man pulls the paper over the dog's head so that the whole animal, except its tail, is covered. Twisting out from under the newspaper, and tied to the dog's tail, is a singed rope with six pierced and blackened oil cans fastened along its length. There is a strong and peppery whiff of gasoline about the dog. With disgust the man stands upright and pulls a tissue from his pocket. Heads, arms, and elbows begin to appear at windows in the apartments flanking the road, pressing against bowed and ripped screens.

The man with the newspaper has gone. Standing behind

the empty chair the boy leans against the wooden door frame, hands folded, quiet, watching.

Having covered the dog the driver returns to his car, wanting only to get away. Rolling the tissue into a ball, he switches it nervously from hand to hand.

"Hey, mister. Hey. You can't just leave it there." A woman leans out into the street. "You can't leave it in the middle of the street." She is wearing a dress, faded and blue, with a pattern of large white chrysanthemums. Her stiff black hair is pulled back by a broad blue butterfly clasp. Shielding herself with the screen door she points at the dog. Her arm is long and slender, a deep ruddy black.

"That puppy just ran out here, and it was on fire." The man shakes his head. Refusing to touch the dog, he sits heavily back into the car, one foot on the street as he searches through papers on the dashboard for something to wipe his hands on.

"Hey." Her hand stays level. The woman's face shines with sweat, a paper fan is tucked under the shoulder strap of her dress.

"It isn't my dog," the driver replies, closing the car door.

"It isn't my dog either," the woman complains, "but you can't leave it there." She snaps her fingers and the driver turns back toward her, her stare holding him fast.

The man with the newspaper has returned to the doorway, and stands close behind the boy in the white shirt. Still watching the street he stealthily slips his hand into the boy's trouser pocket. It is a small gesture, so small that having seen it, I cannot be sure that it has happened until the boy steps down onto the pavement and the man's hand slips out of his pocket.

Blood, wet and black, seeps quickly into the newspaper and puddles down the street, winding between the grit and the sand in the road. The man starts up his car and backs slowly up the street. The woman shakes her head, and calls resentfully after him. "It's not my damn dog."

Closing the screen door behind her, the woman walks into the road. Squatting on her haunches, she lightly lifts the newspaper. Her dress pulls tightly over her knees. The dog's tan hindquarters are bloody and scorched.

The woman curses and complains again that the puppy is not hers. She shakes her head and gently pats the air above the sorry package. As she scoops the dog up into her arms, the blackened cans clatter dull and flat against themselves.

Across the street, the door is closed, the lobby is empty; both the boy and the man have gone.

A broad flat of sunlight reflects into the restaurant causing me to squint at the waiter. I cannot see his face or his hands as he sets the coffee on the table. The air is thick and adhesive and full of light. A fax from my brother curls over the lip of the saucer and sticks to the side of my hand. The paper is buckled, and I have not yet had the heart to read it. A sweet and pungent steam rises from the small coffee cup; the smell is reviving. It is a relief to come here. I am unable to work at the hotel.

A slender elderly man, with a shock of white hair, sits in shadow by the door reading a newspaper. He holds the paper stiffly up and out, almost as a barrier to repel the heat, and turns the pages without bending his elbows, closing the entire newspaper as if it were stiff and hinged. Curled in the shade under his chair is a small tan-colored dog.

Sunlight cuts obliquely across the narrow room, halving the tables, the checkerboard mosaic floor and the white milk tiles along the walls, dividing the room into bright watery sunlight and deep shade. At the back of the restaurant, almost in darkness, two waiters rearrange a second room, lifting the tables up and over between rows of chairs to form one long table. Apart from the man with the newspaper, I am the only customer.

Condensation runs quickly down the water glass and over my fingers. I am surprised by the waiter's hand, barely a shadow as it crosses the painfully bright white of the tablecloth. As he reaches to refill my coffee cup his starched cuff catches the glass. The glass tilts forward out of my hand and water slops onto the table. In an attempt to both stand up and step back, I jolt the table. The glass falls abruptly free from his cuff and strikes the coffee cup. Hot coffee gutters across the linen cloth, running over the fax and onto my trousers. A purple stain blooms instantly across the paper, obliterating the text. The waiter leans quickly forward, hands cupped to prevent more coffee from pouring onto me. Light shines up from the table to the young waiter's face, and though I cannot be certain, I feel sure that I have seen him before.

"It was my fault." I apologize and nudge the table with the flat of my hand. "I should have caught it, I had my hand on the glass." The waiter pauses, as if startled by my accent. Purple dye seeps through the fax paper and into the tablecloth. My notebook is drenched, fresh ink spangles across the open pages.

"Let me get you some towels," he offers. The coffee has stained his shirt-cuffs.

"I'm afraid I'm soaked." I apologize again.

The waiter wipes his hands clean on the tablecloth and smiles at the broad wet patch on my crotch. "Here, we can dry those in the kitchen." He picks up my notebook and I follow him across the restaurant, weaving between tables and chairs, holding my damp trousers away from my skin, pinched between finger and thumb. In the back room the two waiters set down a table and spread out a cloth, working quickly and quietly together.

The waiter swings back the kitchen door and holds it open for me. The kitchen is as large as the restaurant, with shiny and scratched quilted tin lining the stoves, refrigerators, and cabinets. Thick white plates and bowls are stacked in tall slinky columns on a cabinet facing the door. There are two men in the kitchen. One stands beside a sink scrubbing vegetables; the other, a tall thin man dressed in a short-sleeved shirt, apron, and checkered trousers, looks up and smiles at the waiter as he enters the kitchen.

"Hey," he calls for the boy's attention.

"What's up?" The waiter sets my notebook down beside the sink. The front of his shirt is soiled with coffee grounds. The stained linen sticks to his stomach, pink and hairless and wet. "For me?" He points at his stomach.

The chef fractionally inclines his head, birdlike, and smiles again. "Up? Up?" he repeats, imitating the boy. He does not speak English.

"Up. Food. What's up?" The waiter points at the diced mushrooms and onion on the cutting board, and then points at his mouth.

The chef nods and arches his eyebrows, suddenly serious. Untucking a towel folded about his belt he offers it to the boy, insisting that he take it.

Another waiter returns to the kitchen. Leaning through the double doors he briskly sorts through a basket of tablecloths. "Why aren't your tables ready?" he asks, looking directly at the boy. They are perhaps the same age. "Change your shirt and get back out here. I'm not covering for you."

The door snaps behind him as he returns to the restaurant.

"I hope I didn't get you into trouble," I apologize.

The waiter indifferently tilts his head and rinses the cloth in the sink. His neck and cheeks are flushed red. The Mexican washing vegetables steps quietly aside without being asked and returns to the sink when the boy is done.

"There's the bathroom." The waiter hands me the towel and points at a door across the kitchen.

We busily clean and dry ourselves standing together by the door, the boy apparently unbothered or unaware of how close we are standing. His short hair is heavily oiled and still tracked with the lines of a comb. He is sweating slightly. The chef looks up frequently from his cutting board; each time he smiles and nods at the boy.

"How are your pants?" the waiter asks. "Here." He hands

me another towel, thicker than the first. Above the door is a small fan fastened to the wall by a wire armature. He reaches up and twists the armature so that the fan faces down. "I've had to do this a couple of times." There is a switch beside the door. The fan clicks against its buckled guard as it gathers speed, and warm, stale air billows down upon us.

The waiter squats down to wipe his trouser legs. "Your first time in Chicago?" He looks up at me.

I nod.

"English, right?"

I nod again.

"Where are you staying?"

"At the Halifax." I point at the door in the vague direction of the hotel.

"I know it."

The dog nudges through the kitchen door and pauses, keeping its eyes on the chef, waiting to be shooed away. Squeezing between me and the waiter, it skips past my hand, cowering as I reach to pat it, and walks a full slow circle around an island of stoves. The chef turns and, seeing the dog, whistles and claps his hands. The animal nonchalantly completes its route and trots slowly back into the restaurant.

"Not a very friendly dog," I say.

The waiter reaches up to redirect the fan.

"The dog. I said he isn't very friendly."

"She's old, and she shouldn't be in here." He shrugs and smiles, and stepping away from me he untucks his shirt from his trousers. He tosses the dish towel back into the sink and walks to the bathroom at the back of the kitchen.

I wait in the kitchen until my trousers are almost dry. The chef ignores me, it seems deliberately, and talks to the Mexican in Spanish, but the man does not reply. Pushing the mushrooms to the side of the cutting board, he places the knife carefully in the sink and then walks purposefully into the restaurant. I try to picture the boy in an attempt to place him; I have seen him somewhere else. But already he has dissolved into parts: small brutish ears, a narrow nose, a thick neck, broad and rounded shoulders, and blunt square hands. It is only when I recall the strange looseness of his arms, a slack swing as he walks, that I remember. I have seen him at the railway station.

The waiter is still in the bathroom, and on the pretext of thanking him I walk up to the door. The bathroom door is ajar. The room is dark, and the boy stands in front of a sink and mirror, half dressed, his shirt tossed onto the floor. A fresh, clean-pressed shirt hangs from a towel rack beside the sink. Sunlight streams from a small square window above the mirror and falls flat across his shoulders, chest, and stomach; his skin shines as white as polished silver. Dust rises and sparks in the darkness. He moves his head in a particular way, to the side, as if stretching, and I realize that in his hands, resting on the side of the sink, is my notebook, my diary. I watch as he slowly turns the pages, reading the notes that I have kept about the prostitutes at the station.

"Adrian," a voice calls from the kitchen. "Come here and clean off this table. Now."

I step quickly out of the doorway, but the boy has already turned, surprised by the voice and surprised to see me watching him. One of the waiters is leaning through the kitchen door. Adrian pushes quickly past me, buttoning his shirt. Behind the island of stoves I can see the dog's tail wagging, but not the dog.

"Watch the front." The waiter holds the door open, and they both return to the restaurant. I retrieve my notebook from beside the sink and wait, unsure of what to do. Sheets of paper towel have been layered between the pages. The waiter returns carrying the tablecloth and my jacket in one hand, coffee cup in the other. I study his face to read some reaction, but he gives nothing away. He seems relaxed, completely untroubled. As he sets my jacket down a postcard slips out from the lapel pocket. He pauses for a moment and I pull the card out to hold his attention.

"It's a postcard from my sister." I hold the card up. "Happy Birthday Paul, much love, kisses, Katherine," is inscribed on the back. On the front is a drawing of T. E. Lawrence. I have received the same image as a birthday card from her as long as I can remember. "She thinks he looks like me." The waiter looks up from the card and studies my face. There is no recognition in his eyes. "I don't believe her either." I place the card down on the table. But the waiter picks it up. "You can keep it if you like," I say. The waiter hesitates, then, without thanking me, he curves the card in his hands and slips it into his pocket. Walking across the kitchen he checks the coffee machine.

The chef returns to the kitchen. "Nice." He smiles at the boy. "Nice."

The waiter picks up a full coffeepot and smiles back at the chef out of courtesy or interest, I cannot tell. "You're my girlfriend aren't you? Aren't you my girlfriend?"

The chef cocks his head, aware that he is being teased, and seems for a moment genuinely hurt. But as the boy walks past, he squeezes the chef's elbow and the man again smiles broadly.

The boy backs through the double doors, shielding the coffeepot with his arm as he turns toward the restaurant. As the door swings to behind him he looks back over his shoulder, and with his head not fully turned he quickly cocks an eyebrow and winks.

I have spent the whole day at the hotel, determined to work. A second fax has arrived asking me to respond to the first, along with a third fax notifying me that a package will be arriving overnight. The bulk of the shipping happens in October and I must confirm the schedules. I must, it reads, complete what I have started. But my room is small. Two entire walls are glass, and by midday the air-conditioning cannot compete with the intense heat magnified by the windows. I have set a work table beside the bed, but I am distracted, as stupid as it sounds, by the boy's wink, and the afternoon is spent pacing lethargically back and forth between the bed, the television, and the desk.

By four o'clock I have written only three brief letters: two personal and one business. In each I have described the view from my room. Immediately to the east is the flat and leaden Lake Michigan and an expressway, and to the south, about five miles distant, are the blunt towers of downtown Chicago. In the past week I have taken several walks and discovered, within a six-block radius of the Halifax, several restaurants (three Mexican, one Vietnamese), a launderette, a barber shop, and four liquor stores. The supermarket has recently closed, and there is only one small corner shop, a super mercado, and a Mexican bakery. There is a synagogue and a baptist church with a billboard—"Christ died for our sins"—which faces away from the hotel toward the expressway. The hotel faces Clark Street, and except for the billboard, most of the signage is in Spanish. West of Clark the neighborhood is Mexican.

In my brother's letter I have doggedly refused to respond to any business inquiries. Instead I have described the journey, the forced friendliness of strangers, and my troubles at the airport: one piece of luggage arrived late and was delivered to the hotel with no apology or explanation. To my sister I have described a city grown so large and so boundless that like lichen, patches of it are dead. Only in the letter to my sister have I described the railway station beside the hotel, which is a haunt for male prostitutes and thugs. I have described the wild prairie grass that grows in pockets on the station's sloped glass roof, and the boys at the station house steps, sauntering late at night, in and out of view between the stout stone columns.

At five o'clock another boy returns to the station, and finally, frustrated with the room, I persuade myself that there would be little harm in taking another walk.

Behind the station is a vacant yard, a flat gravel plain overgrown with thistle and clover. The fence about the yard has been pulled down, and most sections of it lie flat to the ground. Except for irregular stacks of railroad ties, there is no boundary between the station yard and the scrubland behind the hotel. There is a sweet scent in the yards. The wasteland is thick with heat and flies and bees.

A young boy, Mexican or Puerto Rican, I cannot tell, stands beside a car at the foot of the station house steps, and points ahead at the hotel. The car rolls slowly forward and the boy walks beside it, treading carefully through the scrub and debris.

I stand aside to allow both the car and the boy passage. The boy watches the path ahead of him, looking purposefully past me. He is older than I had imagined, perhaps seventeen, and his skin has an even, olive hue, as smooth as a child's. There is a slight uneven stubble on his chin. Inside the car is an older man, perhaps thirty, thirty-five, clean-shaven except for a small sharp beard. One arm hangs out of the window, fingers tapping to a tune on the radio that he has just turned off. Neither of them talk. On the man's arm, plumped by resting on the door, is a tattoo of an eagle.

The car turns out of view behind the wing of the hotel, and the boy stops beside a line of dumpsters and looks candidly back toward me. We watch each other until he walks away, toward the building and the car.

The building folds around a loading dock. A corrugated tin roof extends out over the courtyard, protecting and concealing the car from view. Collapsed cardboard boxes and crates litter the enclosure. The lower windows of the hotel's kitchens are closed and barred and painted white. The upper windows are also closed, many of them blocked with air conditioners.

The boy is pressed facedown against the car's black bonnet as if he is being arrested, his arms are stretched out in front of him, and his shirt is hitched up over his shoulders. He is standing on tip-toe, his shorts loosely hooked about one ankle. The man is immediately behind him, fully dressed, thrusting so hard against the boy that the car jolts. The man's hair is black, crow black, greasy against the boy's soft skin. Losing his momentum, the man stands upright and rolls up his undershirt, still pinning the boy to the car with his hips. His arms are tanned and his back is white. A small gold cross on a slender chain catches in his shirt as he pulls it over his head. With his undershirt wrapped around one hand, he leans back over the boy, nudging his legs apart with his knees. One hand grasping the boy's hair, he begins to thrust again in fierce, rapid bursts.

Turning to walk back through the yard, I am surprised to see the boy from the restaurant standing close, less than ten steps behind me. I exclaim in surprise, and he places his finger to his mouth. I had not heard him approach. His mouth is set in a fond, clipped smile. Embarrassed, I step past him, stirring flies up from the scrub, and the boy turns to watch me, still smiling. His shirt is untucked and unbuttoned, and he stands with his hands deep in his pockets, squinting into the sun.

I return to my room. Looking out of my window I can no longer see the boy, only the white colonnades of the railway terminus. I sit for a long time watching the station and counting cars on the expressway, and decide not to post the letters that I have written.

Falling asleep at my desk, I awake confused, certain that I can smell something burning. I stand beside the window, picking frantically at my clothes, believing that I have dropped a cigarette. Sitting back down I scratch at the carpet, still looking for a burning cigarette, not sure if I have been asleep for several hours or several minutes. I have a headache, and as my hands find an ashtray, a glass, an empty cigarette packet, I remember that I have smoked the last of my duty-free cigarettes. Beside the chair leg is my notebook, lying open, pages buckled and creased. I pick the book up, and running my fingers over the pages, I close my eyes and attempt once again to picture the boy at the restaurant. But I cannot clearly remember his face.

There is a storm over the lake, and the rain on the window obscures the view. For no specific reason my heart is racing and I feel anxious. Outside, in front of the hotel, is an American flag, and although I cannot see it, I can hear it crack loudly against itself in great wet slaps.

I spend the morning unpacking my books and return to the restaurant in the middle of the afternoon, hoping to see the boy.

The door is open but a single chair bars the way. A handwritten sign taped to the door explains that the restaurant will not open until noon. Inside the floor is wet and the ceiling fans are turned on high, stirring up the corners of the tablecloths. Further back inside a waiter stands behind the bar, arranging coffee cups, saucers, and napkins on shelves in front of a mirror. The boy is not here.

I stand in the doorway out of the sun, trying to decide whether or not to return to the hotel, when the waiter turns about and suddenly starts, surprised to see me. He laughs at himself and apologizes and asks if I would like to see a menu. I walk up to the bar and ask for a coffee. The man slowly wipes the counter and sets out a cup and saucer and coffeepot. He is sweating. Despite the fans, the air seems impossibly thick and humid.

A faint clean chemical smell rises from the floor. The man wipes his brow with a dampened towel. "It rained last night." He points up at the ceiling. "Flooded the kitchen." There is a rusted brown line running between the white tin tiles. "It's a mess back there." He folds up the napkin and returns to his work.

The coffee is scalding hot but I drink it quickly; having wanted to see the boy, I am a little disappointed, but perhaps also a little relieved. What would I have said anyway?

It is still light outside when I wake, addled by the heat. My head is wet with sweat; my fingers and tongue feel fat; the room is so close that I feel smothered. I sit up intending to call the front desk to complain about the poor air-conditioning.

Tucked under the door is a note, a postcard, the postcard that my sister had sent me. I pick it up and unfold it. Written in pencil in small capitals is a name—Adrian—and a telephone number.

At nine o'clock, I return to the restaurant intent on talking to Adrian, but I do not have the courage to enter. It is late and perhaps they will be closing soon. I decide to return to the hotel without walking past the restaurant, promising myself that I will call him, that it would be better to call him, that after all, why else would he have given me his number? A telephone is ringing on the street corner by a bus stop. Having disappointed myself once I decide to answer.

"Hello?" The voice is male, young and soft, with a rounded midwestern accent. I am learning to distinguish accents. "Tony?"

"No," I reply.

"I'm looking for Tony. Do you see anyone?"

I look about. "No."

"He might be on a bicycle. Dark hair. About five-foot-eight. He's got short dark hair."

"No. There's no one else about."

"Are you English?" he asks.

"Yes."

"What's your name?"

I look cautiously up and down the street to see if there is anyone watching.

"So you don't see anyone else around?"

"No."

He asks me for my name a second time, and repeats it several times. "How old are you, Paul?"

"I'm forty-two. Why?"

The voice is quiet. Scratched into the metal hood of the telephone booth are names and telephone numbers. Without exception all of the names are male.

"You don't mind talking to me, do you, Paul?"

"No. Not at all."

"Then ask me a question."

I stare at my feet for a while. "Why are you calling?"

"I wanted to talk to my friend. You know. And maybe make some new friends." The voice again becomes quiet. I can hear him breathing, soft and pensive. Beside the telephone is a bench, and painted across the back in white lettering are the words, CONFIDENTIAL, TEENS IN TROUBLE, TALK TO SOMEONE YOU CAN TRUST. A telephone number is listed beneath it. The bench is sponsored by the Chicago Public Library, at Clark and Lawrence. After a while he asks, "If I tell you where I am, do you want to meet some people?"

"Well I don't know. It depends."

"On what, Paul? What does it depend on?"

"I don't know."

"Are you married, Paul?"

"No."

"Do you have a girl?"

"No."

"My friend, he doesn't like girls either."

I hang up the telephone. On either side of the road are high-rise apartment buildings. Suddenly self-conscious, I look up, wondering if in fact the caller is watching me. The postcard is in my pocket. It is as easy as that, I convince myself. All I have to do is call. I place the postcard on top of the telephone, certain now that I am being watched.

As I dial the number, the traffic lights change on the street corner, and a bus pulls up beside the booth. I can no longer hear the dial tone. The bus is empty except for one man, his head leaning against the window as he looks down, watching me, tired and disinterested.

The bus roars as it pulls away. I realize that someone has answered. "Hello? Can I speak to Adrian?" I ask. The receiver is rested on a counter. In the background I can hear voices, and closer, much closer, is the sound of ice being ladled into a pitcher. I have called the restaurant.

"Hello."

I recognize the boy's soft voice. "Hello, Adrian?"

"Yes?"

"You gave me your number. You spilt coffee on me two days ago."

"Aha."

I close my eyes to concentrate. "I thought we could meet."

"I can't hear you."

"I said I was thinking that perhaps we could meet."

"I'd like that," he pauses, perhaps changing the receiver to his other ear. "But I can't tonight. How about Sunday? I'm not working on Sunday. Where do you want to meet?"

I look about, worried. Where would make sense? "How about the library."

"The library?" He sounds surprised. "Which one?"

"Clark and Lawrence. At four? Four o'clock?"

"Okay."

"Okay." He hangs up, and I am left nonplussed, but delighted that I have called him. As soon as I hang up, the telephone begins to ring again, but I walk away, contented, no longer concerned that I might be being watched. I hold the postcard folded, closed in my hand, believing for the moment that the telephone number is a talisman, and that by exposing it to the night air I might somehow spoil the charm.

Sunday. I arrive at the library a full hour earlier than we had agreed. As I enter the reading room I am surprised to see that Adrian is already here, alone and asleep, and slumped forward on the table. A laundered white shirt in a clear plastic cover is draped over the chair beside him. His head rests against the table and his hand covers his face. His hair is freshly cut, cropped short, clipped so closely on the sides and back that I can see his scalp. His forearm is white, and smooth dark hairs rise up on the skin. It is cool in here, considerably cooler than outside.

I sit opposite the boy and take out my pen and notebook, as if I were taking notes. He stirs, and between two fingers I see the black of an eye. He is awake, and he is watching me. Turning slightly and opening his hand, he watches without apparent interest, his mind elsewhere.

"Nice pen." His chair honks against the floor as he drags it closer to the table. "Can I?" Taking the pen from my hand he examines the nib. Resting one hand on the table he draws a dotted line about his wrist. "I didn't think people used these any more." I sit silently watching him as he embellishes the lines, turning them into spikes of either thorns or barbed wire. The boy admires his drawing, then extends his arms, stretching, returning the pen to the table.

I lean forward, unsure of what to say.

"Maybe the library wasn't a such good idea," he smiles and points at the book. "It's hard to talk. Is this your diary?"

I shake my head and hold open my hands, offering the book to him, unable to speak for a moment, alarmed by his frankness.

"Do you mind?" he slides the book across the table, and looks up at me as he slowly turns the pages. He puffs out his cheeks, and scans the pages, his head resting in his hand as he reads. There is a clock on the far wall above the boy's head. As I look at it the second hand appears to slip backward. "Wow." He turns back a page. "What happened to the dog?"

"I'm not sure."

"Who set fire to it?" He rests his head back onto his arm and closes the book. "I have to go to work soon."

I look quickly about the library. Not far beyond our table a man searches through the periodicals and newspapers. There are other people reading at tables farther away. At least one person appears to be sleeping. I pull the postcard out from my pocket.

"How did you know which room was mine?"

Adrian reaches for the card. "It wasn't hard to figure out." He smiles, obviously pleased with himself. He sits back and stretches and softly brushes his leg against mine under the table. His hands fidget in his lap. "What did you come here for?" he asks.

"To the library?"

"No. Chicago."

"I don't know."

"How come? You don't work?"

"No. Yes." His leg is deliberately resting against mine. "I have a job, but I might not return to it. I've worked there a long time, and I've taken a leave of absence. I can return if I want. But I might not want to." The boy slides his feet between mine and slowly, stealthily parts my legs. "It's family. A family business." I explain.

"You haven't done this before have you?" he asks.

I shake my head. Embarrassed I look down at the table and apologize. "I was hoping that you didn't have to work today." I slouch down and our knees touch.

The boy scoots his chair further forward and whispers, "I think we're being watched."

"By whom?"

He looks over his shoulder. "The fat guy in the jacket."

I nod.

"What do you think he thinks he's watching?"

"I don't know."

The boy snorts, as if suppressing a laugh, but asks kindly. "Go on. Take a guess."

"I don't know."

He sucks in his lower lip and looks directly at me. "Maybe he thinks you're picking me up."

"Is that what I'm doing?"

Our knees are pressed hard together, his inside mine. The boy smiles broadly, and in his voice there is a trace of real surprise. "You really haven't done this before."

I reach my hand about his neck to draw him closer, but he stiffly resists. He will not kiss me. I take his hand and place it firmly on my thigh, all the time watching the station house and the road, worried that we can be seen, nervous for the police, concerned that the car doors are not locked. Mixing with the smells of a new hire car are the smells of the kitchen, of cold grease, cigarettes, and sweat still clinging to the boy's clothes. The boy quickly pulls apart the folds of my shirt and trousers. I cannot help from shaking, and cannot settle my hands or hold them still without touching him. I barely dare breathe. Surely someone can see us. The night is so clear that even the stars can be counted. I am counting the boys at the station house steps and watching for patrol cars from the expressway. My tie rests and bobs upon the back of the boy's neck, and I want alternatively to pull him away or push him harder down—until everything shudders and rushes, and the railway station, the night, and the very stars fall and fold loosely in upon themselves, and there is nothing, nothing other than the boy's mouth.

I awake suddenly from a dream that I am skinning a dog. The sensation of gripping it tightly between my knees as I force my hand between the pelt and warm muscle stays with me as I sit up in bed, shocked, too frightened to turn on the lights and look at my hands. Neither the sensation nor the image will go. The creature had followed me through a field, flinching as the tall grasses scratched against its red-raw flank. However far or fast I had run, the dog had persisted, and still persists, pursuing me out of my dreams. Months of no dreams, months of numbness have abruptly ended, and I wake and find myself alone and terrified, terrified by my own hands.

2

Everything done, he rests, nestled between my legs in a light slumber. "The bed," I lift his head from my lap, "let's move to the bed." Adrian drowsily shuffles backward on the carpet, avoiding my hands, and lodges his head uncomfortably between the chair arm and my thigh. His mouth hangs slightly open. My shirt is stuck to my stomach where he had spat out my come—a thin, clear, viscous stream from his mouth to my belly.

Carefully, cradling his head, I slide down onto the floor beside him. A faint, warm, acid knock of urine hangs between our clothes and skin. He stretches and yawns and pushes his hands and feet out, superb and athletic, as if he is preparing to dive or row, and slowly rolls his head from side to side. He continues to stretch, and gripping his toes until he is fully doubled, he buries his face between his knees. Bright bands of sunlight rim the closed curtains, and in the half-light I can see several, perhaps five, dark round patches, sores, on his back, each as broad as a fist.

"I need a towel." I stand up and fondly run my hand over his shoulders. The skin over the blemishes is smooth and unbroken. I creep past the boy into the bathroom, holding my shirt over my thighs, and softly close the door behind me. As I undress I carefully fold the shirt, resting it beside the sink, trying to concentrate, not on the marks upon the boy's back, but on the shirt.

"So you're English?" he calls from the bedroom.

Syphilis? No. Perhaps? Too large for chicken pox or shingles. "I'm from Yorkshire." I reply. Stepping out of my shorts I rest my prick on the lip of the cold porcelain sink. There are purple teeth marks tracked over its sorry pink head. There is no antiseptic. Mint mouthwash is all I have.

"My mother's from England," he says.

"Where does she come from?" I ask, cringing slightly as I rinse the scratches with a capful of mouthwash.

"Some place near London," he replies. "Are these all your books?"

"Some of them." I peer about the door. Adrian has opened the curtains and lies naked on my bed, running his hand across the bookshelves. A slim band of sunlight lights across his lower back. "Have you read all of these?" he asks, twisting about to see me.

"I just bought them. Or most of them." I reply. Even from this distance I can clearly see the round red blotches on his back.

"How come they're all travel books?" he asks.

I shrug and return to the sink leaving the door ajar so that the boy is reflected in the mirror. "I like to read about traveling." I reply. Gonorrhea? Scabies? Ringworm? I have no idea. The mouthwash is gone. I pour aftershave onto the toothbrush, remembering from somewhere that, as a last-ditch effort, you should use aftershave as an antiseptic because it contains alcohol. I attempt to brush my teeth, but instead stand numb, stupefied, staring at the boy's reflection, appalled to see sickness blooming so healthily, so outrageously upon such young skin. He half-sits, half-lies quietly on my bed reading my notebook, with no attempt to disguise it.

"I was surprised, well actually, more than surprised," I babble. "I am always being mistaken for an Australian, which is funny because I assumed that you were American, but I couldn't quite understand your accent. There's a hint, a faint hint of something English. And then I thought, at first, perhaps, that you were Australian." He is silent, engrossed in my diary. I have written almost daily about him. I wait in the bathroom, expecting the book to be thrown across the room, expecting to hear the boy's disgust, expecting him to leave.

When I step back into the bedroom, the notebook has

been returned unmolested to the side table. Adrian is lying on the bed leafing through my papers on the floor. He picks one of the dockets.

"What's this?" he asks.

"It's a manifest," I explain. "And please, they're all in order."

The boy grimaces and apologizes and carefully sets the paper down. "A man called Joe walks into a club," he begins, "and Frank Sinatra is drinking at the bar. So the guy walks over to him and says, 'Frank, Frank, I'm a big fan of yours, I've seen you fifteen times, but I have a date tonight with someone who doesn't really like me. But if you came up to our table and said, "Hi, Joe. How's it going?" it would really impress her.' Frank isn't wild about doing this but it's the easiest way to get the man off his back. So later that evening the man is sitting at the table with his girlfriend, and Frank Sinatra walks right up to their table. 'Hi, Joe,' he says, 'How's it going?' But the man turns round and says, 'Frank! Why don't you just fuck off?' "

I am so surprised at his joke that I forget to reply.

"I think I should be going," he smiles, perhaps apologizing, and sits up on the bed, drawing his clothes together. "I have to work." As he slides his feet back into his shoes I walk about the bed to face him. There is another mark, smaller, more like a scuff, on his shoulder. He looks at the blemish without interest and without fear.

"What is it?" I ask. "What are those marks?"

He smiles broadly and looks up at me. "What do you think they are?"

I lean closer to him and look down at his shoulder, unable to think of something to say. Beneath the skin is a fine red network of broken capillaries, as round, detailed, strange, and compact as lichen or moss.

"They're bruises. I box." He holds up his fists. "What's that smell?"

"Aftershave." I explain. Looking closer at the bruise I begin to laugh. "I've never seen anything like this before."

He looks at his shoulder again, "It doesn't hurt," and pokes his finger into one of the bruises. "It's the pattern of the laces from the gloves." He smiles again and slips off the bed, drawing his trousers up over his shoes. There, indeed, imprinted on his arm, is a telltale crisscross pattern.

I do not know what to say to make him stay. Baffled I offer him a small roll of money, perhaps sixty dollars, which he pockets without looking.

When he leaves, I have the feeling that he has escaped, that he is running from me, running with my money.

I sit beside the window, another fax from my brother on my lap. One simple question—Are the schedules correct?—is scrawled in capitals across the page. It is a small request, easily answered, but I resent the intrusion and will not reply. Beside the chair are copies of the schedules and dockets, marked with my handwriting. Everything was confirmed two weeks before I left London, everything was settled. I know the routes and schedules, and the alternative schedules should the quantities be down, by heart. In fifteen years little has changed, and year after year, the reliability of the shipping firms and our commissioning agents have made me appear reliable, dependable, indispensable.

It is past two o'clock and there is still traffic on the streets, but the station house is quiet. On an impulse I pull out my suitcases, and opening the drawers I begin to pack, laying down my trousers first, and then a layer of books. I should not, I think, see Adrian again, and for a brief while I should go far away from telephones and fax machines, to somewhere where my brother cannot reach me. With one case packed, I sit back down at the window.

At the foot of the bed, reflected in the window, is a small white shirt. Picking it up I wonder how he could have left it, and I wonder where he is now.

Adrian sits in the same seat I sat in all night, and stares blankly down upon the railway station. "I should have a bath first, I smell like the kitchen," he says, hoisting his shirt out of his trousers, undressing in front of the window. "I hate that place." He turns about, bearing a smooth white stomach. "Let's go see a movie."

I say that I would not mind.

"What's the cake for?" he asks.

"Yesterday was my birthday," I lie. My birthday is today.

"You should have said," he smiles unexpectedly, dropping his shirt onto the floor.

"What do you mean?" I ask, drawing my chair closer to him so that our knees touch.

"I don't know," he smiles again. "It's one of those things you say when someone tells you it's their birthday." The bruise on his shoulder is now a flat vivid purple. "Pants on or off?" he asks.

"Off." I tug at the material. "Do you really want to see a film?" I ask.

He frowns and begins to unzip his trousers, "Why not?" Still frowning, he looks squarely at me as he opens his trousers. "Something's different. What happened to all your books?" His hands drop slowly to his side as he looks about the room. "You aren't leaving, are you?"

I shake my head and kiss him softly on the lips. Carefully he turns away and the kiss becomes a hug. I slip backward so that he cannot nestle into my shoulder, and attempt to kiss him on the mouth again. He does not know what to do with his tongue. The boy abruptly sits back and shivers.

"I don't." He stops and huffs, his head twitching with agitation. "This is too pussy for me." He stands up, exasperated, his pants open wide, and looks again at the empty bookshelves.

"What would you rather do?" I ask calmly, trying to look him in the eyes. He is not wearing shorts. "If it's money, I'll pay you for your time."

Out of surprise he begins to laugh. "Sure," he says. "You

can give me money." He shrugs again and sits down, slouching back in the chair. "You know my sister married an Englishman."

Seeing no reason to stop myself, I lean forward and kiss him again on the mouth.

"You don't have to do anything," I say stroking his neck. He sits stiffly upright and flinches, perhaps at what I have said. I kiss his mouth, half expecting him to pull away. This time he leans purposefully forward, pressing his mouth hard to mine, flitting his tongue nervously, without experience, into my mouth. For a surprising moment, as he withdraws, his kiss becomes sweet and gentle, his hand touches my cheek in a fond, unpremeditated gesture.

Equally surprised the boy sits shyly back. "No shit," he says wiping his mouth. "So what's your name?" Raising his feet up onto the seat he hugs himself, hiding his head behind his knees. "When are you going?" he asks. I shake my head and say that I am not.

He lowers his knees so that I can see his face. "I wouldn't blame you," he says looking about the room. "I'd be out of here tomorrow."

Adrian lies on the floor facing the window, looking out over the lake. A pillow tucked under his stomach hitches his backside up. He breathes in as I sit upright, taking my weight off his back. His buttocks are slithery with gel, and I kneel between his legs looking for a towel. He had brought the gel with him, and a packet of condoms, but at the last moment he had decided against it, asking me to "hump, dry hump, between my legs," insisting that I still wear the rubber. As I reach for the wastebasket I cannot help but shiver, although the room is quite warm. Adrian did not come. Instead, his attention was fixed on a comic book open between his elbows.

In place of the usual bruises is a new mark, a single plum-colored bite, on the back of his neck.

"You know, I heard that this neighborhood used to be Irish," he stretches out, pushing the magazine away from him. "Back when the station was still open. Men used to wait there for work first thing in the morning."

"How long ago was that?" I ask.

"Maybe fifty years. It's been closed for five. They'll be developing this whole area."

"Who told you this?"

"The barber. He said everything will go. In a couple of weeks they'll start knocking it down."

My nightcap was a whisky spiked with half a sachet of Theraflu. Sleep comes instantly, heavily. I am woken at three o'clock by a soft, persistent knocking. I am surprised—too sleepy to be delighted—to see Adrian leaning against the door. As he walks stiffly into the light, he holds his hand out to stop me from saying anything. At first I think he is drunk, but he has been severely beaten. His left eye is so swollen that it is almost entirely closed. I follow him into the bathroom.

"Not now," he says, softly brushing my mouth with the back of his hand. "Ask me tomorrow."

Leaning forward over the sink he spits into the drain. Slowly, stiffly, he straightens up, watching himself in the mirror, and carefully lifts his T-shirt over his head, pulling the neck wide, away from his face. Half-stripped he inspects himself. His left eye weeps involuntarily. New bruises bloom on his back, harsh and red and sore.

I swab his back with a cold flannel to draw out the swelling. Water puddles on the blue-tiled floor. He twitches and tightens his shoulders.

"It's cold, that's all." He shakes his head, his voice is husky and nasal.

I hold the cloth away from his back, his skin is hot and supple, with a dull waxy sheen. There are bruises everywhere, on his shoulders, upper chest, lower back, all reflected in the bathroom mirror. There is no avoiding them.

"How did this happen?" I ask. "Who is doing this to you?"

Adrian winces and spits, the saliva is pink. "It's called hardening." He tests his gums with a finger, rubbing and then spitting, he checks his finger for blood. His nose is swollen, the bridge is scuffed. I ask him if he can breathe through it and he shakes his head. "It's part of the training," he explains. "It looks much worse than it is."

"But it doesn't look like you defended yourself."

"That's the idea," he says.

Adrian stays the night. It is his first whole night with me. He assures me that it is no big deal, and turns to face the window, with his back to me, arms wrapped tight about a pillow. His skin smells soft and warm and faintly of eucalyptus balm. Rolling close beside him I whisper, "You can tell me anything, anything at all." The boy gently rocks himself to sleep.

When I awake, Adrian is sitting at the end of the bed, stretching his arms, stretching his neck and shoulders. The bruises are denser, darker than last night, purple and rimmed with yellow, looking strangely like dahlias. The bite that I gave him yesterday afternoon has all but faded.

Laying a towel out on the floor, he begins to exercise. First push-ups, then sit-ups. He completes the exercises without hurry, and when he is done, he folds the towel and sits beside the window holding the curtain open a crack, looking down at the station house.

"How are you?" I sit up in the bed.

"I think my nose is broken." He opens the curtain and half turns; his swollen eye is black, wet, and completely closed. The swelling extends under his eye and across the bridge of his nose.

"Who did this to you?"

"He's called Bruno." He carefully presses the swelling. "No, really," he insists as if I do not believe him. "It's his nickname. I don't know his real name."

"Is he the trainer?" I attempt to sound indifferent, and try to keep my voice dead, flat, unreadable.

"No." He shakes his head. "He's an amateur. One of the best," he briefly smiles.

"How many times has this happened?"

Adrian stands up and shrugs, throwing the towel onto the floor. "Look, I wouldn't worry about it. You don't box. You won't understand. It's to harden me." He pinches the skin on his upper arm. "I'm too soft, my skin is too soft. If I am going to be any good, I have to learn to take it."

"Has he hurt you in any other way?"

At this he falls laughing backward onto the bed. "I give up. What do you want me to say?"

I run my hand down his chest and stomach to the soft nest of his pubes. The boy rolls stiffly away, turning his back to me. "You know, it wasn't so bad until he saw that hickey."

Is it guilt that has brought me here? I am not sure. Standing in the men's-wear department, I avoid talking to the clerks. One of them refers to Adrian as my son.

Adrian has a particular suit in mind. Something gray, not sharkskin but close, and square. Square, square, square. Row upon row of suits, but none are square enough.

While waiting for him to make up his mind, I buy myself some socks. Placing my card and traveler's checks on the counter, I tell the clerk that I will pay for the boy's clothes separately.

"Harris?" The clerk holds the card closer to his face. "I need a photo ID."

Adrian looks quizzically at me in the mirror as I search through my wallet, and I realize that he is as much in the dark about me as I am about him.

*

I wait for two hours in a café on Clark and Wilson. Adrian is at work. Opposite, in a squat two-story building, up one flight of stairs, is Adrian's boxing club. The Uptown Young Men's Boxing Club. Beneath the boxing club is a chemists, a drugstore. The coffee is weak and bitter, and the greasy table reeks of disinfectant. The street outside is littered and busy. Newspapers, dirt, and paper cups fly up against the window. Colored bunting and flags strung across the street bluster in the wind as if there were recently a carnival here.

A group of teenagers, skinnier and younger than Adrian, come out of the boxing club's door, sports bags over their shoulders. They say good-bye and part, two heading south and three heading north. Fifteen minutes later a man appears in the lobby, pausing, leaning against the door, talking to someone out of my view, back up the stairs. Leaving money on the counter, I hurry into the street.

The man is wearing a suit: a light gray suit, cut square, very square. Without a doubt, this man is Bruno. Adrian and Bruno could be brothers. The boy has modeled himself on him. His body is a double for Bruno's: the same sloping shoulders, the same cocky swagger, the same close-cropped hair, and a deliberate brutish set in the face. I overtake Bruno, half-running, bent against the wind to outpace him. Crossing the road, the light changes to red and traffic divides us. I wait on the opposite curb and watch him approach. The late afternoon sun cuts obtusely between the buildings, periodically blinding him, so that he has to squint or shield his eyes. He is wearing a white shirt and a black-and-red-striped tie, black shoes with thick soles and a thin gold signet ring on the little finger of his right hand. His jacket flips open in the wind, one lapel caught under the strap of his sports bag. His chest is square, angular, tight, and his tie flaps fishlike, hooked one-third down by a simple pin. Bruno is a strong strapping man with an athletic build. I had expected this physique, but not the suit. And this is how Adrian sees himself, as a svelte, well-trimmed brute.

Bruno crosses the road, watching himself in shop windows, a sure and level, unreadable stare. For three whole blocks I follow closely behind, walking in air filled with the sharp sting of his aftershave. Finally, realizing I have nothing to say to him, I allow him to walk ahead and away from me.

The restaurant is very different at night: busy, dark, and full, and surprisingly noisy. The whole room smells of fennel, red wine, and coffee. I eat on my own at the bar, facing the back of the restaurant so that I can watch Adrian as he works. He seems awkward, out of place, disorganized in comparison to the other waiters, who move quickly and efficiently between the tightly packed tables. Several customers ask him about his eye, and each time his hand goes up self-consciously to his face.

Returning to the hotel I try not to think of Adrian and Bruno. But I see it all so clearly that I can feel it in the pit of my stomach, tight and burning. Unwittingly Bruno and I have a pact, a contract written on the boy's body, and Adrian is in love with the man. They do not fuck. They do not even kiss. I am sure of it. But the beatings are sex, sex of a kind. And what I had taken for inexperience and shyness in Adrian's lovemaking is perhaps indifference.

I am soaking in the bath when Adrian returns. He drops his bag in the doorway and sits down on the side of the tub.

"Hi." He smiles, unbuttoning his shirt. "How was your meal?"

"Good." I am surprised, I thought that he had not noticed me. "It was very good. How was it tonight?"

"Busy, I guess."

I ask him if he has eaten yet.

"Uh-uh. I'm starving." He settles down on the floor, and leaning against the bath he unzips his bag. Inside is a carefully wrapped foil package, a small brown paper bag, greasy and torn along the bottom, and two beers. He sets the parcels on his lap. There is a whole braised bulb of fennel in the foil, and a sandwich in the paper bag. "This is the only reason I work there. Free food." He points at half a sandwich. "Free decent food." He corrects himself, and opens up the sandwich so that I can see, chicken breast, basil, and mozzarella. "And no one minds if you help yourself."

I stand up in the bath and reach across for a towel, trying not to drip on him as he eats. "How long have you worked there?"

"Four months. About. Maybe longer." He looks up from his sandwich, his mouth and cheeks full. "I've worked at other restaurants. A place called Jimmy's, and a bar before that, serving tables. But they had to let me go when they found out I lied about my age."

Age. The word smarts between us. Adrian wraps the paper back around his sandwich and scoots aside to let me out of the bath. "Leave the water in. I'll have a bath in a minute."

I wrap the towel about my waist and follow him into the bedroom. He switches on the TV and strips down to his T-shirt and shorts, dropping his clothes at the foot of the bed. Sitting down at my table he watches a sitcom while he eats, picking the fennel apart with his fingers.

"You ever seen this?" he points at the screen. "This is a repeat. You wouldn't recognize her now. She's a mess. She had her face done, everything. She was better fat, but she's still funny."

The family on the television are also eating. Adrian watches without laughing. I watch him eat, and when he is finished I place a gift-wrapped parcel on the table in front of him.

"What's this?" he asks.

"Open it." I reply.

He opens the box distracted by the TV. "Chocolates," he says flatly, unimpressed, letting the lid fall back.

Opening the box I select one of the dark chocolates and slip it into his mouth, withdrawing my finger slowly.

"Have you ever fucked a man?" I ask. "Have you ever fucked a man in the mouth?"

Adrian shifts uncomfortably in his seat. "Sure," he says, licking chocolate off his lips and looking back at the television.

Taking another chocolate, I again place it in his mouth, sliding my finger between his teeth and cheek as he chews. He grins and swallows. "It doesn't take that much," he grabs at his crotch.

"Which is your favorite?" I ask, reaching again into the chocolate box. He quickly chooses, still paying more attention to the television. I close my hand about the small black candy, as black and shiny as a beetle, and squeeze. Sweet fragrant liqueur breaks through my fingers and drips onto his shorts. "Spit into my hand."

I slip my hand, sticky and black with chocolate, into his shorts and kneel between the boy's legs.

"Don't," he huffs, scooting his chair back.

I sit back down on the floor.

"I'm sorry," he apologizes. There is laughter from the television. He reaches over my shoulder and switches it off. "It's just I have to wear these tomorrow."

He stands up, and stepping carefully about me, walks to the bathroom.

"I've been planning a holiday," I cough to clear my throat. "A drive. Will you come?"

He pauses in the doorway, hands tucked inside his shorts, legs apart, back arched. "How long?"

"Eight, ten days perhaps."

"What about my job?"

"Tell them that you're sick, and I'll make up the difference."

He nods and steps into the bathroom. I listen as he runs the taps and washes his shorts. I stand up and undress, watching a cluster of figures down at the station house steps. Adrian shakes out his boxer shorts and steps naked into the bedroom. "I've been thinking I'd quit there anyway."

The windows of the gym are covered. It is early, and apart from a janitor who opened the doors for us, we are alone. There are two full-sized raised rings, one small punching bag, and three larger bags all banded with silver tape hang in a row. Along one wall is a series of mirrors. The room is divided by a row of gray lockers. Taped on the backs of the lockers are yellow newspaper clippings and posters of fights. In each photograph the boxers either scowl or smile, fixed and dazed, fists up or arms extended in victory. On the other side of the lockers is weight-lifting equipment. Beyond that are the toilets and changing rooms. Throughout the gym small blue padded mats are strewn on the floor. The walls are painted a glossy pale green to shoulder height, above that the yellow paint peels back to the plaster. I sit on a slatted bench by the door, keeping an eye on both the boy and my watch.

"Two more minutes." I am keeping time.

Adrian increases his pace. Standing on tip-toe he stealthily darts about the leather punching bag, hitting it hard enough to cause the whole apparatus to shudder. Sweat pours down his back, staining a dark semicircle in the high-waisted shorts at the small of his back. His eyes are glazed and steady, focused on the center of the bag. With each punch sweat sparks off his forehead. Soft divots, imprints of the gloves and his fist are left in the leather bag, its skin as dull and heavy as lead.

"30, 29, 28." As I count down the last seconds Adrian redoubles his efforts, redoubles his assaults upon the bag. So concentrated and furious are his blows that I blink at each smack. "2, 1."

He breaks, then lunges one last time. As the bag swings back he clutches it. Unable to grip it with his gloves, he reaches fully around it and locks his wrists, holding the bag close to him. Stepping up I unlock his wrists and wrap his arms about me. His body is hot, unbelievably hot and wet with sweat, and he is trembling from the exercise. His eyes are closed and he holds hard onto me.

"Let's go tonight," he whispers. "That trip. Let's just go."

He loosens his grip and steps back offering me his wrists. "Undo these, will you?" He smiles as I pick at the laces. "You shouldn't have stopped, you know. You should have put up more of a fight last night." As I unwrap the cords he playfully twists his hands so that the laces become tangled. With the laces half undone he steps away and walks to the back of the gym, toward the changing room.

I follow after him down a short bright corridor; there are windows along one wall opening into an enclosed brick courtyard. Sunlight slakes down the wall. Beside the changing room is a small dark office. Adrian walks into the office and, pushing aside a slim blue mat, he sits on the side of the desk, pulling the gloves off between his knees. The room reeks of eucalyptus oil.

"You'd better close the door," he says, flexing his free hand. "No one will be around for a while, but you never know."

I shut the door and turn the latch, feeling self-conscious and a little nervous. The door handle is slippery with oil. The office is crammed with boxes, each numbered. It is nothing more than a storage room. The boy settles back on the desk, half resting on a greasy blue mat, slick with eucalyptus oil.

I slide my hands down the back of his shorts. The band is tight and the drawstring wet, a puckered line runs about his waist, and his cock is caught in the shorts' soft folds. I rest my head on his stomach, dizzy with the strong heady smell of his sweat and the fast beat of his heart. He sits up and pulling his shorts open wide he forces my head down into his lap.

I swallow deep, tasting salt. Pushing his shorts farther down, I pinch his nipple. Adrian starts up a thrust, equal in aggression to my grip on his nipple. He slides off the desk and half standing begins to thrust briskly, gripping either side of the tabletop, knocking my head against the table.

It is a matter of seconds, and at the first bolt of jissom, my hands take place of my mouth. For the first time Adrian comes, huffing, bothered, red-faced. Tears streaming from his black eye he begins to laugh; and as the semen thins and trickles through my fingers I feel loved, remarkably loved.

Adrian comes out onto the street still dressed in his boxing shorts, his hair is wet from his shower. He opens the car door and sets his bag onto the seat.

"There's some stuff I ought to get before we leave town. It's not far. You can follow me in the car. I'm going to run."

A car pulls up beside me waiting for the traffic lights to change. There are two boys in the front seats, and two girls in the back. The passenger nods at Adrian. The car is new, expensive, and the driver looks much too young to be driving. Adrian turns away, frowning, and looks up the road, as if he has not even seen them.

"So you follow me. It's not far, about six or eight blocks."

The passenger presses his face against the windscreen, twisting his nose and flattening his lips against the glass. The girls laugh as if this were the funniest thing, and as the lights change the driver pips his horn.

Ignoring them Adrian crosses the road and begins to run. The passenger rolls down his window and hoots after him.

"Yeah. Yeah. Go, go, go."

I park in front of an apartment building, a brownstone, and follow Adrian round the building to an unpaved alley. He waits at a chain-link fence, holding open a shattered wooden gate. At the back of the building is an enclosed porch painted black with tar. The yard is a bare, sandy, dirt square, empty except for an upright metal pole and a loose chain for a dog. The apartment is on the ground floor. An old shaggy yellow sofa without cushions is upended near the door, there are cigarette burns in the pink foam armrests. Adrian reaches about the sofa to the window ledge behind and fishes out a set of keys.

As the door is opened I can smell the dry stale air, a smell of old blankets, not unpleasant, but strong nevertheless. Adrian steps in and gingerly turns on the light, as if expecting someone to be there.

The door opens directly into a kitchen. Yellow waxy blinds are pulled down; there are several black dustbin bags next to the door, all tied except one. There are dirty pans and beer cans stacked in the sink, a single plate with a dried mat of spaghetti on the sideboard. The cupboards above the sink are open and empty. No one appears to have lived here for some time.

"Sorry about the smell," he apologizes, bending down to tie up the dustbin bag.

"What is this place?"

"This is where I live." He holds his hands out and looks down at the floor, embarrassed. Someone has drawn a skull and crossbones on the fridge door.

"Who else lives here?" I ask.

"I'm not sure. There used to be about four others. The whole house is divided. They rent it by the room and you share the kitchen and bathroom. I think I'm the only one left now." He pushes the bags together, then walks down the hall, wiping his hands on his shorts. The ceiling is high, and a long brass pole with a single lightbulb hangs down in the center. There are doors along the hallway, each padlocked. One of the doors has a small piece of paper taped to it. Adrian takes the note from the door, and without reading it, drops it onto the floor. He fidgets with the keys and opens the lock.

The room is small and surprisingly neat. The floor is painted black. There is a single mattress pushed up against the wall under a narrow and barred window. A tartan blanket is folded at the end of the bed. In a doorless closet sits a chair, and tucked underneath is a blue and white sports bag. Adrian takes the bag and sits down on the mattress. He is subdued and perhaps a little sad.

"Are you bringing the blanket?" I ask.

Adrian unzips his bag and checks through it. "Do you want it?"

"It's a Harris tweed. I used to have one of these at my school."

"I took it from my sister." He folds the blanket in half and lays it on his sports bag. "So it probably came from England."

Beside the door is a plain brown cardboard box. "And this?"

"No." He speaks softly, his voice low and flat, the blanket and bag cradled in his arms. "It belongs to the person who rented the room." He looks sadly at the mattress and huffs. "It was never really my place. I sort of inherited it."

As we leave the room Adrian steps deliberately over the piece of notepaper. I pick it up. His name is written on the back. At the top is a logo for a hospital.

"Here, this is for you?" I hold the note out to him. He looks at the paper but will not take it.

I place the note on the blanket. "You never know. It might be important."

"Leave it here," he says curtly, brushing the paper back onto the floor. "I know who it's from."

Back on the porch, Adrian pulls the door closed and leans against it, making sure that it is locked. He holds the keys in his fist for a moment, thinking, and then returns them to the sill behind the raggedy couch.

3

Adrian stands with his feet close to the edge of the gorge.

"What if I jump?" he asks. Holding on to the double rail, he peers over the precipice and spits. "Fuck. That's a long way."

I turn my back against the wind to light a cigarette. Adrian is now standing on the lower rail, arms outstretched, leaning against the wind. The upward draft billows out his shirt. "Did you ever get the feeling that you could just go ahead and do something? Whatever it was, you could just do it."

"What do you mean?" I ask.

"Like jumping. Just plain jumping off this cliff."

"I'm not sure I know what you mean." I instinctively make a step toward him.

"Come on," he insists, and unsteadily raises his arms and leans farther forward so that only the upward draft and the brace of his knees against the upper rail prevent him from tumbling forward. Behind us the land raises in a slow, steep gradient. But here, less than ten inches in front of him, the red rock ends and the land plummets; far below us is a sparsely forested canyon, a river, and a black winding road. Farther west the land is flat and segmented into irrigated and farmed plots, and farther still, lost in thunder-gray clouds and a setting sun are the Rocky Mountains. I reach for the boy to steady him.

He teeters forward in my hands. "Go take a picture."

I walk slowly backward through the scrub to the car, watching his arms dip and sway for balance. The camera is on the backseat, beneath newspapers, T-shirts, and sweaters.

By the time I have the camera ready Adrian has stepped

down from the rail. Pulling off his shirt and T-shirt and holding up his fists, he begins to shadow-box, dancing and raising dust as the sun sets, nothing behind him except for a deep blue, a flat and gorgeous blue sky and a few early solitary stars. I turn on the car headlights so that he can be seen, bleached white against a smooth darkening sky. The wind picks up the dust from his feet, and a thin column of smoke rises up and about him, as if steam poured from his body. Four days ago we were leaving Chicago, and today, I have red Wyoming dust in my hands, hair, and mouth.

Once he has tired of boxing, Adrian stands in the cold leaning against the railing, hugging himself. As I step back out of the car he shouts, "What's this place again?"

"Some Scandinavian drove his wagon over the precipice."

Adrian looks down into the canyon, impressed. "Wow."

I pick up his shirt and T-shirt and shake out the dust. The sky is almost entirely black.

"Smell," I say. "What can you smell?"

"Is it the pine trees?"

"I think it's sage or juniper." We both breathe out. "How long is it since you've breathed such clean air?" I ask.

Adrian shakes his head. "We used to take trips. And I went to camp a couple of times. But they make you do stupid shit." He stares down into the black gorge. In front of us there is nothing, only wind and stars. No other lights, no houses, no cars, and no streetlights. "What a way to go. How far's the drop?" It is easy to imagine: the vision of horses kicking wildly, free of land, turning and falling with their own weight and the weight of the covered wagon, and the surprise on the face of the Scandinavian as he realized that in his rush for land he had literally run out of land, luck, and life. "Even at night you'd recognize that there was nothing there."

"I thought they only drove during the day. Perhaps he was preoccupied."

Adrian begins to laugh. "What difference does it make?"

"There's a phrase, I forget it, something about the evening—that point when it's still light enough to see outside but too dark to see anything clearly—about being unable to distinguish the difference between a dog and a wolf." As I hand the boy his clothes he flinches and steps away from the railing and opens his arms. "But I don't remember."

"I'm cold. Let's go now." He walks ahead of me to the car, shaking the dirt out of his T-shirt. "Thanks," he says, blinking into the headlights. "No. Really. I wasn't cut out for waiting tables."

I like to drive, to drive with no intent of arriving. It is an unexpected comfort to drive at night through a landscape that I do not know with the boy asleep beside me. Adrian likes to stop as often as possible, and each time he returns to the car he asks, "So where are we going?" I like to give the impression that I have somewhere in mind, though I seldom do.

After driving mile upon mile through flat, featureless land, we have, in the past two days been rewarded with spectacular change: sheer canyons of black rock and red rugged cliffs, blood-red stone vibrating with heat, and dry tinder forests reeking so strongly of pine sap that it stung the eyes and stank like petrol. But nothing impresses him quite as much as bloodshed. A quiet warning at night to keep his eyes peeled for deer and antelope—as a collision would total the car—has him pressed vigilantly against the windshield for hours.

We have been driving across country chasing disasters, and in the course of our drive both the newspapers and radio have been reporting the manhunt of David Burkitt of Casper, Wyoming. Within the past three days Burkitt has shot and killed three men and fled into the wilds of Yellowstone Park. Yesterday we visited the post office in Edgerton where Burkitt shot his first man, and the bar in Linch where he shot an oil worker. Today, before the canyon, we visited the site of an Old West gunfight in Kaycee, which is now a flat dusty lot with an enclosed aluminum arena. There's a motel and campsite off the road on the way down to Ten Sleep where some maniac held a group of Cub Scouts hostage, killing three, wounding five. Adrian wants to stay the night, but I prefer to drive. Tomorrow we should make Buffalo, the site of Burkitt's last shooting, and then Yellowstone Park itself. The highlight of our return—if we make good time—will be the Donner Pass.

Adrian stirs beside me.

"Are you awake?" I ask.

"Yeah." He replies softly.

The car's headlights illuminate the dead lower branches of the pine trees on either side of the road. Between the strange white barkless branches is darkness, and warm black night.

"What's the total so far?"

"Five shootings, one plunge," he answers as we descend slowly into Ten Sleep.

We are packed and out of the motel by eight o'clock. Adrian is surprisingly awake, standing by the car with a plastic mug of coffee and a doughnut.

"Morning," he smiles. "The doughnuts are stale and the coffee is butt juice."

"We'll have breakfast in Buffalo."

"Great." He pours his coffee onto the tarmac. "Let's go."

The air is clear and cool. There is still some cloud cover, but already the sun is bright and hot on our arms and foreheads. With Ten Sleep Canyon behind us, the interstate falls into a wide low basin, ribbed on one side by the massive swell and blue crescent of the Big Horn Mountains, and on the other by a distant and gentle curve of black hills. Adrian turns on the radio and scans fitfully and unsuccessfully for a station without country music.

"What time is it?" he asks. "I can't find a station with the news."

He switches the radio off and searches through the glove

compartment. He has a map of Wyoming marked with the sites of the gunman's flight. The killings are plotted in red circles, dates and times written beside them; three probable routes are mapped. The first is marked in red—for the most direct route from one site to another—but also the least likely to have been taken. The second is traced in blue, and is the most likely route taking into account time elapsed between the shootings. Green dots mark the most circuitous route, one which accounts for unsubstantiated rumors—there was talk at the gas station in Kaycee of Burkitt hiding out in an abandoned power station on the Powder River. There are several places where these routes cross. Two of the shootings happened in small towns, Edgerton and Linch, where there is only one route in and out of town. Linch is so small that it barely qualifies as a town, having only two trailer-homes bolted together as a bar, and several mobile homes used by the oil companies as temporary housing. Burkitt's flight has preoccupied most of AM talk radio, and Adrian has kept notes of reported sightings, carefully categorizing them as either implausible, unlikely, or those that have some potential. The backseat is a mess of newspapers, local and national.

"I've another idea why Burkitt's in the Park." This question has occupied many hours of our drive. Adrian explains, "It's obvious. He picked the one last wild place. The shootings were pointless. He didn't know the people he shot. He didn't steal anything. He just walked in and blew them away, and now the whole world gets to watch him go down."

I shake my head.

"Come on," he pinches my arm. "Yellowstone is the last wild place. Next to the Grand Canyon there's nothing left."

"So that's your theory?"

"More or less. Yeah."

"Adrian's big bang theory?"

"Yeah." He smiles broadly. "Pow."

There are no other cars on the interstate. The air reeks of

crude oil, and on either side of the road the land is crowded with slow nodding oil derricks. I press my foot down hard on the accelerator. With nothing to stop us, no cars, no police, no one else whatsoever, I drive in a straight, determined line while Adrian leans out of the window howling like a dog, his short hair flattened to his head, tears streaming down his face, forced from his eyes by the dust and wind.

"What are we doing?" Adrian wakes up and stretches. The map has fallen open at his feet.

"We're here," I gently shake his knee. "Do you want some breakfast?"

He scowls out of the window at the row of small shops. Buffalo amounts to one compact high street with a hardware store that sells western boots, clothes, and cattle fodder; a bank; and two craft shops. There is a small brook running through the town. "Coffee. Maybe coffee," he replies. "Where are we?"

"Buffalo," I answer. Adrian sits quickly upright.

"We're there?"

"There it is. Jamison Hardware and Tackle, and next to it is the place where we are going to have breakfast."

Adrian stares at the storefront. "Look, they're open."

"Are you coming?" I ask.

He steps quickly out of the car and stumbles, disconnected with sleep. "Leg's asleep." He smiles at me through the car window as I lock the door.

The café is a small storefront with whole logs bolted to the front of the building. The windows are hung with fringed drapes and curtains. A simple wooden sign THE HOMESTEADER hangs over the door.

The waitress points us to a booth at the back of the restaurant. There is a telephone by the door.

"I'm going to call the hotel. When she comes just get me a coffee."

I watch Adrian as I call. He leans forward, elbows on the table, his attention at the door. Each time a man with a hat comes in, he turns and watches, until they are either seated or beyond his view.

When I return to the table, Adrian is twisted around in his seat, talking to a woman in the booth behind him. "Wow. Listen to this."

The waitress follows behind me with a sweet roll.

"Here you go, honey." She smiles wide and warmly. "The coffee's coming up."

"You want to split that?" Adrian points at the plate. "But listen to this," he leans confidentially across the table and whispers, "a couple of years ago someone was killing cows and cutting out their assholes."

"Where did you hear that?"

He points behind him. "It's true. She told me."

I turn the sweet roll slowly about, unsure of how to respond. "Don't let me forget, but I have to call back. I'm not certain that we can get into Yellowstone today. I can't get through directly, so the hotel is trying. Remind me to ring them after breakfast."

A woman with pale blond hair and bold red-rimmed glasses smiles across the booth at me. A full breakfast rests untouched on the table between her elbows as she smokes. "Kids," she smiles. "It was kids. We had some big New York newspaper here talking about UFOs, abductions and the like, when it was kids all along."

Adrian smiles. "See, she's talking about the assholes."

The woman pauses to take a long draw on her cigarette, then, blowing smoke up into the air between us, she explains. "Your son was asking if there was anything unusual round here. And I told him there isn't usually much to speak of, we're not much to write home about. We're a quiet and neighborly town. Sometimes in the summer there's some hoo-ha with the tourists, you know, and sometimes someone will get a little out of hand. But we never had anything like this." She squints as she speaks as if even the thought of something bad happening is out of place. "The worst we get is during hunting season. My husband works for the police department, most of the time he just gets complaints about stray dogs or rowdy kids. That's about it. Now they had to close Yellowstone, which is real bad. We get three to four tourist buses a day. The others go through Sheridan. So if it lasts for much longer it could really hurt us. And," she smiles, "we don't want people to get the idea that Buffalo is a violent place."

Distracted by the curl of the woman's cigarette smoke, I look up into the rafters. Mounted on rust-colored wood beams above our heads are the stuffed heads of antelope and deer.

"So we can't get into Yellowstone Park?" Adrian turns back to face the woman.

The woman shakes her head. "They're stopping everyone just outside of Cody. You won't get very far with out-of-state license plates. Give it three days. In three days they'll have that boy either dead or behind bars and Yellowstone will be just as pretty as ever. We've usually had our first snow by this time. Maybe later. So, I guess it could have been worse, at least it's happening close to the end of the season." She stubs out her cigarette and smiles at the ashtray. "I don't mean to pry, but are you English?"

I smile back and nod.

"I have an ear for accents. But you," she smiles at the boy. "You don't have an accent at all." She looks across the booth at me and then Adrian, the question hanging in the air.

"He's my sister's son." I reply too quickly and without a smile. "He's showing me around. Aren't you."

Adrian's hands squeak against the tabletop as he turns fully about to face the woman, a disarming and charming smile across his face. "Yeah. That's right. I've shown him a thing or two. Haven't I?"

*

Adrian lies across the roof of the car on a towel, face up to the sky, his shirt wrapped about his arms. He is wearing a pair of plastic sunglasses that he bought at the hardware store in Buffalo, the site of Burkitt's last shooting.

"Did you see those earrings?" he asks. "You could barely see them for all that hair. She must have known the man who got shot."

"Who are you talking about?"

"The clerk. The woman at the hardware store. They were wooden hoops. Gnarly, like a cow's asshole. Weird." He leans up on the roof looking up to the sky. "And that other woman. How could it possibly snow?"

Both of us are silent, stupefied by the heat. Adrian rolls onto his side and takes off the sunglasses, watching me as I light a cigarette. For a moment he looks directly into my eyes. Heat wavers off the car's enamel roof.

"What would you be doing if you weren't here?" he asks. "If you hadn't called that day?"

"Right now? I'd probably still be in the hotel. And you? What would you be doing?"

Adrian settles slowly onto his back. I imagine him in his small and empty room preparing for work, dressed in his white shirt, his black trousers and shoes.

"I'd probably be in Florida. I've got a friend there. I'd probably be anyplace but Chicago." He cups his hands to his brow, sheltering his eyes from the sun. "So, what should we do?"

"We can still try," I reply. "There isn't much hope that they'll let us into the park, but we could go up and see."

"No. I meant after that. After Yellowstone?" He licks his finger and rubs his eye. "We don't have to go back. We could go someplace else. Neither one of us has to be in Chicago."

I walk around to the front of the car and sit on the bonnet. The question is serious. I had assumed that we would return to

Chicago. "I have to go back. I'd have to make some financial arrangements."

"But you're interested?"

"Yes. I'm interested."

Adrian squints, disappointed, his hand fishes about for his sunglasses.

"Why don't you want to go back?" I ask.

"Because," he replies petulantly.

While we have been talking I have been watching a bird. "Adrian, look. It's an eagle," I say.

"I saw. It's a crow."

"Impossible. Look how large it is. Crows are small, small and black. Eagles are big and brown."

"No way. It's a crow."

We both lean forward squinting up at the massive, flat blue sky. The sun is burning off the clouds, even on the rims of the mountains. The bird swoops from perch to perch, from telephone pole to treetop to telephone pole, never close enough to gauge exactly how large it is.

"No. Look at that. Look at the tips of its wings. It's an eagle." As I talk the bird lights down to the ground with a sound, even at this distance, of an umbrella opening.

I can seldom guess what is on the boy's mind. Although I would hazard that it is less and less Bruno. The bruise has faded to a faint yellow-tan, and the swelling has disappeared, leaving a small bump at the bridge of his nose. Something I suspect he is quite proud of. Adrian laughs in a way that begs the question—What's up? I won't ask. I will wait for him to tell me. He laughs again, shuffling in his seat, jiggling his leg and scratching.

The road follows a river upstream through a canyon. The incline is steady and as the car turns, the pressure pops in our ears. Red earth has given way to golden rock, boulders each as large as a house block the river's passage. Whole tree trunks, dried and silver, line the riverbank, marking its flood line. Adrian laughs to himself again and scratches.

"What's up? Have you been bitten?" I ask.

"Just thinking," he replies.

The road turns and widens, and at the foot of the canyon is a mountain, golden and brittle, sunlight hard upon its crest.

"Were you named after someone special?" he asks. "Were there any Pauls in your family before you?"

"Not living. Not in my immediate family."

"Are you pissed at me?"

"Angry? No. Not at all. Why would I be?"

"I don't know." He winds down his window and hangs his arm out and stares ahead at the mountain. A heady, almost flammable, scent of pine billows into the car. I turn off the air-conditioning.

"I was named after an uncle on my father's side. He was married to my father's sister," I say. "But I never met him."

Adrian rests his head on the open window, slightly turned so that he can watch me as he listens.

"He was killed during the Blitz. He worked on the railways with my grandfather, which is how he met my aunt. During the war the Underground, the London Underground, was used as an air raid shelter. Paul was caught on the stairs at King's Cross, on the escalator, and killed. It was a direct hit." I check to see if he is listening. "There was no reason really for him to be there. Aunt Jessie suffered for years with melancholia. They hadn't been married for long, and it broke her heart. She'd go to the railway station every day, even after the war, every day until she moved away from London. Why are you laughing? It's tragic."

Adrian is smiling broadly and chuckling. "Is this for real?"

"Of course it's real," I continue, "I'm serious. In the war people and things were lost to you quickly. My parents had two houses bombed within one year. It's hard to understand now, but there wasn't a family who hadn't lost somebody."

Adrian shuffles in his seat.

"I'm sorry. I'm lecturing you."

"No. It's all right." He sits upright and stretches, hands locked together.

"My father's father worked on the railways," I continue. "He joined the army after Paul was killed, and was one of the first men in Belsen concentration camp at the end of the war. He disappeared shortly after his return, and that broke the family up. My mother's father came from Cyprus, he was a Greek Cypriot. His family owned vineyards across Cyprus, mostly between Paphos and Limassol, but they also had land in Kyrenia. My parents moved there after the war, and when my mother's father died they took over the vineyards. Have you ever heard of Prastio?"

Adrian lazily shakes his head.

"It's a liqueur. There's a monastery called St. Savvas where the monks produce a very strong liqueur called Prastio, from grain alcohol and currants."

"What happened to the grandfather? The one who disappeared."

"He's around. No one in my family, in my generation, has met him. Some of his brothers are alive. I don't know them, but I think that they have a better idea of what happened to him. Perhaps he has another family somewhere."

The sun reflects up off the dashboard and into Adrian's eyes. He squints sleepily, his head lolling against his arm. "So, did you live in Cyprus?"

"No. Not really. I was raised in Yorkshire. When the Turks invaded the island in 1974 we lost both the house and vineyards in Kyrenia. My sister was there when it happened. The local Turks knew what was coming and they smuggled her out. I've heard that everything is still the same as when we left it. The same laborers look after the vineyards, but the grapes are sold for eating." The trees, the steep road, the whole rocky landscape reminds me of Kyrenia.

"Technically the land is still ours, but it would be impossible to farm. There's no link between the two halves: the Greeks won't allow anything over from the Turkish side, and the Turks have repopulated. So both sides are independent of each other. We still have the vineyards at Plakka, but we don't produce as much as we used to. The monks also lost most of their land to the Turks, so they farm three of our vineyards, which is more than enough for their needs and for ours. We buy the liqueur back from them, for a nominal fee, which we then sell directly to confectioners in England. Those chocolates I gave you the other day, they were ours. We sell some table wines, but Prastio is the moneymaker. We have exclusive rights; you can't buy it even in Cyprus."

For a short distance the forest folds over the road, shielding the car from a hard afternoon sun.

"So that's what you do?"

"Basically. Until two months ago."

Adrian looks carefully at me, with a vague puzzled frown.

"My job was export: licenses, landing, and shipping in England to our distributors. We handle a good forty percent of the total volume of wine produced in Cyprus, and my job was to make sure that the wine arrived when and where it was supposed to, that it got to the right people at the right time."

"Why did you leave?"

I pause for a moment, wondering if, in retrospect, there really is an explanation.

"There wasn't any one single reason. I suppose it didn't make any sense to me anymore." The forest begins to thin, falling away from the road, and sunlight flashes irregularly through the branches. Adrian holds his hand up to shield his face. "Honestly. What it came down to is that there was no real reason to stay anymore."

"Won't they miss you?"

I shrug. "It hasn't made my brother very happy. But it was on the cards for a long time. They have computers now, software which does almost everything that I do, quicker, without error. What I do is becoming redundant; no one is being trained to replace me because most businesses are now computerized. One simple procedure will prepare everything. It's like logarithms, nobody does logarithms anymore because we have calculators. If I return to the company I could either work less hours, fewer days, take on new responsibilities—which I'm not so interested in—or live in some kind of semi-retirement in Cyprus. We've been looking for a new manager there for some time."

We are both silent. Adrian focuses on the road ahead, daydreaming. I wonder if he knows where Cyprus is.

"So who were you named after?" I ask.

"I was named after one of my father's friends, which is where the whole English thing comes from. My parents went to the same university. My mother's English, and she was going to marry a friend of my father's."

"So you were named after your mother's boyfriend?" I ask.

Adrian nods. "He married someone else, so I guess it was okay. And then my sister, Allison, who's a doctor, went to the same college, and she married a doctor and lived in England for a while. I think he was like one of her professors or something. He's really old. Almost as old as my father. Everyone in my family is a doctor."

"How old is your father?" I ask.

The boy looks at me and grimaces.

"We aren't the same age, are we?"

For one moment he seems genuinely alarmed. "No way. He's old. Really old."

"How old is that?"

"I don't know. Just really old. There's a big age gap between me and my sister. I think my mother had me so she could give up her practice." Adrian turns and smiles. "My parents would love you." He begins laughing again. "They're stupid about anything English, you know." He laughs even harder. "No, they really would. They really like my brother-in-law, even though he's a total asshole." He stops laughing, suddenly sober. "So, can I drive?" he asks. "I can drive, you know." He slumps back and pushes his legs straight to the floor, thrusting himself deeper into the seat. Holding his arms stiffly out in front of him, he copies me, copies every movement I make.

Adrian is the first to see the hat sliding in the wind across the road. A new wide Stetson skimming across the tarmac as if there were an animal caught beneath, or a string pulling it. It is very funny, a hat with no head. "Must have blown out of some car," he laughs.

"Do you want it?" I ask, checking the mirror. There is no other traffic. Midday and the motorway is empty. One wall of the canyon has fallen away, and the road skirts about the base of a mountain. There are hazard signs beside the road warning of rockfalls. I pull the car over. Adrian hops out and runs around the front of the car. As he bends down to pick up the hat, I notice a depression in the grass in the meridian. The grass has been flattened. Adrian stands up and waves the hat at me.

"It's just my size," he says, trying the hat on. It slips over his eyes to the bridge of his nose. He turns around to see what I am staring at.

"Stay here," I say getting out of the car. "Stay with the car."

A young man lies on his side in the dead brown grass. His back is toward me. I have never seen a corpse before. In forty-two years I have never seen anyone die, or anyone dead. Despite the absence of blood or any obvious signs of violence, I know that this man is dead. He lies too flat to the ground.

"Is he dead?" Adrian stands beside me, holding the hat in his hands.

The man's mouth is open slightly, as if there is still one breath or word left. His eyes are closed and his hair flattened, keeping the shape of his hat.

"What happened?"

"It looks like he's fallen."

We are both whispering.

"No blood. No blood." Adrian squats down on his knees. "And he's smiling." He reaches his hand out.

"Don't touch him."

"It doesn't seem so bad. It looks like he could just get right up."

Wind blows lightly through the man's hair, "I don't understand what happened." Adrian looks up at the rock face. "If he was climbing he would have hit the road." He leans closer to the man's face. "Anyway, he isn't dressed for climbing."

"I said don't touch him."

"I was just . . .," he turns crossly to me, when suddenly the body sits up, very much alive, eyes wide. "Jesus frigging Christ." Adrian launches up, springing backward like a cat.

The cowboy begins to laugh.

"It's not fucking funny," Adrian continues to walk backward, away from the man as he rises. "Jesus frigging Christ," he shouts. "What's so fucking funny? What's he laughing at?"

I am shaking, rooted to the spot. The man is not laughing; he is trying to speak, but his mouth gabbles silently, and his eyes are not focused. As he sits upright his body shakes with the effort as if there were a strong wind blowing against him.

"What do we do?" I say quietly to myself. "I don't know what we should do." The man turns at my voice, as if he can hear but not see me.

"Do something." Adrian shouts. Again the man turns his head toward the voice.

"I don't know what's wrong with him. I think he can hear us, but I don't think he can see us."

"What's wrong with him?"

"How in God's name should I know?"

The man extends an arm toward me. I walk slowly

forward. "I know you can hear me. Can you understand what I am saying?"

The man's hand stays open and outstretched. "Are you hurt?" I ask. But he responds only to my voice and not to the words. He attempts to stand and tumbles forward onto his hands and knees, and begins blindly to crawl toward me.

"He's probably all right. I think he's all right," I say to Adrian without turning my head, resisting the impulse to laugh. In no sense is this man all right. I step forward and bend down toward him, gently lifting him up with one arm about his shoulder. Without making a sound the man carefully stands. His body is cold, there is no warmth in his hands, and he is trembling. He is weak and barely able to walk even with assistance. The back of his shirt is wet from lying in the grass. It is impossible to guess how long he has been lying here. "Open the door." Adrian runs obediently across the road. "I'll sit in the back with him. Do you think you can drive?" Adrian turns and nods, nervous but excited.

"We're taking you to Buffalo," he says. "Do you understand? We're taking you to a hospital."

Everything is taken out of our hands at the hospital. Adrian and I sit in a brightly lit waiting room, uncertain of our responsibility to the injured man. A policeman is standing in the doorway taking notes as I explain the incident for him a second time. Adrian sits at the edge of a chair watching a television with the sound turned down.

"We were about here." I point on the map. "I can't be exact. But somewhere around here."

"And how did you see him?"

"It was his hat. In the middle of the road. As I said, we stopped for his hat."

"And he didn't say anything?"

"As I said before, I don't think he was able to talk. I think he was trying to."

"But he didn't say anything."

"No."

The sheriff squats down in the doorway and continues to write, resting the clipboard on his knees. He is left-handed. His radio hisses at his side, and he pauses to switch it off. He shakes his head and hands me the clipboard. "If you don't mind, I'll need your address."

"Unless they open Yellowstone Park within the next couple of days, the earliest we would be back in Chicago is Sunday." The sheriff watches the clipboard as I write down the address of the hotel.

"Sunday?" Adrian turns from the TV. "We're going back Sunday?"

"I think they'll have the situation under control in a couple of days." Taking off his hat the sheriff frowns and runs his hands through his hair. Adrian sits forward in his seat.

"So we can go?" he asks.

"Absolutely. And I'm finished here also."

The sheriff walks slowly beside us to his squad car. Our vehicles are parked together, the only cars in the lot. Adrian looks down at the man's gun, snug in its holster and strapped to his hip, and then smiles at me. The sheriff offers his hand.

As I unlock the car door Adrian turns to the sheriff and asks, "What's going to happen to him?"

"It doesn't usually take too long. My guess is he was riding shotgun in the back of someone's truck and they were too drunk to notice him gone. Someone has probably already reported him missing. We'll find out who he is." The sheriff closes Adrian's door and taps a gentle good-bye with his fingers on the roof.

Adrian sits facing me in the motel room. He leans carefully forward and squints, rubbing his thumbs into his temples. "What do you think will happen?" he asks.

"I really don't know."

"Are we going back?"

"To Yellowstone?" I ask.

Adrian nods.

"Do you want to?"

He nods again.

"Then where's that map?"

Adrian unzips the bag at his feet and produces the map. He unfolds it across the bed, and we both kneel, side by side between the beds.

"We'll have to take the same road. Unless we go through Sheridan." I trace the route with my finger. He moves my hand out of the way. Beside the map is a schedule of events.

"You know there's a rodeo here this weekend. I've never seen a rodeo before," he says. "We could stay here and wait for the park to open. Why not?" He sits back on his haunches, and leans against the bed. "I could use a beer."

"Do you need some money?" I reach for my wallet.

"You have to get it. I'm not twenty-one."

"Of course. I forget." Embarrassed, I stand up and fold the map away. There is shouting in the corridor.

"Don't get Coors, if you can help it." He wrinkles his nose. "Butt juice." He slides farther down onto the floor so that his feet are tucked under the opposite bed.

I stand at the doorway counting the money in my wallet. The corridor is empty, but from one of the rooms there is shouting. It is a man's voice, and he is bragging, perhaps drunk, about the rodeo. There are small, framed black-and-white photographs of rodeo and bronco riders staggered along the walls, each picture screwed through its frame into the wall.

The lights in the lobby have been switched off, and there is no one at the desk. Through the glass doors I can see two men in broad-rimmed cowboy hats unloading a pickup. As I turn back toward the stairs I hear a tapping on the glass. One of the men is knocking at the door. He has keys in his hand and a cooler at his feet. The door is bolted shut but not locked. His hat is wide and black, and with the light behind him, he cuts a cartoonlike silhouette.

Pulling the bolts I open the door, and the man squeezes through. He is tall and slender, his clothes are impeccably pressed, and he seems too closely shaved, too well presented to be the real thing, a real cowboy. His shirt is a soft cream color with a delicate red-fringed cuff across the shoulder and chest. In his shirt pocket is the round block of a tobacco can. Both his shirt and jeans are tight at the waist. His belt buckle is a large silver oval, studded with glass and engraved with the design of a brand, a simple Y, a lazy Y resting on its side. He nods his thanks, and places the cooler in front of the door so that it will not close.

"You work here?" he asks, bending down to snap the latches on the cooler. His friend is standing in the bed of the pickup, hoisting a saddle onto the side of the truck.

"No, not at all. I was looking for somewhere to buy some beer."

"English?" He stops and looks up.

I nod.

"No kidding? Vacation?"

"Yes."

"No kidding. Hey." He shouts to his friend through the door. "Opie. This guy's English."

"No kidding," his friend shouts back.

"You here for the rodeo?" He bends back down to the cooler and opens it. The cooler is stacked with cans of beer and packed with ice.

"Yes. Perhaps. I'm not sure."

"Here you go." Without turning the man swings a six-pack of beer dripping with water toward me. "Have a good evening." He slowly straightens up and politely tips his hat.

"Thank you." I accept the beer, surprised at the man's generosity.

"It's nothing. What's your name?"

"Paul." I shake his hand.

He nods and extends his hand a second time. "Pleased to meet you, Paul. My name's Buck." We shake hands again, and I turn to leave.

As I return to the room, the shouting has calmed to a melancholic whine. "Then-I-don't-know-a-god-damned-jack-shit-about-nothing-then-do-I?" the voice drawls.

There are three coat hooks on the back of the door, each fashioned from a single horseshoe. Adrian is lying on the bed with his hands tucked into his shorts.

"You'll never guess." I hold up the six-pack of beer like a trophy. "But this must be where the rodeo riders are staying. I was given these by Buck the Bronco Buster."

"No kidding." He sits up and takes one of the beers. Cold water runs down the length of his arm.

"Buck. Buck." I say quietly, "Buck is the name of a dog."

"What's that?" he asks. I shake my head. Adrian rolls the cold can across his forehead. "Hey, do you know how to drink these?" He hops off the bed and opens the screen door onto the balcony. "Here, we should do this outside. Bring another beer, and I need a pen." I search through my jacket pockets and find a ballpoint pen.

Adrian takes the pen and steps out onto the balcony. Below the balcony is a small kidney-shape swimming pool set in a stone-flagged patio. There are small podlike lights set in portholes beneath the water line. White plastic deck chairs are stacked beside a low wooden fence. Behind the fence is the car park, and from a bar somewhere comes a steady one-two-three-four beat from a jukebox, accompanied by a dog's slow repeated woofs.

Adrian leans against the railing, looking up and about at the other rooms and balconies. "You'd better take your shirt off." He smiles and holds up his beer. "Okay, so punch a hole in the can, like this, near the bottom." As he pushes the pen through the tin, beer sprays across his arm. He holds his thumb over the puncture and hands me the pen. "Watch me first. Now, hold it up to your mouth," he raises the can high above his head, "and open the tab."

A thin spout of beer spatters over his face as he aims the stream toward his mouth. The beer pours in one even golden stream, splashing over his face each time he closes his mouth to swallow. He gulps quickly trying to drink as much of the beer as possible, but when the can is empty his face, throat, and chest are wet.

"It's good. It's cold." He laughs as he crushes the can in his two hands. "You can get really wasted doing this."

I follow Adrian's example and hold the can up over my face. But when I pull back the tab, he wrestles with me, fighting to get hold of the can. Beer splashes over both of us as we duck and struggle into its stream. "Pussy," he shouts, shoving me out of the way, "you're a pussy." Being taller, I am able hold the beer out of his reach, but all the same, Adrian jumps up, and grabbing my wrist, he shakes vigorously until we are both soaked.

Adrian falls laughing onto his knees. "I told you to take your shirt off," he laughs. "You should see yourself."

Adrian sits on top of me, his thighs perched above mine, his hands holding down my shoulders. He gradually eases his backside down, his brow creased, registering every twinge, every faint movement. I lie motionless, unable to move, pinioned to the bed, powerfully aware of the painful dig of his thumbs in my shoulders and of an unbelievable pressure and heat. He pushes down harder, and we tremble together.

"It's okay," he breathes. "Can you come?" his face is flushed, dark round red blotches bloom on his cheeks and neck.

His brow is wet, and as I wipe my hand across it, he rests his forehead in my palm.

I move his hands down to my stomach. He sits upright,

trying to balance, and feels between my legs and his backside. I roll my hips slightly and the boy leans backward.

"How does it feel?" I ask. "All right?"

"Aha. You?"

"Tight. It's very tight. Like a fist."

He falls forward onto my chest and wraps his arms about my neck. His skin is hot and he shivers against me, rolling his hips and chuckling into the pillow. "It's kind of weird. Right in my guts."

With some rearranging we clumsily roll over so that Adrian is on his back, and the backs of his knees are crooked into my elbows. I move slowly, carefully, pushing into him, trying to be gentle, but he looks scared. I ask him if I should stop, and he shakes his head and locks his hands tightly behind my neck.

Adrian sleeps with his back to me, strangely indifferent, his head resting on his arm. My lower back has started to ache, and I try not to shift around, try not to disturb him. The room is cold, and I draw the blankets up over us. He flinches as my hand brushes his shoulder.

"Are you all right?"

"Aha."

"I was thinking. There's no reason to stay in Chicago if you don't want to."

He mutters, "Aha," and tucks the covers about his neck.

The music from the bar has long since stopped, but the barking persists, dull, hollow, insistent coughs. I lay on my back, with my fist supporting my lower back, and my elbow resting in a damp patch. The sheets smell of washing powder, beer, and a more acid smell of sex.

I wake up to hear Adrian's voice outside. It is warm again and bright. The curtains and screen door are open onto the balcony. Adrian is sitting by the pool with his legs in the water, his trousers rolled up, and his shirt by his side. There is a small group about him. Men in jeans, with hats and no shirts, lounge beside the pool drinking beer. Buck stands slightly apart from the group, dressed in the same clothes that he wore last night, his long and lanky shadow reaching across the pool. The cooler is open and empty; crushed cans litter the flagstones beside their chairs. I look at my watch: it is nine-fifteen. Adrian has just finished telling them about the man we found by the roadside.

"No shit."

"Shit."

"That's the god-darned truth, all right," the men agree in unison.

My shirt smells of stale beer, and I return to the room to change. Adrian's clothes are scattered across the carpet. When I return to the balcony, less than five minutes later, the situation has drastically changed.

"Why don't you go right on ahead?" One of the cowboys stands with his back to the pool pointing at Adrian, his chest cocked out as a challenge. Adrian stands close to him, unbothered by his shouting.

"Go ahead," one of his friends encourages.

"Hold on." Buck steps between Adrian and the cowboy. "We need to make some rules here."

"We already did." Adrian sounds frustrated. "If I don't knock his hat off, then he can try to knock the hat off me."

"I'm not hitting any boy," the cowboy protests.

"I'm telling you, I'll knock your hat off," Adrian insists.

"Okay. Okay." Buck stands back, holding his hands up in surrender. "I'm with him, if he says he can do it."

The cowboy looks down at his feet, then shaking his head he spits onto the flagstones, "But I still say you can't."

"Will you do it?" Adrian asks.

The cowboy nods.

"Okay. Two of you take hold of his arms," Adrian instructs,

"and pull them out." Two of the cowboy's companions stand on either side of their friend, each take an arm and stretch him out between them. "And if you relax you won't feel a thing. Okay. Relax. Ready? Now breathe out."

The cowboy scornfully puffs out his cheeks as Adrian swings and punches him square in the chest. With a loud smack the man's head jolts sharply back, then forward. The hat flips up and falls behind him, landing beside the pool. The whole crew hoot and clap their hands, laughing as the cowboy rubs his chest.

"That's just weird," he laughs, and turns about to pick up his hat.

"Opie? Opie-boy? Are you hurt?" Laughing, Buck playfully wraps his arm about his friend's neck and ruffles his hair.

"Kinda knocks the wind out of you."

"Hey. Do it again." One of the cowboys holds Adrian's hand up. "Who's next?"

"Uh-uh. Not me." Opie steps back, and another cowboy steps forward, pulling his hat down firmly onto his head.

"Take a shot," he says, raising his arms up by his side for his friends to hold.

"Remember. Breathe out and relax. Ready?" Adrian instructs before he punches the man. Once again the man's head snaps back and the hat tumbles off, and once again the small crowd clap and laugh.

"Where in hell did you learn that?" The second cowboy reaches for his hat.

"I told you. I box." Adrian explains.

Buck doubles up laughing. "Well I guess we should have listened."

Opie reaches forward and shakes Adrian's hand. "We have to go now. Come on." One by one each man shakes the boy's hand, then walks about the pool toward the car park, each carrying his shirt or getting dressed. Adrian watches as they walk away, then looks up at the balcony.

"Did you see that?" he asks, squinting up at the balcony. "One of them was saying how he punches cows out. Knocks them out cold with his fist. I bet him that I could knock his hat off." He shields his eyes and smiles. "So how about some breakfast?"

Adrian returns to the room. "Ready to go?" he asks.

"Do you want to?" I ask.

"Sure. Just a minute though." He steps back into the corridor.

I fold up his clothes and pack them into his small kitbag. Checking the room one last time, I make sure that we have left nothing behind. As I lock the door I look up the corridor and see Adrian trying to force open another door.

"What are you doing?" I ask.

He steps away from the door.

"I just wanted to see what was in one of their rooms."

"Whose room?"

"One of those broncos."

"What for?"

"What for?" he replies, his hand dropping from the door handle. "For nothing. For a laugh. Just to have a look. Aren't you curious?" He leans against the doorjamb.

"How are you?"

"Fine."

"I mean about last night."

"Fine."

The road runs flat and straight, sectioned with barbed wire and wire fencing. Gates either side of the track are padlocked. The land is impoverished, almost barren, the grass so sparse that the powdery red earth can be seen between the dead yellow stalks. Tonight will be our last night in Wyoming, and we are heading toward a campsite near the Grand Tetons. Adrian asks if I am hungry, and we agree to stop. I pull over next to a new road sign saying POWDER RIVER. Beside the sign, new railings are the only other indication that there is a river here.

Adrian cuts the bread with his penknife on the car bonnet as I fetch the beers from the cool box. The cheese is a sickly white, the color of marzipan.

"How do you feel?" I ask.

"Fine. A little sore."

"You know, it won't always feel like that." I press up against him and kiss his neck.

Adrian nods and suggests a swim in the river. "Butt naked."

Thinking of an ice-cold mountain stream, I look down over the railings. The river bed is white and dry, a darker thin trail of mud slumps in its center. Fat and deep crazed cracks are baked into the bed. Branches washed down—who knows how long ago— poke up from mud baked into stone between the bridge's pylons.

"I wouldn't bank on that swim." I say.

Adrian hands me a sandwich and looks down over the parapet. "Jesus. They weren't kidding when they named this, were they?"

The riverbank is a steep and brittle shale. He takes a swig of his beer, rinses his mouth, and spits over the side. "Farther than you'd think. I guess it's nothing more than a runoff. Doesn't even look like it rains here."

There is a wasp's nest built of mud set in the crotch of a beam beneath the railing. The wasps are black, easily an inch long, with fine gangly legs. Adrian spits down on them.

"I watched this movie once where this guy was held down and fucked with a beer bottle." He grimaces and shakes his head. "I saw another where this guy had two pricks up him. I mean two pricks. One, two." He sticks his hands into his shorts and crudely rearranges himself. "It's funny. I can still feel it. That was your first time, wasn't it?"

"Was I that clumsy?" I ask.

Adrian shakes his head. "I thought it would hurt more." He leans against the railing with his hands in his pants, staring hard down at the riverbed, thinking. His mind somewhere else.

4

I watch as Adrian walks into the light. Tall pine trees line the river, stripped of branches and leaves for two-thirds of their length. The brittle sound of running water comes deceptively from the wind breaking through the trees, although there is a cold, fast-running brook through the center of the campsite. Behind him is a scrubby baseball diamond. Small, white-painted rocks set in the pine needles define the pitch. I am sitting at a picnic table; surrounding me are several wooden huts and vacant lots for campers. Except for one trailer parked behind the cabins, we are alone. Rocky hills rise on either side of us. It is noticeably cooler tonight.

Adrian sets a bottle down on the table. "Tequila," he says.

"How did you get that?"

"I brought it with me." He smiles, pulling one small thick shot glass from his pocket.

"All the way from Chicago?"

He twists off the top and fills the glass. "Here you go."

I swallow quickly and see stars up above us, many stars in a clear black sky.

"Look," I point up as Adrian takes the glass from my hand. "Just look at that sky."

Adrian looks up and stares silently for a while.

"I used to know what most of them were called. It's a little different here. Different from the sky I see at home, everything is turned about."

I watch his Adam's apple bob as he swallows. He sits opposite me, banging my knees.

"I know a game." Adrian places the shot glass between us and digs into his pocket for a coin. "Ever played this?"

I shake my head.

"It's really simple. It's called quarters. All you have to do is bounce the coin off the table and into the glass. If you get it in, then I have to drink a shot, and if I get it in, then you get the shot. Okay?"

"We just take turns?"

"There's a story that goes with it, but I forget how it goes. Usually there's more people and whoever gets the shot has to continue the story. Okay . . .," Adrian places the shot glass in the center of the table, and holding the coin between finger and thumb, he practices as if he were aiming to throw a dart. The coin spins up off the table and falls short of the glass.

"Aim about four inches in front. You can't just throw it in. It has to bounce." His finger taps the table several inches in front of the glass. "Aim here and look at the glass." He picks up the coin and passes it to me.

On my first attempt the coin rolls off the table. Adrian takes the coin again, and on his second attempt, the coin bounces and spins successfully into the glass. "Hah. Okay, okay." He claps his hands and opens the bottle, pouring me a shot with the quarter still in the glass. "Don't swallow the coin." He smiles. "And just make something up."

"There was a man," I hold up the glass, "an old, old man. A tattooist, who thought he was the luckiest man in the world. Not only was he famous, but his apprentice was the most handsome boy in the town." I swallow the shot. "How am I doing?"

"I think you have to take it further." Adrian folds his arms on the table.

"Well, this tattooist," I continue, "this famous tattooist was very much in love with his apprentice, but because of shyness, fear perhaps, he never expressed his love to the boy, and perhaps because of this he was also very possessive and jealous. The tattooist was often forced to travel for business, and of all of his possessions he was most concerned about a diamond, which he kept hidden in his bedroom in a closet. Now the whole town knew about the diamond, though nobody knew where it was hidden. Anyhow, every time the tattooist left on a trip he'd tell the boy to be careful not to let anybody into the house, most particularly, into his bedroom. So, one day, returning from one of his trips much earlier than he had expected, he discovers the boy in his bedroom. Is that far enough?"

Adrian takes the coin out of the glass and hands it to me. "You get to throw again."

"I think you should let me practice." I take the coin from his fingers. After three attempts it stands miraculously upright beside the glass.

Adrian pours another shot and pushes the glass across the table. "Usually you get an extra shot when you do that."

"So," I continue, "the tattooist returns home early to find his brother—who happens to be a jeweler—and the apprentice alone together in his bedroom. Believing that they are planning to steal his diamond, he hides behind a screen to watch. But the tattooist is mistaken. His brother, in fact, is propositioning the boy. The tattooist watches and listens as his brother promises the apprentice money, every kind of enticement, but it doesn't work, and the boy resists, until the jeweler tells the boy how good he is, how good he is in bed."

I push the shot glass still full of liquor back across the table. Adrian takes the glass and throws his head back, swallowing in one gulp.

"Anyhow," I continue, "the tattooist is trapped behind the screen and he can't do anything, except watch as his brother and boyfriend make love right in front of him. And his brother, as he had said, is very, very good."

Adrian fishes the coin from the glass. At his first attempt

it spins back easily into the glass. He fills it up and pushes it across the table to me, sucking the spilt liquor off of his thumb.

Copying Adrian I take the shot in one gulp. It is impossible not to grimace. "So, the tattooist watches the whole episode without being discovered. Once his brother has departed and the boy has fallen asleep, he sneaks out of the room and begins to plot his revenge. Jealous and angry, the tattooist creeps back to his workshop and begins to prepare a poisonous dye. Later that day, the boy goes to the tattooist's shop, and, although he is surprised to see him, he doesn't realize that the tattooist saw him in bed with his brother. So when the tattooist asks the boy to reach for a jar of pigment high on a shelf, he doesn't suspect a thing."

I turn the cup over.

"Take it a little further." Adrian smiles.

"So, when the boy reaches up the tattooist pricks him in the backside, poisoning him. As the boy tumbles from the chair onto the floor, the tattooist pretends that it was a scorpion, and points under the bookcase saying, 'Look, look, look. There it is.' Now, the poison doesn't kill the boy. It puts him into a deep sleep. And while he's asleep the tattooist scores his back in exactly the same way that you would score a rubber tree, bleeding the boy so that he becomes weak and sleeps. The boy sleeps for three whole days, during which the tattooist draws the most perfect, exquisite diamond in the pit of his back. Underneath it he writes a riddle about a treasure being sewn inside the boy's intestines. It takes about a week for the boy to recover, and, of course, he knows nothing about the tattoo. While he is convalescing, the tattooist tells him that he will be leaving town again, and that he should not go into his bedroom. One week later the tattooist's brother returns."

Again we take turns with the coin. On the third round the coin knocks against the glass and Adrian concedes. After drinking his shot he grimaces, "This is really foul," and takes up the story. "But this time the tattooist is watching on purpose. He's hiding in the closet so he can see everything. They get down to it pretty fast, and as the brother is plowing the apprentice he sees this tattoo. What's this? he thinks, so he asks the boy. 'What's this about a diamond?' And the boy says, 'What diamond?' The brother thinks that he's just being smart, so he plows harder and harder and asks, 'Is this how I get to the treasure?' and the boy's screaming 'Yes, yes, yes,' out of his mind. The jeweler is still hiding in the closet. Anyway, the brother is getting nowhere so he decides to stick his hand in to see if he can find the diamond, and meanwhile the apprentice is going wild. But, anyway, of course, the brother doesn't find a thing and he starts threatening the boy, saying things like he's going to kill him."

"How long does this go on?" I ask.

"Till the bottle's dry."

Once again I win the toss and Adrian takes the shot. He slams the glass down, "Man, this burns," and vigorously shakes his head. "So, anyway, the boy doesn't have a clue. And he's really sore. And the tattooist thinks, well, that's that. He learned his lesson. Oh yeah, and the brother, the brother's long gone. He's pissed, he's out of there. So a rumor spreads around town about this boy having a diamond up his ass. And everyone is making a pass, even straight guys, so pretty soon he can't leave the house. One night the tattooist's cousin arrives and he sneaks into the boy's room, and he's sweet and nice and makes like he really likes him. Now he's big, really big, and uncut, and the apprentice can't resist him. And when the cousin gets going the boy thinks he's going to split in two, it's so huge. The tattooist is asleep in the other room, and when he hears all the commotion and banging around, he sneaks into the room and hides. Same thing as before. The cousin finds nothing, and the boy is half dead. But he still doesn't really know what's going on. So the tattooist thinks that the boy has learned his lesson and things cool down for a while, until one night, about a month later, three sailors come into town. These sailors were sent by the brother and the cousin to find the diamond, and they break into the house and sneak into the boy's bedroom and tie him down. They take turns all through the night trying to fuck the jewel from the boy's asshole. Finally, early morning, sun's coming up, and one of the sailors collapses on the bed, and says outright that he doesn't think that they will ever get the jewel out unless they cut the boy up."

Adrian turns over the glass and drops the coin into it and pours a shot. "Your turn or I'll puke."

"The boy is confused about what the sailor has said, so he questions him." I pick up the glass. "And he soon learns about the tattooist's hoax. Instead, he tells them that the tattoo was a diversion of sorts, and that the tattooist in fact conceals his diamonds in his own mouth, and that there are a number of diamonds cunningly concealed in the tattooist's gold teeth. Now the tattooist had watched the whole thing as usual from the boy's wardrobe, but being an old man he had fallen asleep and missed the sailor's revelation. And just as the boy and the sailors are sneaking out of the room to search for the old man's diamond, the boy hears the tattooist snoring."

"So he knows it's the old man?" Adrian interrupts.

"Yes," I continue. "And the boy shouts, 'There's a snake in the wardrobe. There's a snake in the wardrobe.'"

"So the tattooist wakes up," Adrian breaks in, "and realizes that he has been discovered, and he swallows the diamond to prevent the sailors from stealing it."

"And he's too nervous—"

"Or greedy—"

"To leave it lying about the house—"

"In a safe—"

"Or a safety-deposit box—"

Adrian clumsily pours himself a drink and hands me the bottle. We toast each other. "So the tattooist sneaks a look through the keyhole to see what's going on," I continue.

"But one of the sailors has a knife, and the old man is so frightened—"

"That a tear trickles through the keyhole," I whisper.

"And thinking that this is the venom from the snake, the sailor stabs his knife into the keyhole."

"The doors burst open."

"The tattooist falls flat out on the floor. And he pukes up the diamond."

With the curtains drawn, the darkness is absolute. The cabin smells of tobacco and old wood. The mattress reeks of old feathers, old sweat, dust. The wind in the trees echoes deceptively as if we were in a cavern. I sleep uneasily, aware of Adrian stirring fitfully on the cot beside me.

There are two small separate beds. Adrian had fallen asleep, fully clothed, as I was outside using the campsite's meager bathroom and shower. Not wanting to wake him, I left him clothed and sleeping, and took the second bed.

"Are you awake?" he asks in a soft, uncertain voice.

"I thought you were asleep."

"No. Maybe we should open a window or something." I listen to the sounds of him sitting up, the creak of the bed, covers being pulled back. "It stinks in here." He sounds tired. "I wonder what's happening in Chicago right now?"

"Everyone will be asleep."

"What time is it in England?" He speaks slowly, as if perhaps he is not awake at all.

"I don't know. But they're six or seven hours ahead. So they'll be up. Probably halfway through their day already."

"Yeah. Probably. Do you think we should go back?"

"To Chicago?"

"No. To see that cowboy."

"Why?"

"Maybe you're right." He coughs and becomes silent

again. The wind whistles under the door and the covers seem too thin. "When was the first time you saw see me?" he asks.

"I don't remember exactly."

"Honest?" The bed springs squeak as he turns over. "I followed you once," he pauses, as if wondering whether to tell me. "All the way to your room."

"When was that?"

"After you came to the restaurant. So what got you interested?"

"That wink. You winked at me. And then seeing you outside of the hotel."

Adrian laughs, causing his bed to shake. The room is suddenly quiet.

"Are you still awake?" I ask.

"Yeah."

"Ten places. Play ten places."

"Ten places where?"

"Name ten places in England that we both know."

"Okay."

"King's Lynn."

"Never heard of it," he replies.

"Grantham."

"No."

"Staines."

"No."

"Leeds."

"No."

"I thought you'd spent some time in England."

"Only in London," he replies.

"Name the borough."

"Easy. Clapham, Brixton, Camberwell, Peckham Rye, New Cross, Deptford, Lewisham." He reels off the names, describing a sweep across London as if he were reciting the states across the forty-ninth parallel.

"How do you know those places?"

"I stayed with my sister in South London, after she got married." Even in the darkness I can tell that he is smiling. "They used to live in Clapham, then they moved to Peckham."

Again we become silent.

"So who was the first person you fucked?" Adrian asks.

"The first? It was a woman actually."

"You dated women?"

"For a while, yes. And you?"

The boy pauses and asks cautiously, "You're not married, are you?"

I can't help but laugh. "No. I never even came close."

I listen as Adrian settles into his bed. "If you could choose, which would you be? Queer or straight?"

"I don't have the choice," I reply.

"No." He huffs, dissatisfied, doubtful. "If you could, what would you choose?"

"I can't imagine the choice. Not anymore. Not now."

Outside the wind has quietened down. I reach across to Adrian's cot and feel nothing, the gap between our beds is too wide.

"My cousin was the first. He's older than me. He, you know . . ."

"How old were you?" I ask.

"I was ten I think, ten the first time. Every time he visited he stayed in my room. So it went on for a while. I think they know, but then they don't."

"Who?"

"My parents. When I got older we did more stuff, and that was kind of weird too. He still expects something when I see him. So who was your first man?"

"It was about five years ago. Odd things had happened before, nothing to speak of. I didn't think that men liked me very much. I thought I was the wrong type. But it was a man on a train.

Going from London to Oxford. Nothing happened on the train, but he found out where I was staying, and he came over."

"Did you like him?"

"He's married now. It wasn't much. I felt ashamed at the time. Degraded. And yes, I liked him very much."

"Did you see him again?" he asks.

"I saw him, but it was only the once, that one time that we slept together. It was a long time ago."

Once again we fall silent.

"What about your parents?" I ask.

"What about them?" Adrian pauses.

"Don't they worry about you?"

"You saw where I was staying," he replies. "The farther away I am from my family the better."

I wake up before Adrian and watch him as he sleeps. He is fully dressed and lies on his stomach with his hands tucked uncomfortably beneath him. He sleeps with his mouth open. His hair, as short as it is, is disheveled.

As I sit up the bed creaks, waking the boy. He turns over and looks at his shoes, puzzled.

"How did you sleep?" I ask.

"Terrible. Felt like I didn't sleep at all."

"What's wrong?" I sit beside him and run my hand up under his T-shirt.

Adrian sits up on his elbows. "Bed's too short." He pulls a face and drops back onto the pillow, his head hitting the wood paneling. I unbuckle his belt. "Room service isn't bad though." His clothes smell musty. I trace a blue vein running down from his abdomen to his crotch.

"Am I tickling?"

"Uh-uh." He rubs his eyes. "Have you ever done anything you regret?"

I think for a while. "Not really. Nothing serious. Why?"

Adrian sits upright, setting his chin against my neck. "You like this, don't you." He scratches the small patch of stubble under his lip against my neck, giving me goose bumps.

"And what do you like?"

"Breakfast," he chuckles. "Unless you're worried about too much protein."

5

Adrian is asleep through most of the drive back. It is difficult to return, difficult not knowing exactly what we are returning to. My excitement at having the boy live with me is edged with dread. Despite moments of genuine tenderness between us, it's my money that keeps him with me.

"How long do you think it will take?" He stirs and sits upright, scratching his head with both hands. "To get your money, straighten everything out?"

"A week," I say. "A week to ten days. They have to open a new account, and transfer the money. I don't know how long these things take here."

Adrian looks hard out at road, frowning.

"Have you thought of where you want to go?"

"That man," he says, ignoring my question, "the guy on the train, remember. How long ago was it?"

"Five years. Six years. Seven years."

"And he was married?"

"I suppose he was engaged at the time; but yes, later he married."

Adrian turns to face me. "What was his name?"

I point at a service sign and ask if he is hungry, if we should stop. Adrian shakes his head asks me a second time. "What was the man's name?"

"It was a long, long time ago. His name was Robert. Rob. Before I moved to London I lived in Oxford, just outside in a small village. I shared a house, a small cottage with my sister, and two or three times a week I would commute up to London. I'd seen him before, noticed him, usually on the train coming back. We never spoke. I was spending more and more time in London and had decided to move, so I was looking for a place. Anyhow, one Friday, my sister had guests and wasn't expecting me. I was late, it was the last train. There weren't many people on it. In the compartment there was only Robert and me. He sat opposite and was watching me for the whole journey. I think he had been drinking. When the conductor came he didn't have a ticket, so I gave him the fare. He promised he'd pay me back."

The sky is a sickly yellow, clear on the horizon.

"I said it was all right, that it didn't matter, that the next time he saw me he could buy me a drink on the train. You can buy alcohol on British trains."

"Did he?"

"No, actually, he never did, not on the train. In fact when we arrived at Oxford he was behind me, following me out of the station down onto the street. I asked him if he needed money for a taxi. He said he was fine, that he was happy to walk, and I asked him if he would like to come for a drink. We went to the White Hart. It's close to the station, but we had missed last orders and they wouldn't serve us. I thought that was it. Since my sister was having a party, and I was tired, I decided to take a room for the night. He came round several hours later with a small bottle of Scotch. He said that he wanted to thank me, and offered to pay for the train. We drank it sitting on the bed. He was there for less than an hour."

Adrian sits watching me, turned awkwardly in his seat.

"I'm not certain that he really liked men that much. And I'm not certain why he came round. I think he knew I liked him. After that I didn't see him for a while. Every time I traveled to Oxford I would wait at the station just in case he might turn up. Finally I did meet him. It was after I'd moved up to London. I was visiting Kate, and he was on the train. After that we met a number of times in London, though we were never intimate again. I loaned him money, and sometimes he would stay over. He would disappear for weeks, months, and then I'd get a call, and we'd meet at a pub, or he'd come over. He was careful for me not to see any of his friends, anyone he knew. Actually, I did meet a friend of his once, when we were drinking; and after he disappeared the last time, his friend told me that he was married. He called me up, left me a message. I think Robert wanted me to know but didn't have the heart to tell me. Up until then I'd always hoped that perhaps something would happen between us. It was so long ago, it seems irrelevant now, but at the time it was very difficult."

"You know what?" Adrian stirs, and sits upright. "I left some stuff at my parents' I'd like to pick up." His hands slowly rub his thighs as if he is cold.

"Where do they live?" I ask.

"Glenwood. Where are we now?"

"We'll be in Chicago in about an hour."

"I'll tell you when we get closer." He sinks back into his seat, and tucking his legs beneath him, settles down to sleep.

The city rises from the plains. Visible from some thirty miles away, until it becomes lost, swallowed by train lines, expressways, and tract upon tract of orderly suburban bungalows. I wake Adrian at the last tollbooth.

"Which route should I take?"

"Stay right." He yawns and leans forward on the dashboard. "Follow the signs for Milwaukee. You want Lake County Road."

Half an hour north of Chicago, the city center is lost and the suburbs blend gently together. The farther we drive—past Evanston, Winnetka, and Lake Forest—the parcels of land become progressively larger, and the houses more elegant.

"How long have you lived up here?" I ask.

"Forever. Take a left." Adrian sits forward, almost hiding

behind the dashboard, and smirks up at me. "Don't drive too slow," he warns. "The neighbors will call the police." The road backs away from the lake toward a small grouping of houses. "Look over there." He points to the crossroad. "See the squad car? They're always there. See that house?"

"Which house?"

He points vaguely toward the estate. "A woman was murdered there about fifteen years ago. The Great Lakes Naval Base is about twenty miles up the road. Her husband walked in on her and some cadet, shot them both and then himself. Okay, turn here. The one on the left."

The house is one of three set at the end of a cul-de-sac. Adrian looks carefully about and sinks back deep into his seat. "If I see one of my parents' cars, get ready to turn around."

The driveways to all three houses are empty. "That's good. Here is good." He bites his lower lip. "You should check it out."

"What if someone answers?" I protest. "What am I going to say?"

"You'll think of something."

As I walk up the driveway, Adrian opens the car door and hoarsely whispers, "Whatever you do, don't pretend you're a salesman. They'll call the police."

The house is pretty, two-storied and wide, built of red brick with small shuttered windows. A tall, bushy, variegated privet hedge sweeps away from the drive and about the garden. To my left is a garage built to resemble a dovecote, topped with a delicately detailed weathervane of a racing horse. The garage is large enough to fit two cars. To my right is a swimming pool sheltered by the hedge. The path is wet, the plants have been watered this morning. I am worried that someone is at home.

I ring the doorbell and turn back to the car, but it appears empty. "Hello?" I call and ring a second time, wondering if Adrian is hiding behind the seat, when I hear someone inside the house.

The door is opened wide, and to my relief it is a maid, a

Mexican woman, clearly not Adrian's mother, who has answered. The woman is young and short, her dark hair tied back by a plain yellow scarf. She is wearing a blue pinafore and carpet slippers.

"Hello, I'm looking for Adrian." I point over her shoulder, into the house.

The maid shakes her head. She does not understand me.

"Are his parents in? Are either of the doctors?"

The maid looks down at the steps. She is puzzled. "Doctor? No doctor?" Her hand plays with the back of her scarf. "Adrian? No." She shakes her head and begins to close the door, then suddenly brightening, she smiles and points across the way, perhaps at the car. "Adrian," she smiles and nods, then politely cocks her head and firmly closes the door.

I return to the car, much relieved. "You can go in. I think she saw you anyway." I call to the car. I stand by the door and look back up the cul-de-sac. Adrian is not in the car. A small toy truck is thrown at my feet, a blue Dinky van, hitting the pavement with a snap. Looking back at the house, I see Adrian leaning from one of the upper windows, pointing frantically to the side of the house.

Checking that the maid is not watching, and that there is no one else about, I sneak alongside the hedge. There is a break in the hedge beside the swimming pool. There is an open door at the side of the house. By the time I have sneaked through the hedge, Adrian is standing in the doorway, impatiently waving me toward him.

"How did you get in there?" I whisper across the paved side of the swimming pool.

"It was open already."

"But this is breaking and entering."

"Only if we get caught," he grins. "Now come on."

Worried that I can be seen from other windows in the house, I hurry into the doorway. Adrian pulls me inside and carefully closes the door behind me. "What would you be doing now?" he asks.

"What do you mean?"

"In England. What would you be doing now?"

I stand lost in the doorway, puzzled, unable to answer.

Adrian grabs my arm and hurries me farther into the house. "Quick. Up the stairs. I need a hand with some of my stuff." He explains. "Come on. It's all right."

"Why don't you just tell the maid what you're doing?"

"Because she'll tell my parents. And I don't want them to know that I was here."

"Won't they notice that some of your things are missing?"

"They won't notice a thing. Now come on." Adrian tiptoes along the corridor. His shoes squeak on the waxed floor. Turning about he presses his fingers to his lips and sniggers, then points to the end of the corridor. "We're in luck. She's watching TV in the kitchen." Sure enough the thin tinny sound of a television carries down the hall. "Come on." Adrian disappears around the corner, and I am obliged to follow him. Taking the stairs two at a time, he walks sideways, crablike, hugging the walls. "Hurry. She's in the kitchen." He walks along the hallway on the upper landing, opening the doors to each room.

"What are you doing?"

"In here."

"What's this?" I ask, following him into the room. Adrian closes the door behind me to a crack. I am standing in a bedroom, large and sparse, with a balcony overlooking the garden. The mauve carpet is evenly tracked with lines of the vacuum cleaner. Either side of the bed is an open doorway leading to a dressing room.

"How about this?" Adrian stands beside the bed and pokes at the wall above the headboard. The walls are coated with cloth, perhaps silk, and padded with a hand-painted trim of vines, leaves, and birds along the skirting board. "I wanted to show you this." There is a photograph on a wooden stand beside the bed. Beside the photograph is a set of clip-on earrings studded with pearls.

"Your parents?" I ask. Adrian smiles. "They're much younger than I thought. Now, let's get out of here."

Adrian sits back on the bed. "Come on then." He opens his arms.

"Come on then what?"

"Let's fuck." He smiles broadly and leans back on his elbows, sinking into the duvet. I stand motionless in front of him. Sitting upright the boy unbuckles his shorts. "Come on. She'll never hear, she's watching *The Young and the Restless* for Christ's sake."

"No."

"Why not?"

"This is your parents' room."

"That's the whole point," he replies tersely. "Come here."

I approach the bed, and he wraps his arms about my waist.

"We might not have the chance again." He rubs his hand crudely between my legs.

I lean forward over the boy. "What if she comes in? What if we get caught?"

"She won't. I'm telling you." He squeezes softly, then quickly opens my trousers and unbuttons my fly. "See. You can't say no." Adrian shuffles back onto the bed and shucks off his shorts. I kneel on my hands and knees, reaching across the bed for his shorts. Adrian lies on his back and crudely raises his legs, so that his elbows are tucked under his knees and his knees are level with his chin.

"No." I kiss him. "Absolutely not." I kiss him again. He grimaces as I lay on top of him and folds his legs about my hips, pulling me tightly down on top of him. "No," I say.

"Do you like me?" he asks.

"I like you very much."

"Then let's fuck. Come on."

"No. Get dressed and get your things."

"What things?" He releases his grip.

"Your things. The things we came here for." I push myself free from him.

"That would be a little difficult. We're in the wrong house. Remember the woman who was caught with the sailor?"

"What are you talking about?" I am sitting upright, buttoning my trousers.

"Well," Adrian sits up on his elbows, "this would be that house. And this is where he shot her." He points his fingers like a gun into the small of my back.

I am forcing the wrong button through the wrong hole, puzzled at both the boy and my trousers.

"I don't live here. Never have. We live next door." He falls back on to the bed again and laughs. "I can't find my pants."

"Whose house is this then?"

"I don't know. I used to go to school with someone who lived here. But they moved out a couple of years ago." He begins to laugh. "How do you like these earrings?" He holds up the pearl earrings to his ears. "What do you think?"

I stand beside the door, peering out into the corridor. "This is a terrible thing. What will happen if she catches us?" Adrian stands close behind me.

"She's probably still watching TV." He pushes by me and walks boldly down the steps. I follow carefully behind. The television is still on in the kitchen.

As we sneak down the corridor, with the outside door just in view, a toilet flushes in a room ahead of us. Adrian breaks into a run, his shoes squeaking as he sprints. I reach the door just in time to prevent it from slamming shut, and as the toilet door is unlocked I step quickly outside, carefully closing the door behind me. Adrian squats behind the hedge, laughing into his hands. He motions for me to stay where I am. The maid walks up to the door. I cannot see her, but from Adrian's gestures I guess that she is standing close behind the door, looking out at the pool. And for one long delicious moment I want to laugh, and laugh loudly, until the woman steps away back into the house, and the moment is lost. Adrian waves his hands, beckoning me out. The coast is clear, and we run along the hedgerow arm in arm, barely able to contain our laughter.

6

Adrian comes out with some fairly stupid things. This morning I find him stretching his mouth in front of the bedroom mirror, waggling his tongue, looking for mouth ulcers. I ask him what is wrong. He says that he thinks he has trench mouth. I begin to wash as he continues his search. I ask him if he thinks he has much longer.

"Much longer what?" he replies, pulling at his mouth.

"Many more days. How much longer do you think you'll live?"

Adrian ignores me.

"I was making a joke," I say.

"Very funny," he replies.

I walk through the bedroom, drying my face with a hand towel. He sits on my pressed white shirt, and with both hands grubs through his pubes, inspecting himself.

"If you're that worried, I could cut it out here and now," I offer.

"I said it isn't funny," he argues, and calling me to the bed, he opens his mouth as wide as he can and sticks out his tongue for me to inspect. There is a small, sensitive rash running along the side of his tongue.

"You have bitten yourself."

He shakes his head. He can't remember when.

"Then it must have been in your sleep. What else could it be?"

Adrian half rises so that I can pull the shirt out from under him, and sits back down upon my tie. Yesterday, except for his morning and evening exercises, he lounged all day on the bed, watching TV and reading magazines, wearing only a waistcoat from one of my suits and a pair of y-fronts. There has been no talk of Bruno, and no talk of returning to either the café or the gym.

"Aren't you going to dress today?" I ask.

"No thanks." He turns onto his stomach, and lying on his arms he pushes his hands into his underpants. With his chin tucked into his shoulder, he watches me as I dress. I zip the tie out from under him.

"The bed needs to be changed." I reply.

"What are you going out for?" he asks, smiling. "Why don't you stay here?"

"I'll be back in an hour," I say, kissing him on the nape of his neck, "probably before you are dressed."

I return later than I had promised. Adrian stirs, cuddling the pillow; my notes and books lay spread about the bed. I sit beside him and place a gift between us, certain that he is not asleep. Rousing himself he yawns, exhaling hard. Curling about the package he begins to unwrap it, picking delicately at the tape. I have bought him a Polaroid camera and several packets of film. As he unwraps the gift, I talk about the new fence that has gone up around the station house. "It looks like they're going to knock it down," I explain, but he is not listening. An atlas, open at Brazil, lies on the floor close to the bed. "What are you reading?"I ask.

"Nothing special." He holds up the camera, and I lie down on the bed beside him.

"Brazil?"

"It was just something that was on TV."

"You didn't get dressed?" I lift up the covers. He is still only wearing his underpants.

"I used to have one of these," he smiles, "years ago," and snaps open the camera and stares at the ceiling through the viewfinder. "Neat. Thanks. What's the occasion?"

I point down at my briefcase. "This is it. My money. It came through today."

"Already? You said it would take ten days." Suddenly animated, he sits up and resting the camera on my chest, he leans across my stomach. "How much?"

I hold my fingers up one by one, letting him count.

"Fifteen? Fifteen what? Hundred?"

I shake my head.

"Thousand?" He reaches over me for the briefcase and pulls it onto the bed. I turn the case about for him and snap the clips back. The money is in a small manila envelope.

"Doesn't look like much, does it?" Adrian weighs the package in his hands. "Did you count it all?" He opens the envelope and takes out a bound stack of money. "How much is this? Five thousand?" He rests back on the bed, running his thumb through the crisp hundred-dollar bills. "Is this everything?" he asks. "Is this all of your savings?"

"It's what I can get my hands on right now."

"So this is everything you have?" Adrian frowns. He sits back up and quickly returns the money to the envelope, placing it carefully back inside the briefcase.

"What's the matter?" I ask.

"You shouldn't have brought it here."

"No one will know." I laugh.

"No one has to. It just means trouble." He is in earnest. "This isn't a good place to have fifteen thousand dollars stuffed in your sock drawer."

I take the envelope out and tip the three blocks of money out onto my stomach. I snap open one of the bands, and the flat, stiff, impeccably clean stack of one hundred-dollar notes fans out, spilling across the bed.

"No, I'm serious." Adrian sits upright and gathers up the money.

I take hold of his hands. "It's for us, for our holiday."

"I can't use this. It's yours."

"Don't you want to leave Chicago?"

"I said I can't use this."

The boy slides off the bed and stands beside the curtain, looking down at the station house.

"I don't understand."

Adrian turns from the window and shakes his head.

"This money," I pick up a bound stack, "is for our holiday. That's what I saved it for, for something like this." I begin to laugh. Adrian looks puzzled. "This is for that rainy day."

He sits back down onto the bed and looks at the briefcase. "I don't believe it," he mutters. "And I still think you're stupid to keep it here."

On Adrian's insistence I have cleared the money away. We have been talking about places to go, and he is in a considerably lighter mood.

"So if this is Chicago," he points at my ear, "then this," he runs his hand down my front to my crotch, "is the Panama Canal." He laughs and tugs back the covers and rolls on top of me sitting upright across my hips, his legs straddling my thighs. As he laughs he rocks gently back and forward, shaking the bed.

"My back. Watch my back." I shuffle forward under his weight until my head is supported by the bedstead.

"Come on, take a picture." He places the camera into my hands.

Bracing his arms like a strongman and puckering his mouth, he strikes poses; pointing to parts of his body, he names distant cities and countries. The room is dark except for a brilliant ginger strip of late afternoon sun across the wall, reflected by the mirror onto the floor. His skin is pale, light, almost made of light, fluorescent.

I place each picture on the carpet and wait for them to develop. Adrian kneels on the bed beside me. "Look at that," he laughs. In one photograph he has his knees up tight to his shoulders; his fingers point at the small tight walnut of his asshole. He is laughing as hard as can be imagined. "Boy-pussy," he sniggers as he skips off the bed and into the bathroom.

I sit up wondering if I can trust the valet to have my suit pressed. Photographs lie scattered about my feet. The bathroom door is open, and Adrian stares at himself in the bathroom mirror, unaware that I am watching. His expression is almost hostile. With a shudder he brings himself out of his daydream, checks his mouth and searches the bathroom cabinet for the mouth-wash, which he brings with him to the bed. I motion for him to come and sit with me.

"It's all right," I reassure him. "It's perfectly safe. We don't need this." I place the bottle on the floor.

Adrian stands beside the bed, ready to disagree.

"It's perfectly safe," I insist. "You're the only person I've ever done this with."

He straddles my lap for a second time and unbuttons my shirt. I cradle his head into my shoulder, cup my hands about his back, and whisper into his ear. "We should celebrate somewhere nice this evening."

Adrian bends toward the mirror, stretching out his tongue, squinting into the cold fluorescent light. The sharp light throws a shadow across his cheek, making his nose appear to be crooked. I ask him what is wrong.

He steps back and replies flatly, "Nothing."

"Then can I shave? What's all this hair in the sink?" I step about him to get to the sink. There are small dark hairs tufted in the drain.

"I shaved my armpit." Adrian holds up his right arm and stares at his armpit in the mirror, stroking his hand over the uneven stubble.

"You shaved only one armpit?" I pull the hairs from the

drain. "Don't do this, please don't leave hairs in the sink. Did you use my last razor?"

He tuts under his breath and marches out of the bathroom. I hear him turn on the TV and jump on the bed. I find my razor in the litter matted with hair.

"It's just that it's my last razor. That's all. And why are you shaving your armpit?" There is no reply. I peep about the bathroom door. Adrian is sitting on the bed with his back to the wall, his legs spread wide. A long red cord stretches across the bed, just touching the floor. As he watches television he binds his hands, wrapping the cotton tape tight about his fists. Flexing his hand he fidgets with the band, ensuring that the wrapping is neat. I repeat the question and walk over to the bed. "What is the matter?"

"Nothing," he smiles at the tape woven about both hands and raises his fists to his face. "Nothing. Everything is just fine."

"Hurry up and get dressed, or we won't be able to get a table." I squeeze his foot. "Unless you want to go somewhere different?"

Adrian drops his fists and shakes his head. "I'm not hungry." Binding his red hands behind his head, he settles onto his back, his legs spread wide, and looks into my eyes. Switching focus from one eye to the other he winks at me. "Where did you get that money from?" he asks quietly, one eye open, one eye closed. I stand at the end of the bed, and he repeats the question. "I'm serious. Where's the money from?"

"I've told you. It's from my savings."

"So when it's gone, that's it then?"

I laugh holding the razor in my hand. "Then? What do you mean then?"

Adrian shrugs as if the question were obvious enough.

"I suppose that when the time comes, I'll have to get more."

"That wasn't what I was asking." He crosses and uncrosses

his legs. "What will you do after that? What will you do when all of the money is gone?"

It is dark outside. The boy's reflection is held in the window above the lake and the station house, porcelain pale. I do not have an answer. My hands hover uselessly above him. This is the first time that we have had to consider anything beyond the next couple of months. "No. No." I assure him. "It isn't like that at all. I don't have a plan for anything. Nothing is planned. If we need more money, then one way or another I will get some. This is what I could get immediately, but it isn't everything. I have the means to stay here for a very long time."

Adrian half closes his eyes and squints at his feet.

"Tell me what you want." I ask, shaking his feet. "What do you want me to do? What do you want to do?"

He swings his feet away and suddenly rises, sitting upright with his back to me. "I just don't want to be here." He stands up in front of the window and looks down at the street. "That's it, that's all I want."

The waiter takes the menus from our hands, and we both watch him walk away across the restaurant. Adrian looks at the door, and drums his fingers on the tablecloth.

"You know. We don't have to eat. We could go straight back."

He shakes his head. "It's all right. You eat. I'm not hungry." He turns his chair so that he can watch the other diners. The sides of his neck are blotched red, he is still irritated. "We're being watched. That couple," he nods, indicating a table to my left. "See. Now the guy's taking a good look. Don't look."

I straighten the silverware in front of me.

Adrian frowns, then leans forward. "I was reading about these military camps in Utah where they're planning to keep people with AIDS, like prisoners. So everyone will have to take a test, and if you're positive you'll be taken to one of these camps."

He pauses, flipping his spoon over between his thumb and forefinger. He stops and stares at his reflection. "Uh-oh, she's staring again."

I turn about too soon and catch the woman's eyes. She looks quickly away, a harsh expression of disgust is fixed on her face. Adrian laughs openly.

"You don't know them, do you?"

He shakes his head. "It's the same thing in Cuba." He stops talking as the busboy refills his water glass. "Except they're already doing it."

I look over my shoulder again. The couple have been served but both are poised, cutlery in hand, and stare down at their plates as if the food were rotten or tainted. The woman shakes her head, clearly upset, and I catch a second quick look.

"I think my mother has hired a detective." Adrian tugs my shirt cuff for attention. "He's been outside the hotel for the past couple of days."

"Whatever for?" I ask.

"Either my mother or my brother-in-law." He lines up his unused cutlery, and points from the knife to the fork to the spoon. "My parents kicked me out and then I lived with my sister, and then she kicked me out, and I never told them where I was or what I was doing or anything."

"Why?"

"I was seeing someone my parents didn't like. And my sister's crazy." He waves his hand behind his head.

"But how do you know that they're looking for you? I thought they didn't care about what you do?"

Adrian frowns as if I have said something very stupid. "They don't care," he replies scornfully. "It doesn't have anything to do with caring."

"Why wouldn't they search for you themselves?" I ask.

Adrian purses his lips and then replies, "That note. Before Wyoming, remember that note when we picked up my stuff? It was from the hospital my brother-in-law works for. I know he's looking for me."

There is a small commotion behind us as the couple summon the maître d'. The plates are swiftly removed, the table is cleared, and trouble is avoided, but the eyes of the whole restaurant are upon them. As the woman leaves she walks a longer route than necessary, deliberately avoiding our table.

By the time I am out of the bathroom Adrian is already asleep, outstretched naked on the bed. He wakes as I prepare for bed. The soft bathroom light falls square across his calves, thighs, and buttocks. Plumping up his pillow, he watches and smiles as I undress. For the first time since he moved in I am embarrassed to be naked. From outside comes the sharp hoot and holler of a fire engine.

"What's the noise?" he asks.

I stand in front of the window, drawing the curtain about my waist, and watch the boy's reflection as he climbs under the covers. The street is empty. "It must have been heading somewhere else." I close the curtains and step quickly back into the room toward the bed. "There was an accident in front of the hotel yesterday." I explain as he draws the blanket up to his chin. "I couldn't quite tell what had happened. The car was on the pavement, blocking the garage entrance." I draw a diagram in the air with one hand as the car, and the other as the hotel. "I've never seen so many firemen. One of them had on gloves. Rubber gloves."

"That would have been the paramedic."

"Oh. I don't think anyone was hurt."

"Two people were killed," he leans up on his elbows. "I saw it on the news."

Bending at the end of the bed, I catch my reflection in the mirror. With my hair tufted up, my head appears out of proportion, huge—skinny arms, skinny legs, round back, and shoulders. I look like something pulled from the ground. I look like a long, flaccid, lanky old parsnip. I untuck the sheets and crawl beside the boy, climbing between his legs.

When I wake Adrian is already up, kneeling on the carpet by the window with an atlas on his lap. His towel is folded by the curtain, he has not exercised. Except for last night's meal, it has been three days since he has left the hotel.

"Morning." He smiles and rolls his shoulder, keeping his head angled as if his neck were stiff. "I couldn't sleep. Look. I bought you a coffee."

"What's wrong with your shoulder?" I ask.

He shakes his head. "Nothing. I'm fine." He pushes the atlas onto the floor and looks out the window. "They've started tearing down the station already. They started at about six this morning."

I stand beside the bed. A gate has been opened into the new fence between the hotel and the station, a small white boxed portable office and a row of yellow port-o-toilets face the facade. Already the station yard is a different place. The gravel wasteland is churned up, the dirt tracked and black. There is a large orange crane nestled in the bays between platforms. The crane unloads sections of itself or of a larger crane from a flatbed, and lays the metal sections on the concrete platforms. The sound is muted and delayed, deadened by the distance and the glass to a soft dull blow. At the front of the station in place of the prostitutes are workmen in yellow hard hats and black-and-orange jackets.

"I had an idea this morning," Adrian leans forward over the map, "we could drive to Brazil." He pauses briefly. "I've checked it out. We drive from Chicago to Memphis." He tilts the page so that I can see, and traces a route down through Illinois. "Then from Memphis to Baton Rouge and take Route 10 across Louisiana all the way to Houston." He looks up from the page. "Route 10 runs on pylons through the bayou. From Houston we go to San Antonio. Then from San Antonio to Mexico at Nuevo

Laredo, then Monterey, Ciudad Victoria, Tampico, Mexico City, Oaxaca, Guatemala, Santa Ana, San Salvador, San Miguel, Managua, San Jose, Panama. And then, if we want, take a boat to Buenaventura. Then we're in Brazil. You can drive the whole way. Pretty much." He closes the book with a snap, and then opens the cover to a smaller map and turns the book about; North America on the top page, and South America on the bottom. "There are two possible routes. Illinois, Mississippi, Louisiana, Texas, Mexico, Guatemala, El Salvador, Nicaragua, Costa Rica, Panama, Colombia, Ecuador, Peru, Brazil." His finger strikes the page, punctuating each word, plotting the route. "Or Illinois, Missouri, Arkansas, Texas, Mexico, Belize, Honduras, Nicaragua, Costa Rica, Panama, Colombia, Brazil. Either way."

"Why Brazil?" I ask, sitting back down upon the bed, pulling my dressing gown closed over my thighs. "Why not China or India?"

Adrian shrugs. "Because you can't drive to China."

I pick up the atlas. Adrian has drawn thick lines over the potential routes to Brazil. Written in the margin in pencil, in his handwriting, is a note, "San Antonio—24th."

"In the rain forest," he leans forward, digging a finger into the carpet, "for every pound of human flesh, there are three hundred pounds of insects."

7

Adrian sends me out in the morning to buy books about Brazil, explaining that he feels under the weather. I return with four books, one *A Modern History of Cyprus*, written by my sister. As I open the door Adrian starts shouting for me. "Come here," he says. "Here. I'm in the bathroom."

I hurry into the bathroom to find him sitting on the tiled floor beside the toilet, with his arm inside the bowl. The water is almost up to the lip and his shirt is wet. His face is bright red. There is a familiar stale smell in the room.

Slowly and with difficulty the story comes out. "I bought some dope. And I was smoking when the maid walked in on me. I thought she was going to call the police, so I dumped it down the toilet. And when the police didn't come, I thought I'd try and get it out. And I got my hand stuck." He shrugs trying not to smile. His face is scarlet, and his forehead hot.

I set the books down in the doorway and ask him if this is a joke. He sternly shakes his head. It occurs to me that the dope would be useless wet. I stand behind him, looking incredulously at his arm. "How much did you manage to smoke?" I ask. "Have you tried any soap?"

Adrian holds up his free hand and points at the bath. An empty shampoo bottle lies without its top beside the drain. "Didn't work. What about that stuff you put in your hair?"

"Brylcreem?" I open the cabinet above the sink, find the small round tub and reluctantly unscrew the lid.

I hold the container out and Adrian scoops the white grease into the toilet bowl, pushing it down onto his hand. He is sweating. "It's not working. We'll have to take the whole thing off the floor." He smirks as he attempts to rotate his hand.

Kneeling next to him on the blue-tiled floor, I take off my jacket and roll up my sleeves. There are small green flecks, flakes of cannabis in the water. The water is cold and milky, and for the first time I believe that his hand is honestly stuck.

"This is absurd. You're like a monkey. You know that? What possessed you to do this?"

Adrian elbows me out of the way and shuffles closer to the toilet bowl, bracing his feet either side against the wall. Grimacing, he tugs twice, as hard as he can. On the second pull his hand pops free and he topples backward spraying water across the room. He lays back, laughing, covering his mouth with one hand and holding his stomach with his other. He sniggers like a little boy, and I realize that this was some kind of a joke.

I sit beside the toilet, arms folded, obviously displeased.

"Jesus." His hand falls away from his face. "It was only a joke."

I flush the toilet. "Where did you buy the dope?" I ask.

His face flushes a deeper red. "I got it at the gym."

"I thought you weren't going back there?"

He shrugs and belligerently folds his arms.

"You bought it from Bruno?"

Adrian pulls himself up onto his feet and walks into the bedroom. "What do you want to know for? Bruno's gone. He isn't there anymore."

"But you were you looking for him?" I follow him into the bedroom. Adrian puffs out his cheeks, and hands cupped behind his head he flops backward onto the bed. A magazine slips from the bed and onto the floor. There are three parallel red lines, each about an inch long, etched into the soft white skin of his right underarm, close to his shoulder. This is the same armpit that he had shaved.

Seeing my concern he folds his arms over his chest. "I was

looking for something to smoke," he replies sharply, "and then I came back here, just like I said, and the maid knocked on the door so I flushed it down the toilet, and then I thought I'd play a joke on you."

"How long did you sit there with your hand in the toilet?"

"I don't know." His eyes seem slightly askew and his forehead is shiny with sweat. "Jesus, I was just playing a joke. I thought you'd think it was funny."

"What happened to Bruno?" I ask, bending down to pick up the magazine. Adrian turns his head and shrugs, refusing to answer. The magazine is folded open to an article, the article is about AIDS. Bright blood-red script covers the entire page. There is a brochure, also about AIDS, tucked inside the magazine.

"And what's this for?" I hold up the brochure.

"Because," he replies defiantly.

I thumb quickly through the magazine looking for the cover. "You shouldn't read this nonsense." I hold up the magazine. "It isn't reliable."

"It isn't nonsense," he shakes his head slowly, his face suddenly stiff and serious.

"Why?" I ask again, but there is no response. "I feel like I'm missing something here. Something is wrong." I clear my throat and ask quietly, looking at the magazine. "Do you think that you have AIDS?"

I am surprised that I have asked such a question. Adrian looks up soberly, equally surprised. The room seems suddenly foreign, the air thicker.

The boy folds his arms tighter, and avoiding my eyes, stares at his feet. He nods and then shrugs, and then closes his eyes. "I have a lump," he speaks softly, almost in a whisper, "here in my armpit."

I walk about the bed and draw the curtains. "Is this what's causing trouble with your shoulder?" I ask.

He nods again and sits upright. I sit on the bed beside him

and unbutton his shirt. It is the armpit that he had shaved. On the first attempt I cannot find it. Only when his arm is at his side can it be felt; a hard swelling about as large as a hazelnut.

"Is this what you're worried about? Everyone has those. Here. The other side. Let me feel." There is no swelling under his left arm. "How long have you had this?" I ask.

"I don't know," he replies sullenly.

"A while? Several days? Several months?" I quiz him.

"Maybe a month."

The lump moves slightly when pressed and rolls under my fingers, a solid and round nub. Adrian cringes, shrugging his shoulder up to his ear.

"What is it?" he asks.

"Honestly, I don't know. Does it ache?"

He nods and relaxes his shoulder.

"Maybe you have glandular fever."

He says that he does not like to touch it as it worries him, and that it sometimes keeps him awake.

"As far as I know, if it was AIDS then there would be other things wrong."

"That's not what this says." He points at the magazine. I pick up the magazine again and give it more consideration so as not to offend him. He flops back onto the bed as I read, his hands gripping his forehead, his thumbs rolling into his temple.

"How old are you? Seventeen, eighteen?" I hold the magazine out to him. "Well, here, in the very first paragraph, according to this, you would have had to have been, infected when you were between six and twelve years old, and I don't think this disease was even around then."

"I have a temperature," he says flatly, obstinately.

I sit down beside him. "Listen to me, there are a thousand possible reasons. Everyone gets swollen glands; it's probably just sex," but he stubbornly shakes his head. "Listen to me. It can't be

AIDS. It isn't AIDS. I promise you, it isn't possible. It's not as if you've exactly done anything to worry about, have you?"

He sinks back onto the bed and folds his arms over his eyes. "I don't know anymore what I've done."

"Then if you're that worried, I think that you should take the blood test."

He scowls at me, horrified by the suggestion.

"Well at least you should see a doctor."

Adrian's eyes widen as if, for some reason, the second suggestion was more outrageous than the first.

Adrian sits on the side of the bed as I undress him. His trousers are unzipped and unbuckled but he will not stand up so that I can pull them down. I ease him backward onto the bed and he stares up at the ceiling.

"You shouldn't worry. Really." I carefully pull down his trousers and underpants. "Are you certain that all you smoked was hash?"

He looks puzzled. "You mean dope? Right?"

"Do you think you can sleep?"

He gives three small nods.

"And what about this?" I inspect the fine lines, cuts, lightly scored under his right arm. "What was this about?"

Adrian shrugs his arm free. His face flushes red again. "I was seeing how numb the dope had made me."

"You cut yourself? Deliberately?"

"It's not like I was hacking off my arm. I was messing around. It didn't even bleed."

I lay out a row of tablets on the bedside table.

"What's that?"

"Paracetemol."

Adrian squints.

"Same thing as aspirin."

Lazily reaching his hand out he flicks one off the table.

"You know. That probably came from the Amazon." He coughs and twists himself about on the bed. "I feel like a total piece of shit."

I stand up in the bath and watch my reflection in the mirror as I dry myself. The water is hot, and my skin is unusually red. There is a small dry rash on my shoulder, which I know to be an allergy to the deodorant soap, but I cannot help looking at it, or from stretching the skin to see if there is perhaps something worse developing. The bathroom door is open a crack, and I can see Adrian's bare legs stretched out on the bed. The television is on, the sound is turned down, and he is half asleep, fitfully dozing. Setting the towel in front of the sink, I sit on the side of the bath and carefully check for swollen glands under my arm, my crotch, and at my neck. Adrian coughs.

"Are you interested in this?" he asks. "Then could you switch it off? I don't feel so good."

On the floor, hidden behind the toilet is an open penknife. A Swiss Army pocketknife. Leaving the knife where it is, I fold the towel back over the rack and switch off the lights. *Johnny Carson* is on, and I crouch in front of the TV, looking for the button to turn it off. I find the switch and the man's silhouette hovers for a moment on the blank screen, his hands stretched out as if for money. The boy stirs in his sleep.

Adrian wakes me at five o'clock, pulling the sheets over to his side. He tells me he is cold. Within ten minutes he is hot again. I try to convince myself that this is not so strange. He reaches for my hand as I rise from the bed.

"Don't call a doctor. They'd contact my parents."

"You should try to sleep," I hand him two paracetemols from the side of the bed. He drinks from a bottle of water. I consider asking why he didn't tell me earlier about his arm. "We'll see how you are in the morning." I tuck the bedspread around him.

He pushes the blanket away and pulls the sheet up to his ears. Hiding his face against my arm, his whole body shivers. "Maybe it will just go away," he whispers.

I cannot sleep. The curtains are open and the room, although dark, is saturated with a dim acidic yellow from the street lamps fourteen floors below. The air conditioner hums, just loud enough to insist that the room is never silent and never dark. I lay awake wondering about finding a reliable doctor. Adrian is asleep. I check myself again, and trying not to disturb him, I press each hand flat into an armpit searching for lumps, but there is nothing. Adrian stirs, kicking back the sheets and shivering himself awake.

"Is that dog in here?" he mutters, drawing the covers back over his chest.

"What dog?" I ask, trying not to laugh.

"Get that frigging thing out of here." His hands move fitfully beneath the sheets.

I lean over him, drawing the covers over his shoulders. His eyes are closed.

"Hey," he says urgently, suddenly opening his eyes. "Get your fucking hands off me."

Adrian frowns, his pupils are wide and black beneath half-closed lids. "Yap, yap, yap."

I am awake, bathed, and dressed before Adrian. I sit beside the bed and watch him sleep. "How do you feel?" I ask. He opens his eyes wide, as if surprised. "And how's the shoulder?"

He nods, the bedspread is wrapped about his face, free of his feet.

"Would it help if I rubbed it?"

He shakes his head and yawns, his voice is gruff with sleep. I couldn't reach it, he says, it's right in there, right in the cleft between his arm and his shoulder. "I wish I hadn't shaved," he complains. "It really itches."

I ask him if he hurts anywhere else, and he nods again.

"Show me. Show me where."

He points to either side of his jaw, and to both elbows.

"You should stay in bed today. And I think you should see a doctor."

He nods indifferently, to humor me.

I roll up my sleeves and run a bath, a steaming hot bath, and make him bathe. Thankfully he is too tired to argue. I stand over him as he lies sulking in the water. His hands cover his crotch, and the water comes up to his chin. His skin flushes red.

"See this," I say sticking my finger into the water. "See how my finger bends?" He looks at my finger and yawns. "Someone I was at school with was born with a hole in his urethra. They operated on it, but it left his penis permanently bent. When it was hard he could hook it round a corner."

Adrian huffs. Sweat runs from his brow. "You went to boarding school?" he asks.

I nod and sit him upright and begin soaping his arms and legs.

"Might be useful if you're really ugly, no one would have to see your face." He screws up his face and slaps his hand on the water, complaining that there is soap in his eye. He raises himself from his bath, pulling on my tie.

"Thank you." I say. "Very nice. Very nice indeed." I wrap a towel about him, feeling the warmth and wetness seep through the flannel as I rub him dry.

I spread a fresh towel on the bed, and have him lay on his stomach. He says that he is becoming cold again and that his eyes still sting. Taking some baby oil into my hands I begin to massage his back. The bath has done little to relax him, his shoulders are tight. There is a small rash on his back below his right shoulder blade, he complains that it itches and reaches to scratch himself.

"Boarding school, huh?" he says, slightly mocking me.

"That's right."

"Figures."

"Have you slept with many men?" I ask.

Adrian stiffens. "What do you mean many?"

"I'm not really talking about sex. It might be that there's nothing wrong. You could be unduly worried. That's all. It's just that the first time you're involved with someone, someone of the same sex, in a relationship, that's essentially what we have here, and well, the first time is particularly hard. That's all."

Adrian half-turns, resting on his elbows. My hands rest on his buttocks, slippery with oil.

"Sometimes you say the weirdest shit," he says.

I snap the top back on the bottle and wipe my hands on the towel. "I had the hardest time, my first time. It could just be that. That's all I'm saying." Walking back to the bathroom I tell him, "You were talking in your sleep last night." I return the bottle to the cabinet, avoiding my reflection in the mirror. "Do you remember?" The cabinet smells of baby powder.

"What did I say?"

"Something about a dog."

I lean in the doorway. Adrian is under the covers, tucked into a small tight ball.

"You shouted at me."

"What?" he asks. His voice is hoarse. He coughs to clear his throat.

"You told me not to touch you."

Adrian turns and frowns. "I must have been dreaming. I don't remember." He half smiles, a little embarrassed. "Did I really shout?"

"You were very explicit."

He blows out his cheeks. "It must have been a dream."

"I wasn't touching you."

Adrian sleeps while I spend the early afternoon on the telephone calling the representative consulates for the countries along our route down to Brazil. In most cases Adrian does not need a visa.

The British Consulate advises me not to travel through El Salvador, but otherwise the trip is not as capricious as I had imagined. The more information I gather, the more likely the trip seems. Adrian wakes at two o'clock, sweat matting his hair and damping his pillow. I sit him up and exchange his pillow for mine. He leans heavily forward, hot and tired.

"This stinks," he croaks. "Stinks. We should be gone already."

I ask him if he is hungry. He shakes his head.

"My eyes ache," he complains and squints at the light.

I close the curtains and draw my chair closer to the bed. Adrian turns onto his side and kicks back the sheets. I sit beside the bed watching over him, listening to him breathing, and there is, I realize, little else that I would rather do today. Given the choice of a whole possible world of activity, I would still prefer to sit here, silent, undisturbed, watching.

Adrian wakes me up and points at the TV. It is already dark. I have fallen asleep beside him, fully clothed.

"What's the matter? Are you sick?" I ask. I check the clock beside the bed. It is seven o'clock. The television is on. Adrian is sitting upright, the bedspread is wrapped about his shoulder, and his face is shiny, greased by the light from the television.

"Watch this. Watch." He insists shaking my leg, his voice is deep and husky.

I sit back in bed, confused and not completely awake. "You're all right?" I ask, searching for my cigarettes.

"Shh. Watch." He waves his arm behind him. Slowly the image on the television becomes familiar. "That's us." He points at the screen. "That's the hotel."

I sit up, pushing my pillow back against the headboard to prop up my head. I can recognize the hotel, but the view is unfamiliar. "It looks different somehow."

"That's us." He points at the screen. "You can see our room."

"Is it live?" I ask.

Adrian steps quickly off the bed and walks to the window hugging the bedspread close to himself. "I can't tell." He turns from the window. "Are we still on?"

"What happened?"

"The building collapsed. The station. They didn't support it well enough so the building fell in on itself." He trips on the bedspread and stumbles onto the bed.

The reporter is standing in front of the boards by the station house steps. Over her right shoulder and above her head, where there should be the station house is the Halifax Hotel.

"Here. Watch this." Adrian crawls over me and hops from the bed to the door. "Okay, now watch," he flashes the bedroom lights on and off. "Here, see if you can see this." I cup my hands over my eyes like binoculars and stare at the television set. Sure enough a small light flashes, slightly delayed, in the hotel just above the newscaster's left ear. A tiny regular blink.

Adrian begins to laugh, between deep and wet coughs. It is the first hearty laugh that I have heard from him in several days.

"Wild. This is fucking wild. Do you know any codes? We could flash a message. Suck my dick," he says flashing the light on and off with each word. "Suck my dick, suck my dick."

He will not come down to breakfast. Although his fever has passed, his mood will not lighten. Throughout the morning the news has repeated the broadcast from the night before, showing footage of the fallen station house. Each time the light can be seen flickering "Suck my dick, suck my dick" beside the newscaster's ear. Adrian is no longer amused by his joke.

"I'm sick," he pouts, "and my shoulder hurts."

I have room service bring his breakfast up. As I unfold the tray on the bed, I ask him if he needs more Polaroid film. I watch him pick at the plate, slowly turning over each item. Seemingly the camera is broken, and anyhow, what would he take pictures of?

The station house looks like a wedding cake with the top tiers removed. Rubble has been pushed to the side, into mounds around several of the remaining columns, leaving one central, clear area. There are abrupt changes of pattern in the stone floor; it is possible to tell where there had been walls and doorways. What remains is a two-dimensional plan of what had been, until yesterday, an entire building.

"I don't understand why you won't see a doctor."

"Because they don't know shit." He begins to sulk. I remove the tray from the bed and sit next to him. "And there's nothing they can do anyway."

"What if I've already found a clinic, and I've made an appointment?"

His eyes widen in anger. "What do you mean, what if?"

"I didn't say that I have." I slip my hand under the sheets. "But you realize that you'll have to see a doctor in any case."

He attempts to sit upright, clearly irritated.

"You'll need shots, inoculations if you want to go to Brazil. If you're feeling a little better this afternoon we should talk about the trip. You'll also need your passport."

He slumps back onto his pillow. "A passport? Fuck. My sister has my passport."

I have a passport application for Adrian, but he is not in the room when I return. I check the bathroom and regret that I had teased him this morning. I prefer for him not to leave; without him the room is reduced to a foul orange carpet and the sweet cold smell of stale cigarettes.

I check under the bed for his sports bag. This is the bag he arrived with. It is not my intention to look inside but the zipper is undone, and by pulling the bag from under the bed by its strap, the bag yawns open. Inside is a pair of sports shoes, boxing shorts,

RICHARD HOUSE

a skipping rope and a roll of magazines. The shorts are made of a fine white silk with the word EVERLAST stitched into the thick elastic waistband. Tucked into the heel of one shoe is a soft leather purse. Inside, in five-, ten-, and twenty-dollar bills, is perhaps three hundred dollars. I know what the magazines are even before I unroll them. There are two copies of *Manshots*, September and November, and one of *Inches*, November. He has scribbled over the covers, drawing circles about the model's faces and genitals. These magazines had been bought after he had moved into the hotel with me. Tucked inside the cover of *Inches* is a postcard. It is the postcard that my sister had sent me for my birthday, the card that I had given to Adrian at the restaurant. The card has been folded several times, the image scored clean from the edge of the fold. Underneath his name and telephone number is a new name, Reyes, and a new telephone number. I had thought that I had thrown the card away, and I am surprised that he would be senti-mental enough to keep it. I return the card to the magazine, and return the magazines to the bag.

It is a relief to hear his key in the door.

"Where were you?" I ask.

Adrian stands at the door with a suitcase in his hands. He looks tired and agitated. "Nowhere. I just went out. What's the problem?"

"There isn't a problem. I just wanted to know where you were."

He stands beside the door, arms hanging by his side, the suitcase blocked between his leg and the door. "I just went out. Out. What does it matter?"

Adrian sits at my table in his shorts and my suit jacket, drawing over an old boxing magazine. I try to persuade him to dress, saying that when he is ready we will have dinner in the hotel, but he has no interest or energy and refuses to talk. His suitcase has been stashed under the bed, safely away from view. He scribbles around the head of a boxer, drawing a ring, a black halo about the man's head.

"I'm getting ready for dinner. I'll need my jacket." I turn on the shower and begin to undress.

Adrian begins ripping the pencil through the paper, cutting across the boxer's neck, furrowing the lead into the wooden tabletop. I ask him what he is doing and he stares at the pencil, eyes narrowed; the tip is blunt. His mouth is pinched shut.

"Aren't you going to join me?" I ask, standing beside the bed folding my trousers. "You know, I only asked you where you were today."

"Just lay off." He talks quietly and mutters, "stupid jacket." He pulls the jacket off, and catching his arm in the sleeve he tugs until his wrist is free. There are blue and red lines scribbled across his chest and forearms.

"What's this?" I ask.

"What?" he replies bluntly.

"These lines."

"It's a marker pen. I was bored so I drew in my veins and arteries."

"What for?" I ask.

"I said I was bored," he suddenly shouts, bracing his arms either side of the table. "Bored, bored, bored, bored, bored. All right?"

I pick up my jacket from the carpet and lay it carefully down upon the bed. "Did you go to the gym today?"

Adrian stares out of the window, ignoring my question. I straighten the jacket's sleeves. "You were looking for Bruno, weren't you?"

He shakes his head, exasperated.

"What's your problem with him anyway? I just went out to pick up my stuff."

"But your things are here."

"What things?" he turns briskly about.

"Your shorts, gloves, everything. In your sports bag, under the bed." I walk about the bed looking for my cigarettes.

Adrian thinks for a while, his hands set flat on the table in front of him. "What are you doing going through my stuff?" he asks quietly.

"I was looking for my shoes. I just pulled it out by accident and it was open," I stop excusing myself. "If you want to keep something private, then don't keep it under the bed."

"Where else is there?" his head is shaking with anger, "this place is so fucking small." He picks the magazine off the table and walks into the bathroom, slamming the door shut behind him.

"Adrian?" I knock hard upon the door, but he has it locked. There is no reply. I rest my head against the door and look down at my bare legs and socks. "I need my trousers."

I wait again for a reply.

"Adrian?"

The boy is silent. The door will not budge. I press my ear against the door. The shower is running. "Are you having a shower?" I wait for a few minutes and knock again. "Fine. I'm going to call the front desk to come and unlock the door." I say. There is still no answer. I walk into the bedroom and stand over the telephone. "I'm at the phone right now. Think about it. I'm picking up the receiver." This is stupid I tell myself. "I'm dialing the number." I hold the receiver up to the bathroom. "It's ringing!"

"Big fucking deal," he shouts. The door judders as he kicks it.

I hang up and sit on the edge of the bed wondering what to do.

"Adrian, where did you go today? Just tell me where you went. It doesn't matter where it was or what you did."

There is a click as the bathroom door is unlocked.

Adrian sits naked on the wet bathroom floor. His shorts are wrapped about the foot of the toilet. The tiles are slippery with steam, and the magazine sticks sodden to the floor. I sit beside him and offer him a towel. Water bleeds into my shirt as I cuddle him. He shuffles across the tiles, out of my reach.

"So where did you go today?"

He leans back against the bath and stares at me for a long time. His short hair is wet and matted flat to his skull. "It doesn't matter." He coughs to clear his throat. "I went to my sister's to pick up some stuff, and then I went to the gym. That's all."

"Then why didn't you say that earlier?"

He swallows hard and asks quietly, "What would you do if I had AIDS?"

"AIDS?" I rest back against the bath, my shirt sticks to the tiled side. "But you don't." I reply.

He closes his eyes and shakes his head, as if to shake away my reply. "But what if I did?"

"I would stay with you. I would do whatever I could."

Adrian turns away and wipes under his eyes, and we are both silent.

"Last summer," he begins after a pause, "I worked at this restaurant, my father was friends with the manager." He swallows hard and coughs to clear his throat. "I only worked a couple of days a week, and my father would pick me up after work. There was this guy I worked with, this other waiter. Reyes. He was older than me, maybe twenty, twenty-two." Water trickles down his back, running unevenly from bead to bead. "Reyes really liked me, and I liked him enough, but it was just stuff, you know, just stupid stuff. It wasn't anything serious."

Spitting on his forearm he tries to rub away a red felt-tip drawing of a flower.

"Anyway, the manager at the restaurant knew exactly what was going on, and he told my father." He pauses and pinches his arm. "So, one day my father came early to the restaurant. He'd packed a bag with my stuff. He said that I had to make a choice. I could either quit the job, stop seeing Reyes, and come home, or I could take the bag and fend for myself. He also said he'd make me take an AIDS test, that he'd take me to the hospital to see people with AIDS so that I would know what was going to happen to me." Adrian coughs to clear his throat. "Anyway, I took the bag. I think he thought I'd come home. I know he thought I'd come home. After that I went to live with my sister. I didn't have much of a choice." His voice runs dry, and he shakes his head. "I was there for a while, and I kept seeing Reyes, and then, anyway, when Allison found out she kicked me out. So I moved in with Reyes."

All the time he is talking he rubs at his forearm, trying to erase the flower.

"Reyes had this big plan for us to move to Florida. He has a sister there. I think he used to live there. I'm not sure. In the end he went on his own."

He pauses and looks down at his stained fingertips. There is a thick red welt on his forearm. "I told you we shouldn't have come back."

"Why didn't you go with your friend?" I ask.

Adrian groans and hangs his head. "I didn't want to. I was doing all right by myself." Pausing again, he sets his hands between his thighs. "Reyes is sick, really sick. I called his sister after we came back from Wyoming, she said he was sick and couldn't talk to me. He was too sick to come to the phone. I tried calling again but he wouldn't answer. So I went to the gym to see if anyone knew anything, and that's when I found out that Bruno had gone. And then I went back today to see if anyone had heard from Reyes."

"Do you know that Reyes has AIDS?

Adrian shakes his head. "He said that he was tested a couple of years ago, and he was negative. But he used to see these people. He said he didn't do much with them, and he said he was always safe. They paid him a lot; he always had money. He said he wasn't in it for the money. It was a kick, a big kick."

"What about your other friends? Do they know what might be wrong?"

"What other friends?" He looks up resentfully.

"How can you be so sure that he has AIDS?"

"How sure can you be? His sister thought it was hepatitis, because he's had it before," he pauses. "Maybe it was. I haven't heard from him. He won't talk to me."

"But it worries you."

"What do you think?" he shouts at the top of his voice, shaky, high-pitched, verging on tears. "What do you think?" he asks.

I wait in the corridor beside the gym. Through the doorway I can see the corner of a raised rink. Two Hispanic youths wearing bright red leather headguards spar. Bare-chested and thin, with round and corded upper arms, the boys scowl at each other, stepping deftly back and forth, in and out of view. Another boy, also Hispanic, with a small wispy goatee, leans against the doorway, his vest sagging with sweat. He shifts his feet and crosses his arms as I talk to him. I have a small roll of money in my hand, pinched between my finger and thumb, at which he periodically smiles.

"Reyes?" He shakes his head and wipes the sweat away from his eyes and smiles again at the money.

"You've never heard of him? He's about twenty-two."

"There's a lot of people." The boy nods over my shoulder at someone passing by. "I could ask."

I shake my head and return the money to my pocket. If it were not for his name on the postcard, I would not believe that Reyes existed.

"If you don't have a last name, then there isn't much I can help you with," he repeats himself.

Adrian swims surrounded by blue as I watch him from the balcony. The chlorine is so strong that it makes my eyes sting. Having completed his laps he lies on an inflatable raft, kicking his feet so that he spins slowly round. He knows that I am here but chooses not to acknowledge me.

I walk on the running track about the pool and remove my jacket. It is uncomfortably hot.

"How is your shoulder?" I call across the pool.

Adrian tilts his head. He answers fine, and looks down into the water.

"Do you intend to do anything about it?"

He does not reply.

"Or do you think it will just go away?"

"Just give it a rest," he shouts, turning his raft about to face me. His voice echoes back across the pool.

I hear a door beneath the running track open and close.

"What was that?" I ask.

"Somebody else wanting to swim," he replies in a calmer voice. "It's okay, he's gone now." He stares into the water as if thinking.

"I'll come with you. Whatever happens."

"Look, just leave me alone. I know all about doctors."

I complete my circuit about the track and walk down the stairs to the poolside. I crouch beside the pool, washing my hands in the water. "Did you try calling Reyes again?"

Adrian paddles the raft around to the side of the pool. Water catches in the small of his back as he kicks his legs. He pulls himself closer to the pool's side and swears.

"What's the matter?" I ask.

"Look." He shows me his elbow. There is a small red rash about the size of a penny where he has scuffed himself. As he puts his arm back into the water a thin wisp of blood catches on the hairs of his arm. "I tried," he looks up, confused, perhaps annoyed. "He doesn't want to talk to me, and his sister won't say anything."

He slides off the craft and treads water close to the edge. As I reach over he suddenly smiles and slips backward into the water closing his eyes.

I pick up my coat and decide to wait for him in the lobby. As Adrian swims I watch his body change, alternatively stretched and compressed by the refraction of the water. Now he is a boy, now he is a man, once more a boy. Just for luck I touch the water.

8

I return to the hotel lobby with Adrian's coat. "Do you think this will be warm enough?" I ask.

Adrian waits by the window, his eye fixed on a car parked in front of the construction site.

"That's him," he whispers, and points at a man standing behind the car.

I stand behind him, looking over his shoulder, holding his coat open. He slowly slips one arm into a sleeve then points outside.

"The guy in the brown jacket. That's the man who's been following me around. That's the detective my mother hired."

I lean forward and squint into the street. "Who? The man with glasses?"

He is insistent: the man in the wide-collared leather jacket, with slicked-back silver hair, has been following him since we returned from Wyoming. It is cold outside, and the man stands with his shoulders hunched and his hands deep in his trouser pockets, looking up and down the street with the patient air of someone who has been waiting for a while and does not expect anything to happen.

"What makes you think he's a detective?"

"He has to be, look at him." He replies without moving his head. We are whispering. "Why else would he be following me around?"

The man looks down at his feet and pulls his hands out of his pockets. The sun catches on a ring or a key in his hand.

"Why don't we ask him?"

Adrian turns and frowns as if I am stupid. "Are you serious?"

"Why not?" As a dare I walk toward the hotel entrance.

Adrian retreats to an alcove between the elevators and shrugs off his coat. Sitting on a leather couch half hidden by the plush flat leaves of a potted plant, he watches and shakes his head as I push through the revolving door.

The detective sits in the car, his head hangs down as if he is asleep. There is a yellow construction hat and a pair of mirrored sunglasses resting on the seat beside him. From the rear-view mirror hangs an ID card on a beaded silver chain.

"Hello. Excuse me." I tap on the window. "Can I ask you a question?"

The man folds away a newspaper and rolls down the window. One hand steadies a cup of coffee tucked between his legs. He squints up at me, sunlight reflecting into the car from the hotel's windows. A small crescent of steam rims one of his spectacle lenses. He blinks rapidly and I step aside so that my shadow falls over him.

"Can you tell me what they are building?"

"Condos," the man replies. A walkie-talkie cackles on the seat beside him. He pushes aside the hard hat, and picks up the hand-set. And nodding brusquely at me he half-winds up the window, returning to his work. "Okay?" he asks.

"Okay." I reply, and the man winds the window shut.

As I return to the hotel Adrian sits upright and turns in his seat to follow me. He smiles foolishly and allows me to sit down before he asks how it went. His hands are full of cork pellets from the potted plant.

"He's the site manager. The foreman," I reply, pointing in the direction of the station house. "It's going to be an apartment building."

Adrian sucks in his lower lip and stubbornly folds his arms.

"He had an identification card. He's the site manager. He

isn't a detective." I insist. "I'm not sure why someone would be looking for you. And suppose that they were, how would they know to look for you here?"

Adrian ignores me and cranes his head to look at the site manager's car. I sit back into the chair. There is a small dining and breakfast room on the first level, and from its open glass doors comes the rich and fresh aroma of espresso. While he sucks on his lip, still watching the site manager's car, I prepare my breakfast order. A porter sits on a stool beside the elevators, his thin mouth closed, upturned, perhaps in a smile or a daydream. His cap covers his eyes, but he seems to be looking at the boy, lost in his thoughts.

The walls of the clinic are painted a pale swimming-pool blue. The carpet is maroon. There are no windows opening to the outside.

"It's to disguise the blood." Adrian leans forward in his seat, and resting his elbows on his knees he points at the floor. "If anyone messes up then they can just pick up one of the squares and replace it." He splays his fingers, to describe the tile or the mess, I am not sure.

Two rows of chairs divide a small section of the waiting room into a children's play area. The walls are decorated with paper cutouts. Sickly paper flowers curl off the walls, the color bleached from the paper by the overhead lights. A toy tricycle lies tipped on its side between a plastic swing set and slide, and a young boy lies beside it, one foot resting on the tricycle's saddle. The child's arms stretch over his head and he watches us, slowly wiggling his fingers, his black eyes wide and fixed on Adrian. Adrian stares at the floor, concentrating, tapping his thumb and forefinger against his knee.

"What are you doing?" I ask.

"I'm counting the hours till we go." He stares up at the ceiling and then sits back. "Sixty-four hours, if we leave at seven in the morning."

An intern enters the waiting room. Taking our folders

from a plastic tray mounted on the front of the clerk's desk, the intern pauses and carefully reads either side of the charts. There is a large black letter *B* suspended above the intern's head. Behind the clerk's desk is an office.

"Mr. Harris?" The intern looks up and about the room, as if it were full. I stand up immediately. Adrian rises slowly, digging his hands deep into his pockets. "If you could both please come with me."

We follow the intern down a corridor, his white uniform making a crisp zip-zip-zip as he walks. Adrian strides closely behind the man, swinging his arms and backside in a parody of the intern's gait. After turning a number of corners it appears that we are back where we started. But this waiting room has no play area, and there is a large letter *D* above the clerk's desk. Fluorescent lights run in parallel lines across a suspended ceiling, regardless of the walls and divisions. The whole clinic, it seems, has been partitioned from one large room.

The intern points with our files at a row of chairs. "If you'd like to take a seat, I'll just be a minute."

In a small closetlike room the intern prepares our vaccinations.

"Where did you find this place?" Adrian asks.

"The telephone directory. Why?"

"It's just funny that you'd pick this place, that's all." He holds his breath and puffs out his cheeks.

"Why don't you ask him about your shoulder?"

Adrian looks sideways at me. "What's the difference between a mosquito and a blond?"

I do not reply.

"When you slap a mosquito it stops sucking." He laughs, perhaps because I am not. "Did you notice?" He whispers through his hand.

"Notice what?" I shake my head and sit farther back into my seat. They are so smooth it is hard to sit upright.

"The doctor's wearing makeup?" Adrian slouches, his shoulders even with the back of the chair.

I look up into the office. The intern has his back to me and I notice that his hair is blond. "Perhaps it's for a skin condition?"

"Right," he scoffs. "Eyeliner for a skin condition."

"Adrian?" The intern stands at the door. "I'll see you first."

"She would," he mutters. Leaning on my armrest he whispers. "I came here last year, and one of the doctors made a pass at me."

I frown at him.

"Honest. He stuck two fingers up my ass and asked me how I liked it." He winks and walks away. I follow after him, unsure if his story is true or not.

The room is almost too narrow for three people. There are posters on the walls, charts to measure a child's height. There is one plastic folding chair with a swiveling Formica-topped arm; beside it is a metal stool. Above the door is a small wooden crucifix. The medicines are ready: small squat glass vials like inkwells set upright in a white sectioned plastic tray. The needles are wrapped in plastic, and beside them is a small clear container marked "disposal—contaminated waste." The room has a nasty, acrid smell, almost like vinegar.

Adrian sits down and rolls up his sleeve as the intern rereads the chart in front of him. "Hepatitis A, smallpox, and yellow fever?" The intern smiles at him. "So where are you going?" He stands to prepare the syringe. Adrian does not reply. The man moves smoothly, with incredible grace, as if each motion were rehearsed until it became fluid. His hands are beautiful, long and slender, fingernails carefully manicured. Adrian watches the intern prepare the vaccination with undisguised suspicion. Turning to the boy the man sits down again and opens a small packet containing a cotton-wool swab. His features are distinctly feminine. His face is smooth, without a trace of stubble, and indeed, on both the upper and lower eyelids is the finest trace of kohl. An astringent smell floods the room.

"The Amazon." In a vain attempt to block the smell, I fold my arms and casually rest one hand over my mouth as if I were seriously considering my reply. "We're driving."

The intern sits upright and pauses, holding the swab in midair, making the smell much worse. Adrian presses the flesh of his lower arm as if there were no sensation, as if the arm were dead, and the intern begins to swab his upper arm. "Driving?" he smiles.

"Yes," Adrian replies. "Driving, in a car."

"I didn't know it was possible." He turns back to the counter, tossing the swab into the contaminated waste. "How long will it take you? Make a fist."

"It depends," Adrian replies cautiously.

The intern repeats his answer absently, and pinching the skin on the boy's upper arm he pricks and sinks the needle into the flesh. He is listening but not paying attention. Adrian watches indifferently as the needle slides into his arm. "How long will you stay there?"

Adrian turns to me and winks. "It depends. Why did you pinch me?"

"Relax your fist. To distract you." The intern withdraws the needle and immediately discards the whole syringe. "There will be a lump here for the next couple of days." He pats the spot. "I wouldn't scratch if I could help it."

Adrian stares across the room, frowning, as if he is trying to remember something. "This isn't so bad," he smiles. "It really doesn't hurt at all. What's next?"

"Smallpox." The intern smiles again. "It will take about ten days for you to build up an immunity. And you may feel some flulike symptoms, but they should pass within twenty to forty-eight hours."

The injections are completed in silence. Despite standing in a cool air-conditioned draft, the room feels unaccountably close.

"Here." The intern hands Adrian his receipt, stamped with today's date. "Keep this certificate with your passport. Did your doctor," he looks quickly at the forms on the counter beside him, "talk about a visit when you return?"

I assure him that he has as Adrian stands and offers me his seat with a theatrical flourish. "You look like you're going to pass out," he smiles.

Adrian steers the car out of the compound, appearing extra-small behind the wheel. The passenger seat is pulled too far forward, and my knees are uncomfortably close to the glove compartment.

"I've never seen anyone faint before." He is smiling broadly, obviously pleased.

"I didn't faint." I disagree as I fish under the seat for the lever.

"Then what would you call it?" He lowers his voice to imitate me. "A little nap?"

"I didn't faint."

"You went out like a light."

"Just watch it here," I say, nodding at the road.

"I'm watching," he replies, pooh-poohing me with his hand. "I've driven a stick shift before." He checks the mirror and shuffles forward in the seat. "Didn't kill us then, did I?"

"I think you should be on the inside lane. Try to get on the inside lane."

Adrian looks intently ahead and lightly wets the corner of his mouth with the tip of his tongue. "Does your arm ache?" he asks. "My arm aches." He vigorously rubs his upper arm, and I remind him not to scratch.

There is a van parked at the crossroads, sticking a little too far out into the junction. Hand-painted with red oxide, no rear bumper, and the back doors tied together to keep them closed, the vehicle seems overfull and abandoned. Strapped to its roof is a jumble of metal chair frames, a car bumper, and several barbecues—all dented and useless—and tied to one side is a full-size aluminum canoe. As Adrian pulls up beside the van, two dogs lunge at the window. Startled, he quickly rounds the corner. There is a hard thump against the right fender, a mess of hands, coat flaps, and white skin smear across my window. Adrian immediately stalls the car.

"I couldn't have hit him; I wasn't going fast enough." With his thumbs locked about the steering wheel, he points at the pavement. "Those fucking dogs. He ran into the car. I saw him on the sidewalk. He deliberately ran into me."

The dazed pedestrian stumbles backward, down on the pavement as I open the car door. I step out of the car and over the man. He is wearing a frayed and dirty suit, his shirt is hiked up over his stomach. The two dogs tumble over each other in the front seat, rocking the van; white teeth and black mouths striking against the smeared and greasy window. One is a white Alsatian, the other a pit bull, both fully grown. The man lies back on the concrete and stares straight up at the sky, blinking and breathing heavily, oblivious to the barking and commotion. I bend down beside him, his breath is stale and strong with alcohol.

"Are you hurt?" I ask, trying to keep out of his reach.

He shakes his head and leans forward into the gutter, hugging his head between his knees.

"Can you stand up?"

"He shouldn't move," Adrian says. "He could be in shock." He steps cautiously into the gutter and stoops forward, holding his hand in front of the man's face. The dogs scramble and bark, scrabbling at the window as Adrian approaches the man. "Can you focus on my finger?" He straightens up, slapping his hands at his side, looking nervously at the van. "Let's go. He's drunk. And this is just trouble."

"But I think we should get him to a hospital." I look back up the road; the clinic is barely four streets away.

"Are those your dogs?"

The man looks up, mouth open, and squints at the boy. His wallet lies open at his feet.

"I was robbed." He shakes his head.

"Who by?" Adrian asks. "I don't see anybody."

The man hunches forward as if he is going to be sick. The dogs quiet down and watch side by side, maintaining a low, constant growl.

Adrian turns to hide his smile. "He wasn't robbed at all. Isn't that right?"

The man mutters to himself as he looks through his billfold. "I've been robbed." He offers an open and empty wallet as proof.

It has begun to rain, small droplets begin to spot on the car's roof. The dogs, mercifully, have settled down inside the body of the van. The street is empty. Next to a vacant store is a bar, their windows are bricked up and the doors padlocked.

Adrian draws me away to the car. "Let's get out of here. It's a scam."

"We can't just leave him."

"Why not?" He rolls his eyes. "He's doing this for money."

The man in the dirty suit turns over and carefully levers himself up on all fours until he can stand upright.

"Here, come with us." I grip him by his elbow and guide him to the car. The dogs immediately begin barking again. "I'm taking you to a hospital."

Adrian frowns at me behind his back. "I'm telling you, he's doing this for money."

"I just need some money to get me home," the man implores feebly, locking his arms against the car, refusing to get inside. "Fifty," he says, "Give me fifty bucks, and I won't say a word." He extends his hand out to the boy.

"Oh Jesus Christ." Adrian slaps his hands at his side and looks up into the sky. "There's too much to do already. We don't have time for this crap."

"Here. Take this. It's five dollars." I hold the money up to the man's face, worried that Adrian might hit him. "It's all I have on me."

"Please," he holds his hand out for more money, the word catches in his throat, "please," his expression is frighteningly desperate.

Adrian takes hold of the man's collar, gripping the jacket with his fist, and turns him about, shoving him back on to the pavement.

The man stumbles away, his jacket falling from his shoulders, his mouth and fingers twitch with anxiety. "Look, look." He fumbles with his shirt buttons, and tugs his shirt back out of his trousers, as if his actions will persuade more money out of us. There is a rim of dirt about the man's waist, the dirt is so ingrained that the skin is swollen.

"Oh my god, he stinks." Adrian covers his mouth and pinches his nose.

Running under the man's rib cage and partly covered by his shirt is a scar. The man opens up his shirt, and lets it fall behind him. He stands half-naked in the rain with his arms outstretched.

Adrian winces and turns away.

The man's chest is entirely the wrong shape, as if it has collapsed in upon itself. The perimeter of the depression is lined with a scar, the scar tissue is a glossy pink. The man's arms are different by almost a hand's length. The right arm is shorter, thinner, and uneven, buckled twice below the elbow, as if it had been broken several times and badly set. "My god." Adrian steps back off the curb. "How many accidents has he been in?"

I sit back against the car and turn my head. "I told you. I don't have any more money." I shake my head, but cannot look at the man. "Please. Please. Cover yourself."

There is one single raucous hoot of a police siren. The dogs appear back at the front of the van. The lights of a police car flicker across the storefronts and the man retreats. It is mid-afternoon and already it is becoming dark. The man watches from the depth of the doorway as the police car drives past, lights flashing but no siren, his arms still outstretched.

Adrian walks about the car and opens the door. "He walked in front of us on purpose. It's what he does for money. He gets into accidents and then scams money from the insurance."

"How can that possibly work?" I ask, stunned by the idea.

"I don't know. But that's what he does. And he probably lives in that truck."

I am sweating, and as I wipe my fact I can smell the man's clothes on my hands.

Adrian squats on his haunches beside the bed and pulls his suitcase out. We have both washed and changed, trying to rid ourselves of both the memory and the smell of the recent accident. I am on the phone to the Chicago Passport Agency of the Department of State. After working through their voice mail, I am now holding for an officer.

Adrian snaps the case open and shakes his head. "I couldn't find it. And I went through everything." He smiles to himself.

"You'll probably have to get a new one. They said it takes three to five weeks."

"See this." Adrian throws a stuffed child's toy at my feet. "I bought it in London." The thing is so bald and misshapen that it is impossible to tell what it is. "It was supposed to be a terrier, you know, a Scottish terrier." He stands up next to the toy and rests his foot on its neck. "I bought it for my sister. She thought she was pregnant and it turned out she wasn't. So I bought it for her. It was kind of a joke, but she really liked it. When they came back to Chicago, Alan bought her a real one. The dog loves it to pieces." He grinds his foot down and squeals for the dog. "I should stitch a piece of shit into it and take it back. Only I don't think I should go back there."

I hold up my hand. "Yes. Hello. I'm calling about a passport application."

Adrian sits heavily back down on the bed.

"No. I have a form already." I look down at the table. "DSP-82." I listen to the woman explain information that I have already listened to. She is very polite. "And that's the problem, he can't find his old passport, and we don't have six weeks."

Adrian closes the suitcase and pushes it back under the bed with his foot. He looks vacantly out of the window. I cup my hand over the telephone. "You don't have your birth certificate, do you?"

He shrugs. "I don't know where any of my stuff is."

I hang up the phone. "What did you mean you can't go back?"

Adrian looks down at the bed, toward the suitcase.

"Just now you said you couldn't go back. What did you mean?"

"I made a mess." He clears his throat. "Actually I made a big mess. If I go back now, they'll know it was me."

I sit on the bed beside him. "Isn't there anyone you should tell that you're leaving?"

He shakes his head emphatically.

"What about your mother?"

"My dad would have a fit. She called me a couple of times at my sister's and sent me some money. But I think he found out and stopped her." He looks down at the bald and deformed toy. "She's scared of him. So is my sister."

"What else is in the suitcase?" I ask cautiously.

"Stuff. Just stuff."

"You don't have a Scottish terrier in there, do you?"

Adrian laughs. "Uh-uh. It wasn't there. She has it groomed once a week. I tell you, she's crazy about this dog."

*

Adrian wakes early, anxious to have his hair cut for his passport photograph; by nine o'clock we are at the barber's opposite the hotel. I am feeling much better this morning, although my left arm is stiff from the vaccinations. It is cold outside, cold enough to see your breath, and there is condensation on the barber shop windows. The pavement and road are wet from last night's rain. We are taking Adrian's passport application to the federal building today; if the application is submitted before noon, the passport will be ready within two weeks. We have given ourselves two days to prepare for our trip.

The barber shop is one long single room. There are four stations but only one barber. The man has a handsome and smooth, boyish face, but although his arms and neck are slender, his waist is disproportionately large. My chair is slung back, and as I wait my turn I look up at white tin tiles nailed in uneven lines on the ceiling, wondering if we have everything that we need, if we are anywhere near prepared for this journey. Adrian sits next to me, his haircut nearly complete. The barber wipes his neck with a towelette and unfastens the apron, shaking the hair onto the floor. The boy stands up, leans close to the mirror, and picks hairs off his white shirt, ignoring everyone else in the room. He pays the barber, and the man walks slowly to the till, rubbing the money between his fingers. Adrian waits with his arms folded for the man to return with his change.

There is a television hung above the doorway, and the barber watches a talk show as he works up a lather in a small bowl, the sound turned down to a gentle murmur. I watch Adrian in the long mirror as the barber lathers my face. His hair is trimmed short, very short at the sides. So short that his face takes on a square and defiant attitude, and his small and round ears seem to stick out. He stares directly at his reflection, with an expression so devoid of affection that it might express distaste.

After the shave, the barber presses hot towels upon my face and massages behind my ears. It is so soothing that I almost

fall asleep, lulled by the quiet room and the barber's careful atten-
tions. In two days we will be heading south and all of this will be
gone. I am not prepared to leave Chicago.

"Are you awake?" Adrian whispers into my ear.

I open my eyes and turn to him. I must have dozed for a
moment; the barber is now sitting at the back of the room, feet up
on the counter reading a newspaper.

"If you want I'll go back to that clinic. I'll see a doctor."

The towels have cooled and fall to my chest as I lift my
head. "But you're better now, aren't you?" I stammer slightly,
astounded by his sudden decision.

"My arm," he mutters. "It's not so good today." His face
is close to mine. Small clipped hairs rest on top of his ear. "I don't
know."

"But the fever's gone?"

Adrian closes his eyes. "My shoulder. It's acting up again."

"It's probably the shots, the injections. They said we might
feel a little sick."

He shakes his head. "No. It's the same thing. It's my
shoulder."

"Are you sure? Why don't you wait until we return? We
can both go together."

He shakes his head again, his face set, stern, severe. I rest
my head and watch him as he steps back toward the window. A
pool of light slakes across the floor between us, streaked with last
night's rain. It is a cloudy and blustery day, and the sunlit square
abruptly dims and shifts. Adrian stands at its corner, almost as if his
foot held it down.

The shave is completed, and as the barber sets my chair
upright he massages my shoulders. I pay him and turn to Adrian,
though I cannot think of anything to say. The light shudders
beneath his feet, and I feel a surge of sadness. I have begged for
him to see a doctor, and now that he has chosen, without my

persuading him, to do exactly what I wanted, it seems—though I cannot clarify why—absolutely futile.

Adrian sits quietly in the car, his hands clamped between his knees. The passport application rests in a manila envelope on his lap. As I turn onto the expressway he visibly shudders.

"What are you reading?" I ask.

He looks down at the book. "It's about Cyprus."

"Is it any good?"

"It's yours. You haven't read it?"

I look at the cover. "No, it's one of those I bought for you."

Adrian turns the book over, ending the conversation, and looks up and out of the window, staring into the rain.

"Are you sure you want to do this?" I ask. "We could wait until we come back and both go."

He twists in his seat to face me and shakes his head.

"Why now?"

"You don't have to come in," he says. "Really," he insists. "Just stay in the car."

Rain stalls the traffic on Lake Shore Drive, falling so heavily that the view of downtown entirely disappears.

I lean across the seat to open the passenger's door. The rain will not let up. In the short distance from the clinic to the car, Adrian has been soaked. His trousers are black, sodden from the knees down.

"So tell me, what did the doctor say?" I ask. "What did he do?"

Adrian frowns and takes off his jacket, water drips from his nose and chin. He reaches forward to turn up the heat. "It's cold," he shudders and rubs his hands together.

"So? What did he say?" I ask again.

"Nothing." Adrian points at the clinic as we drive past.

"Except for a bunch of crap about condoms." He grins. "Like I'd never heard of one." Half rising in his seat, he fishes in his trouser pocket and begins to throw the rubbers that the doctor gave him at the dashboard. "How did you know it was a he?" he asks.

"Didn't you see the same doctor?" I collect the condoms and throw them onto the backseat. He shakes his head. "So what did he say?" I ask. Adrian continues to empty his pocket, tossing the rubbers against the windscreen. There is a yellow receipt mixed in with the condoms.

"And green condoms," he continues. "Who ever heard of a green dick?" he rolls open his window and picking the green condoms off the dashboard he throws them out into the street. "They aren't candy, you know, so why do they have to be different colors?"

"What did he say about your arm?"

"The same thing you said. That probably I had swollen glands from some virus, and yesterday's vaccinations probably just brought it back. He gave me a prescription for my back." He pulls a prescription out of his shirt pocket and throws it onto my lap. "I have shingles."

"How can you have shingles?" I squeeze his wet knee. "I thought old people had shingles."

"How should I know? It's the same thing as chicken pox. Anyway, they've just about gone. Doesn't this thing work?" He irritably twists the knob for the heater.

I scoop the remaining condoms from the dashboard. "And what about what you were worried about?"

Adrian frowns at me. "What was I worried about?"

"Adrian? Why are you being so obtuse?" I turn up the fan so that the heat is directed toward our seats. "Reyes. AIDS. Isn't that what you were worried about?"

"That," he replies brusquely. "He said exactly what you said. He said that even if I'd caught it the first time I fucked I'd still probably be too young to have any symptoms, and that just as long as I'm careful I shouldn't have anything to worry about."

"So he didn't suggest the blood test?"

Adrian rolls his head, exasperated. "What for?" he sighs, trying to keep his patience. "Look, there isn't any point. I don't want to talk about it anymore. Okay?"

I turn to the boy, but as I begin to reply he places his hand up to my mouth and repeats with increasing firmness, "No. Get it? I don't want to talk about it." His hand drops, and he waits for a response. I wind down my window and look out at the wet street, wanting to be anywhere but here. Stopped at a traffic light I pick up a receipt.

"So what's this then? What is this receipt for?" I ask unfolding the paper and reading it. The receipt is marked for $120, for unspecified blood work. "What's this about blood work? What did they take blood for?" I hold the paper up to his face. He pushes my hand and the receipt away. "Tell me. What blood test did they give you?"

Adrian turns away, his arms folded. I take hold of his arm and forcibly roll up his sleeve. A car toots behind me. The lights have changed. There is a Band-Aid in the crook of his elbow. "This is an HIV test, isn't it? Why wouldn't you tell me about this?"

"It's nothing." Adrian fights for his arm back and rolls down his sleeve. "It's just a blood count." He buttons up the cuff. "It's just a standard test to see if there's anything else to worry about."

A car horn sounds behind me a second time.

"And I didn't tell you because I knew you'd freak out."

9

Adrian sits on the floor counting out the money. The anxiety of the past couple of days seems to have passed. There is a travel book open on his knees and an accounting book open between his feet. I have given him the task of organizing the money. It is still raining outside. There is a storm across the lake, and occasionally we can hear the distant boom of thunder.

"So, tell me again. What's happening with my passport?"

"They'll send it to the hotel, and the hotel will send it overnight to us, wherever we are. I just have to let them know."

"So this is for gas to Texas." He points at one stack of money with his pencil. "This is for motels. Food for the road. Meals, breakfast, and dinner." He writes a note in his book. "Okay. Put this somewhere." He hands me the money. I am sitting ready on the bed with envelopes and a black marker pen. "Mark that gas to Texas."

"And when will you hear about the blood test?"

"Friday." Adrian frowns, talking into his lap as he totals his figures. "I can call the clinic. It takes about four days."

I place the money in an envelope and seal it. "How much do we have left?" I ask. The smell of the Magic Marker fills the room. Adrian looks down at his books, trying not to smile.

"What's so funny?" I ask.

Counting the money in his hands he continues smiling. "Not including what we've put aside already—" he loses his place and starts to count again. "Nine thousand. We have about nine thousand left. And that's not counting flights and travel. That's nine thousand dollars to keep us going in Brazil." He looks down at his list again. "Knives. You need one of those Swiss Army knives." He counts out the notes. "You should have broken down more of these hundreds." He looks up at me smiling. I am surprised at his efficiency.

"You didn't think I could do this, did you?" He taps the ledger with his pencil, and folds his legs under him, sitting upright and attentive, like a Boy Scout. "Is this what you used to do?"

Our plans have changed significantly. This morning, while calling the car hire company, I discovered that the car could not be taken out of the country. The agent had laughed at the suggestion, but quickly became concerned once he realized that the question had been serious. I can take it only as far as Texas. We will drive to San Antonio, return the car, and then fly to Mexico City, and take whatever transport we can manage once we are in Mexico. Adrian has a little information about train travel throughout Central America, and several of the guides list bus routes. Failing that, we will fly on to Guatemala, and leapfrog our way to Brazil. Adrian is completely unbothered by these changes. "You can't plan something like this. You should just let it happen." I am not so convinced. Lack of planning has also given us problems with visas. In truth only El Salvador and Panama require some kind of visa that cannot be arranged at the border. Transferring my savings into cash has also proved to be unnecessarily expensive. It would have been simpler to have left the money in an account in London. Instead, the money will be deposited in an account here in Chicago, redeemable through checks at American Express offices. If trouble should occur, then we will not lose all of our money at one time.

Adrian holds up the remaining cash. "We can do anything. We have enough to go somewhere else if we want to."

I lean forward and kiss him on the forehead. "This is our last night. Where do you want to go?"

He shrugs, indifferent, playing with his toes, "I've already said my good-byes," and lies back across the carpet, stretching his hands over his head so that his shirt pulls up out of his jeans. "Do you still like me?" he asks, still smiling.

"What do you mean? Of course I like you."

"No. I mean, you know, to fuck and stuff."

"Of course." I kneel down on the floor beside him and slide my hand under his shirt. He arches his back, and I rest my fingers between his ribs. "It's just you've been sick, that's all. I didn't think you'd want to."

His smile melts at the word "sick" and he turns onto his side. I lay down on the floor beside him and hug him close, pressing my hand just hard enough over his heart to catch his pulse. "Have you heard about the boto?" He shakes his head. "In the Amazon there's a fresh-water dolphin that the Indians call boto. On a full moon the dolphins, depending on their sex, transform into irresistible young men. The males have to wear hats to disguise their blowholes. And any man who sleeps with a boto will never sleep with a woman again." I tap the top of his head. "The boto is responsible for all embarrassments: infidelities, unwanted pregnancies." I do not tell him that the boto is also blamed for spreading venereal disease. "So there's no shame in having slept with a boto."

Adrian sniggers into the carpet. "Have you ever heard of flogging the dolphin?" he asks.

I blow into the small dark hairs at the nape of his neck, and the boy folds into me, collapsing his back against my chest.

The prospect of a holiday influences everything. I feel optimistic, happy that tomorrow we will be away from this small and cramped bedroom. We sort through our clothes, deciding what to take, what to pack, and what will need to be laundered. This afternoon we will shop for new clothes and boots. Adrian sniffs at the armpits of his T-shirts and shouts "clean" or "unclean" as he tosses them into the appropriate pile. I send him down with the laundry and sort through the receipts and pieces of paper that I have picked from my trouser pockets.

Adrian's wallet is resting on his pillow. Underneath the wallet is a card, the postcard of T. E. Lawrence, and a newspaper clipping. I throw the receipts away, but immediately return to the bed and pick out the postcard. The word "Reyes" and a telephone number are written in pencil above my sister's birthday greeting. It had not occurred to me before to call Reyes, but perhaps I might reason with him, find some answers for Adrian and some information for myself.

The phone rings five, six times before it is answered. I face the door, ready to hang up should Adrian return. It is answered by a woman speaking Spanish.

"Hello. Can I speak to Reyes please?"

"Reyes?" the voice repeats.

"Can I speak to Reyes please?" I talk slowly and clearly, worried that she might not understand me.

"Reyes?" She speaks quietly, her voice catches the name, rolling the R, as if the word were precious, hard to give up. "I'm afraid that this is not possible," she replies slowly and pauses, "Reyes died."

I sit down, and missing the end of the bed slide awkwardly onto the floor. Reyes is dead, she said. Reyes is dead. Adrian slept with Reyes, and Reyes is dead. "I am sorry. I am so sorry."

The woman repeats again that Reyes is dead, "Who is this please?" she asks.

I look about the room for a clue, for an answer, for an appropriate reply. What would make sense to her? The telephone cord stretches tight across my throat. I switch hands and ask, "I'm calling from Chicago. I was . . . can you tell me how?"

Now the woman is silent and after a moment the phone is hung up. I sit beside the bed listening to the crackling telephone line and look out over the flat, leveled plain of the station house.

Adrian returns to the bedroom. "It will be ready in the morning. Where are you? The laundry," he repeats as if I have not understood. "They'll send it up early tomorrow." He peers about the bathroom door. "Do you want that washed?" He points at my shirt on the bathroom floor. I am standing in front of the mirror. I have been checking the glands under my arms.

Adrian stands in the doorway prying one shoe off with the other foot, leaving the laces tied. "So what time do we leave?"

My throat is tight and dry, and I begin to cough. "What's the matter?" he asks. I sit down on the side of the bath, unable to talk, and lean forward with my head between my knees to calm the cough.

"Here. Get some water." He hops on one foot to the bathroom, tips the toothbrushes into the sink and fills the glass with cold water. He stands aside and hands me the water. I lean over the sink coughing, unable to stop to drink.

Adrian stands back at the doorway, looking concerned, his arms folded. I hold my breath and after a few more sputters the coughing subsides. I smile briefly at him in the mirror. My face is red and wet with tears. I splash water on my face and hold my breath.

"Are you all right?"

I nod into the mirror and force a smile. My face is flushed a deep red, my neck and shoulders are white, unhealthy, and pasty, the pallor of raw dough. Leaning back over the sink I begin to shiver. "I hope I'm not coming down with something."

Adrian steps into the bedroom, and returns with the newspaper clipping from his wallet.

"When do you think we'll be in San Antonio?" he asks.

I shrug, uncertain. He hands me the clipping. In seven days there will be a boxing tournament at the Sheraton Hall, San Antonio, December 24th. The clipping lists participants from Austin, Chicago, Dallas, Detroit, Houston, Indianapolis, San Antonio, and St. Louis. "Texas vs. The Midwest," the title reads. Adrian reminds me that San Antonio is on our route, and that it is somewhere he would like to visit anyway.

*

I return to the room exasperated. I have not been able to buy rail passes or open an account to deposit the money. Adrian is lying on the bed, the sheets pulled up to his chin. His toes stick out from under the sheets. There is a keen, chemical smell about the room. Our cases are packed and ready beside the door.

"Why aren't you up yet?" I search through the bedside drawer to check that we have not left anything. "You know, we should have started this earlier. I can't deposit the money. And an American Express office can't change that much into travelers' checks in one go."

"We'll just have to take the cash with us."

"But it's almost twice as expensive changing money in small amounts, and what if we lose it?"

Adrian is smiling broadly. Grinning, in fact, like an idiot.

"What have you done?" I ask. "And why aren't you getting up? I thought that you wanted an early start? We have to be out by eleven."

"Nothing."

"Then what is that horrible smell?" I get down on my knees and check under the bed. "I can smell something funny. What have you been doing?" My hands find a suitcase. The suitcase Adrian had brought back with him from the gym. I pull the case out.

"You nearly forgot this." I stand the case up on its end. It is new, the leather still yellow and waxy. The case is locked.

Adrian begins to laugh. I sit back on the floor, leaning my arm up on his suitcase, my face level with his crotch.

"No, really, what is that smell?"

Adrian winds the sheet up, slowly gathering it over his chest, gradually exposing his feet, ankles, and calves. He uncovers his legs as gingerly as someone entering a cold bath or pool. When the hem reaches his thighs he pulls the whole sheet off the bed, then holds his hands up, humming a little flourish. His penis has been painted black.

"What have you done?" I bend forward, curious.

"It's black Magic Marker. It should wear off in a couple of days."

We both stare as his penis slowly rises, seeming strangely separate from the rest of his body. It looks poisonous. "It's alive!" He laughs, his head stretched back and his belly shaking. "You should have seen the doctor's face."

"You did this before you went to the clinic?"

He nods. "I just gave it a little touch-up." He smiles. "I might keep it like this. It looks bigger black." He draws the foreskin back and twists the head. "How about it then?"

"How about what?" I look into the boy's eyes. He is laughing so hard that there are tears at the corners of his eyes.

"How about one last time, huh? One more for the road?"

I slip away from the bed. "We have to get going. We have less than half an hour to get out of here."

As he sits up I place his suitcase with the others beside the door and tell him that I will meet him downstairs at the car.

10

For several miles before Marion there are signs for the state penitentiary. When we pass it, the buildings are set on the left side of the road. The walls of the complex are huge, brightly colored concrete squares, more suited to a kindergarten than a prison.

Adrian has stripped the Band-Aid off his forearm. For a while he stares at the tiny blue puncture.

"So," I say, "can you believe we're actually doing this?"

He shakes his head and watches the road. "I won't believe anything. Not until we're clear of Illinois," he says, helping himself to my coffee.

The farther we drive from Chicago, the more relaxed he appears, until he is slumped, his seat pushed back and reclined, his feet scuffing magazines on the floor. An oversize gray Stetson, our first holiday purchase, rests on his lap.

He complains about the Christmas carols on the radio.

I remind him not to scratch.

Adrian points to the road ahead. Against the flat mid-western plains rises a square billboard festooned with colored Christmas lights. ROBERT'S PLACE FOR GAMES, he reads as we pass the sign.

I turn down the radio. "I am a soldier driving through Europe," I say.

"And I am a hitchhiker," he answers, "in the Black Forest, and you stop to pick me up because I'm lying helpless by the highway. A climbing accident," he explains.

"Right. You've taken a nasty fall," I say.

"Did I break my leg?" he asks, his hand itching under his shirt.

"No. I don't think so. But I'll have to make a splint all the same."

He begins to laugh. "All I have on are those tight climbing shorts."

"So I take out my knife and start to cut them apart," I say.

"Come on." He rolls his eyes.

"All I have is my uniform," I protest. "I have to cut the shorts for bandages. I'm really steady with the knife." I work my finger into the boy's fly, unbuttoning his trousers. He widens his legs and smiles. "I roll you over on your face in the road to tie the splint on your leg."

"I start to panic," he interrupts. "But you're right on top of me, and I can feel a gun sticking into my back. People are slowing down to watch. You're worried I'll shout something, so you pull out your gun."

"Adrian," I stop him. "Why does it always have to be violent?"

"It isn't always," he squeezes my hand. "Besides, you're the one who wanted to be a soldier."

Robert's Place for Games is a small two-story wooden motel, built around three sides of a gravel car park. Adrian counts the rooms and turns to watch a man sitting on his own in an office with steamed windows.

"See something you like?" I ask.

"Just looking." He puffs out his cheeks.

The office is hot and smells of eucalyptus. The attendant appears to be sleeping with his eyes open, leaning forward over his desk. There is a door ajar behind him, and I can see through into a room with a punch bag, a bench, and a full-length household mirror. Roused by the snap of the closing door, the attendant blinks and stands. He is remarkably tall, perhaps a whole six inches taller than me. He nods without particular interest as I ask for a room with two single beds. As he replies he slowly rubs his stomach with one finger inside his denim shirt. His skin is an unwholesome white, the sheen of wet soap. There a tattoo on his chest, which I can barely see.

"Why's it called Robert's Place for Games?" Adrian asks, humbly holding his hat in his hands.

"The games room," the man coughs and points out of the window. "Used to have a bar, but we lost the license. We still have the pinball machines and video games."

There is a flat plastic decoration of a fat-cheeked Santa Claus on a parcel-packed sleigh mounted inside the window of our room. Seasons Greetings, the sleigh salutes in alternating red and white lights. The windows are dirty and someone has kicked at the paneling in the door and broken the baseboard.

"What did you think of our host?" I ask. "Doesn't he seem peculiar? He looks like a soldier."

"His name is Frank," Adrian says fitting his foot into one of the holes in the door. "It was on his shirt, on a label pinned to his shirt."

I open the door, surprised that I had not noticed the name tag.

Adrian enters the room and heads straight for the TV.

"Hopeless," he says, "it doesn't work."

I place the bags down and kneel beside him, my hand on his shoulder. "How are you feeling?" I ask.

He groans, twists away from me, and collapses on the bed. "Great, I just managed to forget about that for a while."

Adrian cannot sleep because the plastic Santa is flashing red and white lights directly into his face, and he cannot move as we are both squeezed into the same single bed. Pulling the sheets back so that both of us become cold he bumps his way across the room, swearing at the Santa Claus.

"I can't switch it off," he says. "It's wired into the wall."

"Cover it up then. Pull it off the window. I don't care." I pull back the covers.

"What should I do with it?"

Adrian stands in the middle of the room holding the flat flashing Santa to his chest; a kinked white cable drops between his legs and runs across the floor. Soft red and white light glows over him, touching his nose, his chin, and his stomach.

"Try putting it in the closet," I reply.

He tries this, but the door won't fully close, and light bleeds across the ceiling. Adrian returns to bed muttering "Season's fucking Greetings," and playfully thrusts his cold hands between my legs.

"I am an arsonist," he whispers into my ear.

"And I am a fireman, off duty, very tired, and very asleep."

"It's a three-alarm fire," he says, sidling closer. "It's the motel you're staying in."

"It's a terrible tragedy. Fireman slumbers while hotel burns."

"I try to escape from the basement where I set the fire."

"You trip on the steps and catch your head between the railings."

Adrian sniggers and thinks for a moment, "and I'm bent over, and my head's stuck. All I can do is shout and wake you up."

"There's a whole crew of firemen, I'm the first to reach you," I say. "Your face is bright red, and your backside is sticking up."

"Please help me sir," Adrian grips his hands about his throat. "I tripped on a crack in the sidewalk and caught my head between these bars."

"There's another fireman who's on the other side of the railings, trying to pry them apart. Your face is at his thighs," I explain.

"Then he must be fairly tall."

"He's a large man. And as he's straining against the railings, his jacket unzips down to his navel."

"Please sir, it's hard for me to breathe." Adrian turns onto his stomach and shakes his head on the pillow.

"The other fireman slowly pulls down his zipper," I say.

"What is he going to do?"

I slip down the sheets, tracing my tongue down his back, and the boy laughs into his pillow.

Adrian thrusts into my mouth, and at the first taste of salt I spit into the pillow. He pulls my head toward him and comes in my hair, pushing uncomfortably against my ear. He relaxes his grip and his legs slump against my shoulders. I turn my head away and spit a second time into the sheet.

"What are you doing?" he asks. "You didn't come." It is too dark to see his expression.

"Hairs." I lie, terrified by what we have just done. "I had a hair in my mouth."

Adrian wants to stay another day. He likes being out of the city, he says. It doesn't matter where we are, it's just nice to be away. Tomorrow, he promises, we can get on our way.

The door behind his desk is open. Frank Roberts lies on a black padded bench watching himself in the mirror as he lifts two weights. There is the same strong smell of eucalyptus.

I step back into the office and knock on the door to rouse Frank away from his reflection. He comes into the office, buttoning up the same blue denim shirt, with a towel about his shoulders. The buttons are fastened before I can get a clear view of his tattoo.

"Can we have the room for another night?" I ask.

*

The lotion is helping to clear Adrian's back, a process that would be much faster if he wouldn't scratch.

"It's a tattoo of his first prizefight." He squeezes the pillow. "He used to box for the army."

"How do you know that?" I ask.

"Easy. I asked him," he replies.

"How come?" I pull down his T-shirt.

"Well you saw it, didn't you? How come you got to see it?"

He has a point there.

"He let me lift some weights this afternoon."

"I thought you were playing pinball."

"I was," he explains. "Then I got bored. It's been a while since I did any training."

I look for a towel to dry my hands.

"I don't know if I like you being with this man," I whisper.

Adrian pulls down his trousers and crudely spreads his knees, his feet handcuffed by his underpants. He waggles his cock at me. "Come on then."

I wave my hands at him. "Sticky," I say.

"So?"

I step away from the bed holding my hands up like a surgeon. "I'm not really in the mood right now."

Frank sits naked at the edge of his bench. I cannot completely see him through the slit in the door, though I can very clearly hear him uh, uh, uhing, like a pig. I can see the back of his right hand, stroking slowly up and down. "Come on," he mumbles, "yeah, uh, yeah, that's nice, real nice." His other hand runs along his leg and up his side hitching up his running shirt. I watch the man tease his own nipple. I cannot determine if he is by himself.

"Put the hat on the bench," he says, standing up. Legs either side of the bench, he straddles it, gripping the end between his knees. "Farther back." His chest braces, and his fist works faster up and down. Frank arches over the bench, one hand gripping its side to steady himself. He curses as he comes, and his knees strike the bench, nudging it forward; his belly tightens and loosens as if it is being pumped from deep inside him.

"Did I get it?" Frank leans forward, his face out of view, his cock swaggering from under his shirt. A hat is pushed along the bench, a new gray felt Stetson hat. It is Adrian's hat. It is Adrian's hand, and I can hear him laughing.

"Now how far would you say that was?"

Adrian comes into the room, and stands by the door scratching through his shirt.

"What happened just now, downstairs in the games room?" I ask him.

"What do you mean?" he replies after a pause.

"Where is your hat?"

"Oh that," he screws up his face.

We stand stupid and silent for a moment.

"What's the big deal?" he asks. "What's wrong with watching someone jack off?"

I cannot think of a reasonable reply. "Adrian," I say, completely puzzled.

"What's wrong with that?" he asks again. "I didn't do anything." Then he begins to laugh. "He hit the hat, nearly two feet, his personal best."

"What would you think, what would you think if you had caught me watching someone jack off? What would you think?"

"I wouldn't care," Adrian shouts, turning to the door.

"How can you even say that?" I ask, but he has already gone.

Adrian returns pointing toward the evening sky. He has retrieved his hat. "It's snowing. Look, it's snowing."

A new whiteness falls from a pallid blue-gray sky, slow and

thick. Warm rings of moisture form about the window where Adrian has pressed his face. Mesmerized by the snow, he has already forgotten our argument.

I cannot stop my hands and head from shaking. Even through his imaginings of disease I have not felt so threatened. As the snow falls, I lay beside the bed, resting my face in the rough blankets. There is a map at my feet.

"Memphis," I am stuttering. "I thought we could avoid Memphis tomorrow. We can join Route 10 at Baton Rouge." As I fold the map I repeat to myself. It is nothing. It is nothing. Adrian is right. It doesn't mean a thing.

11

Mississippi. Route 61. The land is flat, unbearably so. We have passed through some temperate line, yesterday's snow is now a cold slow drizzle. The road is black and slick, as wet and shiny as a seal's hide. Branchless trees with thick gourdlike trunks stand in still pools beside the road. Adrian says that he has seen plantations, but I have not. The land is flat and farmed for as far as we can see, but there are no large mansions, no isolated estates. There are surprisingly few buildings, just the occasional sorry groupings of shanty houses, trailer homes, and abandoned cars. Beside the road are pockets of dried and wizened cotton plants. The fields are black, furrowed, and barren.

Adrian sits with the map on his lap, his elbow on the side of the car, channeling in the cold air. He has been studying the map for some time. The boy is cheerful, perhaps deliberately so. I have been silent through much of this morning's drive, responding to his questions with a monosyllabic "yes" or "no." We have not spoken about the motel.

"Look." He runs his finger across the page. "If we get on Route 61 at Baton Rouge, then we're exactly halfway." He holds the book up, but I cannot see clearly. "Route 10 goes all the way from Florida to California." There is something on his mind. "We'll be exactly the same distance from Texas as we are from Florida." I watch the road, aware that Adrian is watching me. "Why don't we go to Florida? It would only take two days, three days. Two days at the most," he pauses. "I'd like to see Reyes."

*

We have pulled into a garage for Adrian to fetch a pullover from his luggage. The garage is a low wood-frame bungalow set alongside a muddy courtyard. A small wooden awning extends from the bungalow over the car. The afternoon has turned much colder. I sit in the car, my seat belt still fastened, staring at the shack thinking, stupid, stupid, stupid. How could I have not told him?

The car shakes as he slams the boot shut. He taps on the window. "Do you want anything?"

I shake my head.

"Look." He leans into the car. "You don't have to worry. There's nothing going on between Reyes and me."

"But why now, Adrian? I thought that we were going to make a new start." I cannot look at him. "You don't even know where he lives."

"I can find out. I can call him." His voice is earnest, eager for me to agree. He looks down at the ground and scuffs his feet. "And that thing at the motel," his voice trails away, and he runs his thumbnail back and forth along the edge of the window. "It's just," he grits his teeth. "We haven't, you know, fucked in a while. I thought you lost interest." He stands upright and looks at the store. "I thought you didn't like me anymore."

"I don't know. I don't know what to think."

I watch him walk into the store. The solution is simple. I will refuse to drive to Florida. I will let him believe that I am jealous. It would be better if I told him after he has the results from his blood test.

Adrian's seat is littered with crisp packets, sweet wrappers, and napkins. I pick up after him, filling almost an entire brown paper bag. Stuck to the seat of his chair and rolled into a small ball is a Band-Aid, the gum blackened with dirt. His pocketknife is open on the floor, sticky with pop. There is an open dustbin beside the petrol pumps. I throw the trash away and look up and down the road. In both directions the view appears exactly the same: flat fields, a straight wet road, and telephone poles.

Adrian has been gone a while. I walk inside the store wanting to hurry him along. Two children sit inside, beside the door; one plays with the tightly bound knobs of hair on the other's head, twisting the hair until the child shrieks. A heater above the door blows warm air onto the back of my neck.

The store is dark, and I do not find him. A woman serves behind a counter stacked with sweet pies, honey pies, pecan pies, and steel tubs of greasy, spiced chicken. She is a deep black, blacker than anyone I have ever seen. I wait at the counter to buy a pack of cigarettes.

I return to the car, believing Adrian to be in the toilet. The children chase each other in and out of the store, banging the door until they are told to stop.

To the left of the car, built beside the store's cracked and whitewashed slats, are two telephone booths. Adrian stands in the closest booth, his arms loose at his side. He stands like a useless thing, like something that has been squeezed or shaken hard. The telephone hangs at his side in his hand, brushing his trouser leg, and he is staring blankly at me through the plastic hood. He has called Reyes. He has heard the news.

Adrian holds the receiver to his chest as I approach the booth.

I attempt to take the phone from his hand, but he will not release his grip. He looks up, blinking, his head shaking slowly, shivering, as if a great weight compressed down upon him. I pry his fingers from the receiver one by one.

"Don't." He moans, his mouth tightens, and he grabs the telephone with his other hand. "I'm still talking to her." He twists about, turning his back to me, hugging the receiver between folded arms. "No." I reach about him, take hold of his wrists, and attempt again to prize the telephone free. "I'm not done talking." Our hands intertwine in a game of slap, one hand quickly replacing another, as I try to hold the boy close to me. Losing his grip, the telephone swings in a wide arc away from him. Suddenly angry, he wrestles himself free and wheels swiftly about, swinging his fist. I stumble backward, tripping over my feet, and catch myself by one of the awning posts.

Adrian lowers his fists and folds his arms, and the receiver, swinging wildly, begins a loud and shrill beeping.

"Reyes is dead." His head quivers. "She said he's dead."

Adrian sits slumped forward, holding his breath. His forehead rests against the dashboard, and with his fists clenched he grinds his knuckles into his knees. I stare ahead at the wooden slats. The telephone still hangs off its hook, and spins slowly, knocking against the booth.

I cough, trying to clear my throat to keep my voice steady. "What did she tell you?"

Adrian rocks his forehead slowly side to side over the dashboard, muttering, "Shit, shit, shit, shit, shit," to himself.

He opens his fists and stares at his palms. His eyes are watering but he is not crying. "I'm fucked." He looks up at me and wipes under his nose with his finger. His voice barely even a whisper. "Everything's fucked." He opens his door, stumbles out of the car and walks away.

I sit beside the road under the wooden awning, waiting for Adrian to return. My upper arm aches with the cold, and my hands are numb. It begins to rain, lightly at first, but enough to drive the children away. I have been counting, repeatedly, up to one hundred and then back down again to nothing. As it begins to rain, I stop counting and listen instead to its rapid rattle on the awning. A strong rich stench of black earth rises in the fields. The woman from the store comes outside and stands at the door. She watches me, and then takes a long look at the car, without interest or concern.

It is raining so hard that I cannot see much beyond the courtyard.

The fields either side of the road disappear into sheets of gray. I am not sure in which direction Adrian had begun to walk. I drive south, hoping that he has the good sense to stay on the road. Five minutes away from the garage the road cuts under the interstate. On one side of the motorway, beside the entrance ramp, is a petrol station, on the other is a motel. There is a sign on an embankment between the motel and the interstate of a large fiberglass crawfish, with bug eyes, a big grin, and ALL YOU CAN EAT, $5.99, written on a bib about its neck.

After booking us in, I drive up in front of the chalet and take our cases inside, running from the rain. Except for a U-Haul the parking lot is empty.

Half an hour later I return to the garage. The rain continues to fall heavily, distorting my view through the windscreen. I drive with the side window partially open and squint out at the side of the road, the cold rain stings on my forehead. Adrian is sitting huddled on the stoop, hugging his knees. He is soaked, his sweater hangs loosely from his shoulders. I park the car on the road and walk across the muddy courtyard.

"I've booked us into a motel. I think we should talk." I squat in front of him and rest my hands on his knees. His face is swollen, his lower lip is bloody. He has been hitting himself, punching his face. "It's all right. It's going to be all right." I rub my hands along his thighs.

"No," he says slowly. "No, it won't." He pushes my hands away. "It won't be all right."

I stand useless in front of him, unsure of what to do. The rain suddenly quiets and settles into a lighter fall. I look around as the sky brightens; the courtyard is saturated, swollen with mud. Adrian leans forward, resting his head on his arms. His knuckles are raw.

"I'll be in the car." I wait for a moment and then walk back through the rain toward the car, the soles of my shoes thickening with mud.

I sit, watching the boy. For a while he does not move, then wiping his face with both hands, he rises and walks slowly through the drizzle to the car pulling his sweater over his head like a hood. He opens the back door and crawls into the seat behind me.

We are silent all of the way to the motel.

The rain has stopped, and it has become much colder. Adrian will not leave the car. I take the blankets off the bed and stand in the doorway. Even though it is not raining, the drain is overflowing onto the curb. The car sits marooned in a puddle. Adrian is awake, but says nothing as I tuck the covers about him. The traffic on the interstate creates a busy hiss and hum of wet tires on wet tarmac, filling the air with something like the sound of a hive.

Adrian stares ahead at the seat, his face puffy and his mouth still bleeding. I shake him by the shoulder. "What do you want to do?" I ask. "What can I do?"

He stares blankly ahead. His mouth is crooked when closed, and his nose is swollen. "You knew, didn't you?" His tongue tests his swollen lip. "And you didn't tell me. And that's why you don't want to fuck anymore."

I return to the room and run myself a bath. Everything is monogrammed with a logo of a smiling catfish: the receipt, the towels, towelettes, and soap packages. On our pillows are two complementary postcards of the sign in front of the motel. I undress in the bathroom and sit in my underpants on the side of the bath, trying not to think, no longer interested in the bath. It is too early to sleep. I sit staring at the front door and a wall covered in a dissonant yellow-and-brown bamboo-patterned paper. After a moment the lines begin to dance and irritate my eyes, but I continue to stare to stop myself from thinking.

A regular thump starts up in the parking lot and quickly dies down. The room becomes warm and fills with steam. I test the temperature of the bath and turn the water down. The thumping starts up again, and there is a shout, a single hoarse cry. Picking up my trousers I hop across the bedroom, one leg at a time. As I open the door, the thumping becomes more frantic.

The car jolts as Adrian slams his hand against the side window. His hand leaves a wet, red, spattered imprint on the glass. It is blood, I think, blood. There is a shrill ringing in my ears as I run barefoot across the gravel.

The boy sobs as I open the car door. "It's all right," he assures me. Blood spews like vented steam from a gash in his armpit and beads like condensation on the seat, the window, the carpet; black on the plastic, scarlet on the glass. I have never seen so much blood, his hands are so slippery with it that he cannot open the car door or pick up the knife to hide it.

I scoop him out of the car and run into the motel, into the bathroom. He is stiff in my arms, his hands twist spastically back in pain. The bath is still running and as I drop him into the water he shouts. Returning to the car I pick up his shirt, his vest, the carpet, the knife, hat, shoes, map, magazine, everything sodden with blood, and run back to the bathroom to throw them into the bath on top of him as he attempts to clean himself.

Only when I am on my hands and knees sopping up watery blood with a face towel do I stop and listen to Adrian's shouting and sobbing, the water running into the bath. It is four in the afternoon, and Adrian is sitting half clothed and bleeding into a scalding hot bath full of detritus. My knees are damp. Pink footprints dirty the floor. I have cut my foot on the gravel outside.

"It won't stop bleeding," he sobs. "I can't make it stop."

I pull him upright, and forcing his arms by his side I hug him tightly. "This will help," I whisper into his ear. "This will make it stop." Adrian rocks stiffly with me, his head thrown back, as I squeeze as hard as I can, whispering, "Stop. Stop. Stop. Stop. Stop."

12

Adrian sits at the edge of the bed with his eyes closed, holding his arm tight to his side. A bedside lamp shines starkly on his face and chest; his shadow crowds up behind him, up over the wall and ceiling. I kneel beside the bathtub and pick out everything that I had recently thrown in. The bleeding, mercifully, has stopped; but he will not allow me to look at the wound. The water drains slowly from the bathtub with a loud and prolonged suck; the drain is plugged with newspaper. The objects seem foreign to me. His Stetson has collapsed and his shoes sit side by side at the bottom of the tub, the leather dull and fat with water. There are coins under the heels, forty-seven cents.

"When I was a boy, I set fire to the garage at my parent's house. After the firemen left, we could only find one of everything." I speak too quietly for Adrian to hear. "Shoes, Wellingtons, gardening gloves. The fire spread so quickly, one moment it was smaller than my hands, and the next, the whole floor was on fire."

I turn toward the bedroom. Adrian's feet are mashed together, toe to toe.

"It needs to be seen to." My voice echoes in the small bathroom. "Someone should take a look before it becomes infected. I think we should return to Chicago."

"No." He hunches slowly forward, exhausted. "I want to keep going."

"I think you should have someone take a look."

"I won't go back."

I wrap the bedspread and towels that I had used to clean

up the blood into a plastic trashbag. Adrian watches as I wipe the floor, his eyes in shadow.

"Promise me."

I stop at the doorway and throw the last of the towels into the bag.

"Promise we won't go back to Chicago."

It is a clear night and very cold. Frost has formed on the window. As I carry our luggage back to the car I am surprised at the night sky, deep and black and full of stars. Yellow lights from the expressway flood the parking lot, and revolving slowly above us is the orange crawfish, illuminated from inside, its claws corkscrewing at the air.

I lay towels across Adrian's seat, which is still damp from cleaning. After loading the car, I set his seat as far back as possible, so that he has extra room. I start the motor and turn up the heat.

Adrian walks slowly from the chalet to the car. When he sits down I wrap his coat on top of him and fasten his seat belt. I give the room one last check. The carpet is wet, and as I walk backward toward the door, I rub my foot over my footprints, erasing them, like a fugitive. By the time the maid comes to clean the room there will be no sign of what has happened. All that will be missing are some towels and a bedspread, which I have stashed in a plastic bag behind my seat.

Adrian huddles forward, fully doubled, his head resting on his knees, his back arched and his hands wrapped about his shoulders.

"I fucked everything up, didn't I?" he asks. His voice, not quite a whisper, sounds hollow and without emphasis.

"It's all right. It isn't your fault." Headlights swoop past, glancing across his shoulders and back. "Tomorrow, first thing, we'll find out your blood results. And then we'll go somewhere you can rest."

"It was a test for syphilis." He repeats himself and coughs.

"I didn't want an HIV test, so the doctor thought he'd rule out some of the other options."

"So what was the blood work you had done?"

"Just the syphilis."

"Is there anything else I should know?"

"Uh, uh." His hand slides over the back of his head.

We drive on in silence, and the forest draws closer to the highway as the road begins to wind.

There is a slight mist, enough to fur the lights from the truck stop. Adrian is asleep, face down on his knees, as if he has collapsed. I step carefully out of the car, and fish behind the seat for the plastic bag of bloodied towels and bedspread. There is a catch of sulfur in the air; behind a black bank of fir trees is a chemical plant. The mist leaves a cold damp film on the plastic. I walk to the toilets past banks of trucks, each with towels, newspaper, or cardboard propped up as blinds behind their windscreens.

A clock is centered over the entrance to the rest rooms. It is nearly two o'clock. I stand smoking by a row of telephones watching people walk toward and past me into a bright cafeteria, waiting for the toilets to become empty. Everyone squints and shields their eyes. My neck is stiff and my arm numb from driving. The coffee is almost undrinkable, bitter, sweet, and scented of almonds. Along one wall is a mural, a map of Texas inset with the state bird, the state flower, and blocks of text. The state is bordered by a thick blue line, as if the Rio Grande were an ocean, and the state an island.

Despite my precautions, the toilets are not empty. A young man, a Mexican, slowly mops the floor and pauses, watching me as I wash my face.

I throw the bag into a trash can in the parking lot, worried that if I had disposed of it in the toilets the man would have looked. It would have been too complicated to explain. From across the parking lot the car appears to be empty.

Adrian is still asleep, still hunched forward. I have brought another coffee for myself and a cold orange juice. As I turn back onto the interstate he slides sideways, so that his head is resting against the door. I check that his seat belt is buckled. For a while I can hear his head vibrating against the door; I am surprised that it does not wake him.

Adrian moans in his sleep. I shake him several times and he wakes slowly, as if rising through something heavy and thick. He stares ahead at the windscreen, head tilted, unfocused, his face imprinted with the crease from his trousers. Even in the faint light from the dashboard I can see that bruises are coming out on his swollen face.

"I was dreaming about him." He lets out a short breath, a huff. "I never dreamed about him before." The words catch in his throat, and his eyes glaze.

"Here, drink this." I hand him the orange juice and run my hand over his head. His forehead is hot. He is running a fever. "Does your arm still hurt? I have some Tylenol."

Adrian nods, dislodging a tear, and settles the orange juice between his legs.

"Over there," I point at the horizon, to a bank of blinking lights, "is the Gulf of Mexico." Small blue flames jump from the stand pipes of the refinery. A strong headwind buffets against us, and the car's headlights glance across regularly posted road signs: DON'T MESS WITH TEXAS, DON'T MESS WITH TEXAS.

13

The expressway sweeps around San Antonio, above malls and industrial strips. Without thinking I continue on Route 10. It is five o'clock and the night sky is a thin and cold sepia, the color of weak tea. Adrian is asleep. I am surprisingly awake, and several times I have wanted to turn on the radio, or more absurdly, to whistle. Several miles out of San Antonio the signs say Leon Springs, Bourne, and still further, Fort Stockton, before I realize my mistake. I am heading west, not south.

Turning at Bourne I make my second mistake and drive onto the frontage road instead of the motorway. I stop at a set of lights beside a machine shop and a Dairy Queen sign. I have no real idea where we are. For a moment I feel a surge of exhaustion; I am hungry and my eyes ache. The car idles and stalls; rain spatters on the windscreen with a dull strike. A faulty fluorescent tube blinks in the Dairy Queen sign. A more modest sign, DINER—ALL NITE—COFFEE/DONUTS/RIBS, handwritten on a single piece of cardboard, is taped to the stoplight. The cardboard is wet and buckled and flaps in the wind. It has been raining since Houston. I start the car, watching the sign flap against the post, trying to remember the last five minutes.

The café is in a small strip mall immediately to the left of the traffic lights. The Dairy Queen is closed, but the lights are on in the diner. Christmas tree lights are strung in a zigzag across the door.

Adrian wakes slowly, his hair flattened and sweaty. His eyes are swollen, the lids are heavy and bruised. He breathes cautiously through his mouth.

"How are you doing?" I ask.

He frowns at me as if he does not understand.

"How are you feeling?" I unbuckle his seat belt and reach across his lap to open his door. The wind catches the door and buffets it open. As he slinks out of the car, he keeps his left hand wrapped about his right shoulder and squints at the lights from the diner.

"Hungry?"

"Yeah." He nods. "Feel kind of pukey."

Adrian sidles slowly onto the pavement, and the wind blows his shirttail up to his shoulders. I take hold of his elbow and open the door for him. Leaning against me like an old man, he slides into the closest seat, a booth beside the window.

"Do you think you can eat?" I draw out two menus from behind a napkin dispenser.

Adrian leans forward onto his forearms and mutters, "Anything. I don't care what." His head is reflected perfectly round, as fat as a balloon on the dispenser's silver side.

"Some eggs?" I ask. "Scrambled eggs and toast?"

He nods into his elbow, and awkwardly sits himself upright.

A kitchen runs along the back of the diner, behind a blue Formica counter flecked with silver. A woman stands behind the counter with her back to the door. Christmas decorations, paper chains, and paper bells, limp and translucent with grease, hang so low that I could pull them all down. There is a mirror above the cash register, and I catch myself looking up. I had forgotten about Christmas. The woman pours oil over a large steel hot plate and vigorously scrubs a brick across it, scouring the plate. She is wearing a blue pinafore, white lacy socks and old trainers, and stands on tip-toes as she scrubs.

"I'll be with you in a minute," she says without turning. "We don't start serving till six. There's coffee on the counter."

I look to the coffeepot; the glass is stained and scratched, cups and saucers with chipped and blunt edges are stacked separately beside it.

"It's fresh. I just made it."

A small black-and-white television is suspended from the ceiling with gold and green tinsel tied about the box; a paper chain has come unfastened and slowly twirls in front of the screen. There has been a shooting in San Antonio. Two men, brothers, have been wounded in a shoot-out with the police. One seriously. The men are charged with the murder of a rent boy. The image slowly rolls: a photograph of the two brothers, both smiling with their arms about each other's shoulders, flickers up and over. A reporter, head down, reading from his notes, announces that Jon Koury, the younger brother, had his entire lower jaw shot off.

I walk slowly toward the booth with a cup in each hand, trying not to spill the coffee. Adrian is leaning awkwardly over, tilted sideways. I scald my thumbs and rest the cups on a table to get a better grip. Adrian suddenly slumps onto the seat, his head protruding into the aisle stiff and suddenly immobile. As I drop the cups, one upsets and spins from the table to the seat to the floor without breaking, scooting across the aisle in front of me. I kick it across the floor in my hurry to reach him.

Adrian is white, a bloodless white, his brow waxy and wet with sweat. He stares myopically at my hand as I feel his pulse, his forehead. His hand is open on his lap. There is a small crease of blood in his palm. He is bleeding again.

The woman stands at the counter holding up the brick.

"I need a doctor." I kneel beside the boy and wipe his brow. "Adrian. Adrian?" I speak softly. There is a small patch of sweat on the vinyl.

The woman deftly skips around the counter and runs to the booth.

"Is there a hospital here?"

The waitress pulls her hair away from her mouth and shakes her head. "There's a doctor. Dr. Hollander." She opens the door and points out, one hand flat to her throat, against the cold and the dark. "It's the first house on Main and Third. Go straight through the lights, one block and turn left. It's the big house across from the post office. I'll call ahead."

Adrian struggles to sit upright as I lift him out of the seat. "Hold on. Put your arm around my shoulder."

He yelps as I hoist him up. "It's okay," he protests. "I'm just tired."

The woman runs her hand across his temple as I carry him through the door. "You're worse than tired honey," she coos. "You need some help."

Adrian's head lolls against my shoulder. "Promise me we won't go back," he asks. "I won't go back."

I stand beside the examination table. The doctor's office is a bright garish green, so bright that I have to squint. I am numb, exhausted from the drive. Adrian fiercely grips my hand, his face creased with pain as the doctor inspects his shoulder. Silent until now, Adrian begins to howl as the doctor raises his arm.

"Ow. Ow. Ow. Ow. It hurts. It hurts." He jolts and attempts to sit upright. The doctor rests his hand flat on the boy's stomach and looks across at me clearly angry. His eyes are almost colorless, almost as white as a wolf's, a clear and indifferent gray.

"There is quite a bit of damage, and it's infected. Why didn't you bring him in earlier?"

I shake my head.

"There are four puncture wounds. I can't tell how deep.

The tips of the doctor's rubber gloves are encrusted with blood. He cleans his hands on a large flat daub of cotton dressing awash with an astringent alcohol. The smell hits me, and I hold Adrian's hand tighter, fighting against nausea and exhaustion.

I sit in the waiting room with a cup of sweetened coffee and stare out at the rain. Stacked neatly on a table beside the couch are old copies of *National Geographic*, *Reader's Digest*, and *House and Garden;* the prices have been carefully covered over with a black felt-tip. The magazines are strangely thin, and when I pick them up, I notice that whole articles have been cut out.

The doctor is standing at the door, his arms folded. He has the strong and compact build of a rugby player. As I rise he waves his hand, patting me back down into the seat. He scratches behind his ear, then smoothes his hand through his hair as he sits down in an armchair opposite me. His hair is black and shorn close at the sides, military-style.

"My sister," he says reaching for a *National Geographic*. "We often have children in here—she likes people to have something to read—but she doesn't always approve." He talks slowly, without inflection, his voice an even tenor, as if he were bored or tired, and runs his hand flat down a dark paisley tie. He has not yet shaved. "A naked Guianan tribe. Perhaps a liquor advertisement." The pages rustle one by one through his fingers.

"How is he?"

"He should be in a hospital." The doctor allows the magazine to close with a quiet slap. Sitting forward he closes and rubs his eyes and yawns; and without the strange impassive lights of his eyes, his face seems handsome, less predatory. His head ticks uncomfortably sideways, and the magazine slides off his lap and onto the seat. There is something on his mind. "I could refer him to St. Joseph's. But I need to know more about what happened." The doctor sits back and rubs his shoulders against the chair. "It's a Jesuit hospital."

I look about the room, at the leaded windows, at the meticulously embroidered covers over the arms and backs of the chairs, and at the doctor, very much at home. Everything is contrived to appear older. The man waits, fidgeting, running his forefinger across the cleft in his chin.

"He had a swelling, under his arm." I tuck my hand under my shoulder. "I think he was trying to cut it out. We aren't certain, but he believes that a friend of his might have had AIDS." I look to the doctor to see some reaction, some response, but the man simply leans forward and nods his head, as if something he had already believed had been confirmed.

"Have either of you been tested?" he asks. I stand up, suddenly angry at the doctor's assumption. The doctor looks up, surprised, and smiles for the first time. Uncomfortable and embarrassed, I sit back down.

At eight o'clock a police car pulls into the small car park behind the house. A policeman hurries through the rain close by the window and around the side of the building to the porch. I have not seen Adrian for two hours, and it occurs to me that the doctor might have called the police and not the hospital. Standing back in view and away from the door, the policeman shakes the rain from his hat and coat. He is stout and the short run has left him out of breath. The man peers short-sightedly into the rain, back into the parking lot, directly at our car. At last he rings the doorbell, a buzzer sounds in the back of the house. The doctor walks unhurried past the waiting room door and greets the policeman by name. There are, it seems, reports of a flood. I turn to the fireplace, and press myself against the seat, attempting to hide. I try to think of a story, something to tell the policeman if he asks about Adrian, but I cannot concentrate, and nothing convincing comes to mind.

The doctor invites the policeman into the house and returns to his office. The policeman apologizes for the rain and waits out of view, inside the corridor. The doctor returns with a note, a prescription perhaps, and with a smile he closes the door to the waiting room. I listen to the rustle of the policeman's coat along the corridor wall and the snap of the lock as the door is finally closed behind him.

The doctor returns to the sitting room. He is flushed and animated and smiles again. "St. Joseph's will admit him. He'll be ready in five minutes." He points outside. "That's my car. If you pull around the house you can follow me there." He clenches and unclenches a pen in his hand. "He can ride with you. No," he pauses and tips the pen at me. "Perhaps it's better if I take him."

It is light outside and still raining hard, the sky is as dull and heavy as pewter. I drive behind the doctor's station wagon. Adrian sits in the backseat, the top of his head just visible in silhouette. I feel tired and dirty and anxious. The doctor stops at a level crossing, waiting for a train. A bell clangs in time with two red flashing signals, the barrier comes down and after a few minutes a train rattles steadily through. The car shudders as each boxcar passes with a slow and hefty trundle. Exhaust from the doctor's car hangs in the air between us. The signal's red light blossoms in the vapor. There is a police car behind me; and once the train has gone and the barriers are raised the police car stays with us. It is a slow procession; the doctor drives cautiously and the squad car sticks close behind, turning away only at the entrance to the hospital's car park.

The hospital is square and solid, built like a Norman keep, with few windows and a deep recessed entrance. For the second time today I find myself in a waiting room. Thankfully, there is no sign of the police. St. Joseph's reception is a wide carpeted hall, bounded on two sides by stairs. A large crucifix is cut into the wall above the reception desk. Painted beneath the cross in a are the words, HOSPITAL DE SAN JOSE—MISSION HOSPITAL OF SAINT JOSEPH. A sign by the entrance requests in both Spanish and English that silence be observed within the hospital corridors at all times. Almost immediately I hear voices and laughter and footsteps coming from one corridor. An elderly man, Mexican, his hair white at his temples, vacuums the carpet and occasionally smiles at me.

At about nine-thirty, after several more cups of coffee, Dr. Hollander returns with a nurse. The nurse stands back as the doctor shakes my hand; he assures me that he has talked more with

Adrian and will be in touch with the hospital once he has contacted Reyes's doctor and family. His manner is brisk and he seems uneasy.

"We should get you a pass."

The doctor takes me aside to the receptionist's desk and signs a form allowing me access to the boy. The receptionist writes a number, 3710, on a sticker marked ST. JOSEPH'S: GENERAL VISITOR and peels the back off, offering the sticker to me with the tip of a finely manicured nail.

"Tell me," he asks, offering his hand. "Your accent, you're English but you're not from London. Am I right?" I tell him that I am from Yorkshire, and he nods. "I thought so." He keeps hold of my hand. "You'll be able to visit. It shouldn't be a problem. You should think about getting some rest." With one curt shake the doctor releases my hand.

The nurse hurries ahead of me at a brisk pace and swinging her arms as she walks she describes visiting hours and visiting policy, assuming, without any word from me, that I am a relative. I turn back to the counter to thank the doctor, but he has already gone. Catching up with the nurse I ask her if she knows Dr. Hollander. She pauses, and raising both hands she declares him a saint. "An absolute saint."

Immediately out of the waiting room we are into the body of the hospital. The first ward is divided into small cubicles with curtains instead of doors; affording the patients some privacy, or perhaps just the notion of it. The nurses' station is crowded with birthday cards, balloons, and a large bouquet of flowers wrapped in cellophane. Despite the bright colors there is a terrible feeling of malaise. Young men sit upright on their beds, bored, looking out at the corridor, watching as we walk by.

On the third floor the elevator opens to a blank wall. The corridors are wide and similar, the walls are painted a pale blue. Hung close to the ceiling are directions to other rooms, other wards, HYPERACUTE, RESPIRATORY, ISOLATION, and CARDIAC STATION. At every corner there are concave mirrors and security cameras. As I follow the nurse I become confused and anxious for Adrian, secluded at the back of the hospital. Finally, the corridor opens out to a set of small cubicles arranged about a central station.

The rooms have wide sliding glass doors and thin nylon curtains. Patients' names are written on white plastic boards beside the doors. Each booth faces out onto the nurses' station. In several I can see the blue flickering light of a television. Unlike the first ward these patients are hidden behind drawn curtains and doors; their conditions seem much more serious.

The nurse turns and stops at one curtain and briskly opens it. I am surprised to see Adrian's clothes folded neatly on a chair beside a bed.

"If you need anything," she points at the call button. The nurse smiles, and as she steps back into the corridor I catch a soft talcum scent of soap.

Adrian's room is small, barely larger than a walk-in closet. He is lying flat without a pillow and does not see me enter the room. There is a cradle over his upper torso so that the blankets will not rest on his shoulder. An orderly carefully organizes the tubes reaching from Adrian's nose to his wrist, and from his wrist up to an armature and drip beside the bed. The man's movements are slow and considered. I stand back in the doorway waiting for him to leave.

Adrian lies motionless. The bed is set dead center against the wall below a strip light and a small wooden crucifix. A long panel fixed with switches, ports, and outlets marked AC, OXYGEN, VACUUM, runs the whole length of the wall. To the left of the bed is a narrow window, recessed like an archer's slit. A Bible sits on top of a cabinet beside a telephone. The hospital name and logo is printed and stamped on everything: the pillow, the bedsheets, the drip bags.

The orderly raises the bed and sets the railings on either side upright. The bed whirs automatically adjusting itself, adding to the soft and constant shush of the air-conditioning.

"How do you feel?" I ask after the orderly has left. The curtain is open, and I can see through the glass to the nurses' station.

He shucks the sheets free from his hands and signals "so-so." His eyes are closed, his face oily with cream. "They have to keep the wound open. It has to heal from the inside out."

I squeeze his hand. His palm is clammy, and he does not return my grip. He is wearing a blue plastic bracelet typed with his name and a number.

"He said I have to stay here for a couple of days." He coughs and frowns. "The police were here." His eyes flutter open and closed. "I hear you passed out again." He smiles faintly. His voice is husky and fades into sleep. "You know what? I'm hungry. Go get me a hamburger, will you?"

I awake stiff and confused, unsure of where I am, the back of the chair pressing into my shoulders. Someone has placed a blanket over me, and there is a tray with a covered plate sitting on the cabinet. Adrian is asleep; the curtain and door are drawn shut, and the lights in the room are out. My watch has stopped. It is still daylight, although it is too dim and overcast to tell the time.

I step about the curtain and stand in the doorway and stretch, cracking my elbows. The hospital is silent as if abandoned. A small lamp lights the desk at the nurses station. A young man sits writing, tracing a line down one sheet of paper as he checks another. I peer gingerly into the booth beside Adrian's, anxious not to be caught prying. The rooms are identical. The patient lies asleep, the sheets folded down to his stomach, his arms rest flat to his side. An oxygen tube and mask is attached to the man's face, and protruding from his chest is a short and stubby clear tube, a plugged catheter lodged into the skin at one end and masked at the other with surgical tape. His skin appears gray and dry. Beside him is a steel-gray machine, the size of a water cooler, which clicks forcefully and regularly, and shudders like a refrigerator. A woman sits behind the machine, head lolling sideways, mouth slightly open, asleep. Her glasses are tilted, and she has slumped deep down into the chair, a lime-green cardigan pulled about her as if she were cold. I cannot see enough of the patient's face to tell if he is her husband or her son.

Returning to Adrian's room I pull the curtain closed. The man at the desk asks if everything is all right. I lean over the boy. He looks like an old man, his face puffy, cheeks and jawline swollen; it is hard to understand how it all came to this. His breathing is heavy and regular, undisturbed, a sure and certain sleep induced by drugs. I sit down and pick up the tray, although I am not hungry. Taking off the aluminum cover I am happy to see that the meal— white boiled chicken, peas, carrots, and mashed potatoes—is still warm. As I pick at the food I hear coughing; the woman next door is awake.

There is one motel beside the frontage road called the Ranger's Lodge. The rooms are small and depressingly familiar, furnished in beige and brown, with tan candlewick curtains and bedspreads. Beside the door sits a squat overstuffed easy chair, porky and creased; it looks too greasy to sit in. Between the bed and the chair is a short three-legged table, pocked with cigarette burns. The walls are painted a dull off-white, yellowed by two small twin lamps fastened to the walls either side of the television. The room reeks of carpet cleaner. Everything seems damp. I think enviously of the spartan and sanitary hospital rooms.

I unpack as quickly as I can, running back and forth from the car to the room, wanting to wash, eat, and return to the hospital by six, although I have no real idea of the time. Evening visiting hours last from five-thirty until nine. It is bitterly cold and the sky is beginning to darken. The drains outside belch up water, one side of the parking lot is flooded, and my shoes are wet. I leave my briefcase with the money in the car.

Wanting to know the correct time I turn on the television.

Clicking through the channels I find the news; it must be close to five o'clock. And while I am stowing cases under the bed a report comes on about the Koury brothers. A title "The Koury Killings" swings across the screen, and there is a shot of a house, a small suburban bungalow with a bare unkept yard. The shot closes in on the police and medical examiners gathered at the open door and steps. Two bodies have been exhumed so far from the crawl space beneath the house.

It is ten past five. I have not washed or changed my clothes since Mississippi; I feel unspeakably dirty, there is a large and dry coffee stain on my shirt. I turn off the television and strip standing where I am, and hurry into the bathroom. The bathroom is cramped, with only a walk-in shower and a toilet; the sink is in the bedroom by the door. I shower quickly, dodging in and out of the lukewarm stream.

As I rinse off the soap I am surprised by a short, almost human, cough. A small dog, a puppy, lies on the mat just inside the bathroom door. It is a mongrel, part Labrador, part Alsatian perhaps, certainly no older than six months. Its pelt is wet and matted with mud, its head rests on the damp rug, eyebrows cocked. There is no collar, no identification tag.

"How did you get in here?" I ask the dog. The puppy rolls completely over, legs thrown all to one side and coughs again. I crouch down and hold out my hand. The puppy uprights herself and scuffles backward, tail pricked up, out of the bathroom to the front door.

There are no towels in the bathroom. I follow the dog into the bedroom, tracking wet footprints across the carpet, shivering, my hands modestly cupped over my thighs. There are two towels, stiff but clean, stacked beside the television. "What happened?" I whisper to the dog. "Did somebody forget you?" The dog watches as I dry myself, and barks, a surprisingly musical bark, prompting me to the door.

As I open the door, she presses her nose into the widening

171

gap, and forces herself through, bounding onto the verandah and into the parking lot. The dog's breath trails behind her as she scampers about in the rain, as pale as a ghost.

Next to the motel is a small restaurant. The facade is crudely disguised as a wooden fort with upright plastic logs. A sign—the branded outline of a pig—reads Hank & Rita's BARbeque.

The interior is divided into small dark booths and smells of beer and vinegar and burnt sugar. Three waitresses in striped red-and-black caps and overalls sit at the bar, and turn in unison as the door bangs shut behind me. Except for two boys sitting at the back beside the rest room doors, the restaurant appears vacant.

One of the waitresses grabs a menu. "Just one?" she asks and swings off the seat, sulky and bored and chewing gum. "Smoking?" Her long brown hair is pulled through the back of her cap in a skinny ponytail. I follow her to the back of the restaurant.

Sitting on his own in a booth opposite the two boys, and almost hidden in shadow, is Dr. Hollander. The doctor half-stands, surprised, his lap brushing against the table, and offers me a seat. He flattens his tie to his chest, and runs his hand down to his stomach, the tips of his fingers tuck under his belt. "Please," he smiles. "Why don't you join me."

The waitress flaps the menu against her leg and grins into her hand. The doctor asks for his check and the girl walks away with the menu. I shake the doctor's hand and slide into the booth. The doctor pulls the table back, and I mutter in a confused way about what a coincidence this is.

"Coincidence? No. Not really. You can eat Mexican, or you can eat here. There are only two choices." The doctor folds his napkin and wipes his mouth. "Or you can eat at the hospital." He smiles again. "My sister is away." He opens his hands faceup on the table. "And I'm afraid I'm not much of a cook."

I turn about in my seat looking for the waitress and the menu. One of the two boys punches the other across the table and points directly at us. The other boy leans forward and sniggers into his arms. I turn back. The doctor has also seen this gesture.

"Look," he smiles and stands up. "It's been a long day. I'll leave you to your meal."

As I unlock the car door outside of the restaurant, a bank of lights flares up across the parking lot. I turn about and squint into the headlights of a small boxy truck. The vehicle sits high off the ground on thick fat wheels shunted out of the wheel-well. Long red licks of fire are painted along its side. There are two people in the cab, the same young boys who were laughing at us in the restaurant. Their chins, noses, and the tips of their wide-brimmed hats are lit by the bright glare of a halogen lamp above the restaurant's door. Opening his window and resting one hand flat to the truck's door, the driver leans out to spit and look behind as he backs up. The rain has almost stopped.

"Hey, you." The boy slaps the side of the truck, shouting at me as I unlock my door. "Yeah, you. Faggot."

The passenger leans forward, laughing, bottle in hand, and shouts, "Go, go, go." The truck punches into gear and lunges forward, bouncing as it hits the rise of the road. The boys hoot and holler; a bottle rockets from the driver's window and explodes at the side of the road.

As I turn onto the frontage road, a shape catches the headlights and floats for a second beside the car before tumbling in the darkness down the scrub-covered embankment towards the motorway. It is the dog, the puppy I had found in my room. The dog returns, bounding up the rise, running wild, caught in the meridian between the two busy roads. Her shadow arcs wildly behind her, wheeling across the embankment as cars and lorries overtake her. I pull onto the side of the road and hurry down the muddy slope.

As soon as I am out of the car the dog cowers in the brush.

Her eyes glint a sharp and bright green, reflecting the headlights from the passing cars. I step carefully forward, my shoes heavy and clodded with mud, and coo in a gentle voice. The dog ducks behind the scrub, laying low. I reach forward, close enough to touch but not grab her, and for one moment I am terrified that she might bolt out onto the motorway. To my surprise the puppy shuffles forward and nudges my hand.

Adrian stares through me at the door. A slender strip light floods the bed, deepening his eyes.

"I'm not too late, am I?" I stand just inside the room, packages still in my hands, and pull the curtain closed behind me. The curtain is too short for the rail and does not reach entirely across the doorway. "I can come back. I can—I'll just leave you these." I look about the room for a chair. "I thought that you might like to look at these." I step further forward into the room and rest the books and maps at the foot of the bed.

Adrian turns his head and looks sideways out of the window. I lean against the plastic railing and look out after him, trying to guess what he is watching. There is a strong wind blowing outside, and the rain runs almost horizontally across the glass, streaked yellow by the street lights. I look at my reflection in the window, wondering what to say.

"Somebody just called me a faggot." I talk quietly, mumbling so as not to be heard by the nurses. The door again is wide open. "Just shouted it at me as I was coming here." I pause and tug at my shirt cuffs. "I met that doctor again."

Adrian smarts and stares up at the cradle straddling his chest, his hands hidden beneath the covers. There is a purple bruise running under his eyes and high across the ridge of his nose. His face, excepting his lower eyelids, has lost its puffiness, and he looks exhausted, drained. Sitting beside the end of the bed I begin to tell him about the dog. I cup my hands to describe the puppy's paws and realize that he is not listening at all.

"So. How is your shoulder?"

"My shoulder?" He winces. "Hurts like fuck."

I reach under the covers for his hand. Adrian looks nervously to the door and shakes his head with an air of exhausted disbelief. "What are you doing with a dog?" he asks. "We can't take a dog with us." He swings his lower arms out from beneath the clean white sheets. He is wearing thick red wool gloves. His right eye is watering, there is a thin, dry saline trail running from his eye to his temple. "I mean a dog?" He shrugs one shoulder.

"Why are you wearing gloves?" I ask.

"I found them," he says defensively, grimacing as he awkwardly sits himself upright. Shuffling up on his elbows and pushing back the cradle he rests his head uncomfortably against the wall. "Everyone who comes in here is wearing gloves." He holds up his hands and splays his fingers as if it were blood or shit instead of wool that covered them. "I'm not taking these off until I leave. I'm not touching anything in here."

"Even me?"

Adrian frowns wearily.

I stand between the bed and the window facing him, still wearing my coat. I feel like a guest.

"They said I came this close to a major artery." He twists his hands in front of his face and curls his upper lip against the plastic oxygen tube. "They couldn't find the lump. So I guess I cut it out." He looks at me through his fingers and smiles maliciously. "What color was the blood?" He asks, pinching his fingers in front of his face. He rolls the back of his head against the wall and tucks his hands away, closing his eyes.

A nurse enters the room and, smiling at us both, she takes Adrian's pulse and asks him if he is comfortable. I take this as a signal to leave and make my excuses, promising to return tomorrow morning. "Is there anything you need?"

Adrian relaxes until the woman has left. He shakes his

head, perhaps pouting. "So what did he want?" he asks, craning his head about the frame on the bed. I step back into the room.

"Dr. Hollander? Nothing. He didn't want anything. I met him by accident. We were at the same restaurant."

Adrian closes his eyes. "The guy's a creep. He had his hands all over me."

I rest my arms on the chair to steady myself. "What do you mean?"

"I told them I did it myself." He rests his head back onto the pillow. "They were asking about my parents, so I said I was nineteen. I didn't know what else to say. Then they started asking questions about the doctor. Like they're after him or something."

"What did the doctor do?" I smile, more for my assurance than his. Adrian stares blankly at the ceiling. I shake his feet. "I'm serious."

Adrian closes his eyes and covers his face. "Nothing," he sighs through his hands. "He just took a little too long checking things. That's all. He just touched a little too much, and seeing as I was bleeding all over the place, it gave me the creeps."

I lean over the front of the car, double up and retch onto the asphalt. The puppy jumps up, banging her head and paws against the window. I lean against the glass, coughing and catching my breath, and the puppy settles down.

I return to the waiting room and check my clothes and shoes, and search through my pockets for my handkerchief and cigarettes, counting quickly from one to one hundred. There is a sharp sting of bile in my mouth. I stand outside the waiting room doors smoking, protected from the rain by the awning. It is all too easy to imagine, the doctor taking advantage of the boy, because he is sick, because he is in need of help. The wind is cold and the cigarette flares, blowing ash into my eyes. Adrian's neighbor, the woman in the green cardigan, stands just inside the door. She is wearing an open navy blue overcoat and slippers, her cardigan is unevenly buttoned. In her hands she holds a lighter and an unlit cigarette. She looks out straight ahead, occasionally blinking, rolling the unlit cigarette patiently between her fingers, waiting for me to leave.

14

I sit bolt upright in bed, unable to sleep, with my hands beneath the covers, wondering if Adrian is still wearing his gloves. The puppy is whining in the bathroom. I have tethered the animal to the toilet as the bathroom door will not lock and I am worried that she will foul on the carpet. At five o'clock I am wakened by a series of lonely and sorrowful howls.

The puppy snaps and yaps as I enter the bathroom; both of us blink at the light. Newspaper torn and chewed and wet with urine sticks to the linoleum floor. The dog lunges at me as I reach about the toilet to untether it. "What do you want me to do with you?" I ask the dog. She cocks her head and huffs, both of us exasperated by her mess.

It is almost dawn. I open the curtains and sit in front of the window beside the television, crossing and uncrossing my legs, unable to make myself comfortable. Water falls in a sheer curtain over the verandah; the whole parking lot is flooded. The puppy runs excitedly about the bedroom and then jumps up onto the bed and settles facing me, huffing as she rests her head between her paws.

Adrian's leather suitcase sits at my feet, the soft cover is flipped open. Lying on top is a collection of dog toys, the bald and deformed terrier, a hard yellow rubber ring, and a soft leather ball. Beneath the toys, and tucked carefully down into the sides, is a well-worn sheath of brown wrapping paper. Adrian's white silk boxer shorts are folded neatly underneath. As I lift them up, the cold and creased material softly unfolds onto my lap. The waistband is as thick and stiff as a leather belt. Beneath a second layer of brown paper is a pair of brick-red boxing gloves. The gloves are beautifully crafted; the leather is new and supple and rounded like the shoulder of an easy chair; they seem large, even for my hands. Tucked inside the wrists are streams of red cotton banding. There are two new plastic protective cups, the elastic is tied loosely into a knot. Among other clothes and shoes less carefully packed are three pornographic magazines and four pamphlets with their covers torn off. The pamphlets are full of stories, some of which have been circled: YOUTH GETS SUCKED BY OLDER BOY, WARNED BY AN OFFICER, PUERTO RICAN SUCKS STUDENT'S HOSE. Adrian's purse is tucked down the side of the suitcase. Folded carefully inside the purse is the newspaper clipping announcing the boxing tournament: "Texas vs. the Midwest, the Sheraton Hotel, San Antonio, December 24th."

At the bottom of the case, folded into a sweatshirt, is a Walkman, along with four tapes tucked together in a sock. Despite a crack in the plastic cover, the Walkman still works. I turn it on, put in the earplugs, and smooth the shorts over my knees.

The tape growls as if the recorder were being dragged across the floor, or a table. Gradually the hiss recedes and the sound clarifies, revealing a young man's voice, soft and flat and without cadence, so much so that it is almost lost in the static.

There is a break in the tape, and then, quietly at first, someone, perhaps the same man, begins to sing.

The voice is low, shaky, and shy. The words are Spanish, and I wonder if this is Reyes. Slowly the voice grows stronger and more courageous. The song is sad and sonorous and slow, and after two verses the low and husky voice falters to a halt.

I return to the bed, the puppy settles beside me, her tail beats softly against the blanket. Sneezing into the covers, she sniffs at my ear and mouth, then nuzzles her head under the pillow. I roll beside the small, warm, bristly body, and the faint, muzzy smell of pee, cradling the boxing gloves in my arms and listen again to a song that I do not understand.

*

I return to the hospital at eleven. Reyes's song—I assume that it is Reyes—is caught in my head. I walk past Adrian's neighbor. The door and curtains are wide open, but neither the patient nor his visitor are there. A woman's soft black handbag rests in the center of the bed. Adrian's curtain is also open, and I stand for a moment out of view. Adrian's chart rests in a plastic pocket between the booths; there is one red star beside a scrawled signature. Visitors are not allowed when the patient is scheduled for treatment, and there is a small timetable clipped to his chart. Treatment hours are blocked out in black.

I reach up to draw the curtain. Adrian coughs. "Don't do that. They don't like it. They'll only think that something is going on." His voice is coarse and brittle. As he turns toward me the bed hums, compensating for his movements. The oxygen tube has gone, and his face appears less swollen and less pallid. He sneers nastily at me, struggling to hold his head up. "Where were you? Huh?" He sits slowly upright, struggling with the cradle. "You said you'd be here." His head is shaking. "Oh, I'll be there for you, Adrian. I'll be right there with you," his voice whines in a high-pitched caricature of mine. "Do you know what I had to do this morning?"

I shake my head and look down at the covers.

"I had two doctors in here asking me who I've been with and what I've done, like I'm a freak." He settles back against the pillow and squints at me as if I were a great distance away. "How many people have you fucked?" His head shakes.

"Did you talk to them about Reyes?" I ask.

"Did you get rid of the dog?" He stubbornly focuses at my collar and stares hard. An orderly pushes a tall trolley stacked with food trays up to the door. He smiles at us through the glass as he walks away.

"There hasn't been anyone else." I reply to the first question.

Adrian shakes his head, indignant, "What about the women you've slept with? What about the guy on the train?"

"I've told you everything about him."

"Forget it." He turns back to the window. "You don't get it, do you?" The cradle severely restricts his movements, and he looks foolish, just a head and shoulders peeping up from under the sheets.

"I haven't slept with many people." I walk about the bed so that he can see me. "Robert was the only man." I am suddenly embarrassed. "I used to have these crushes, terrible crushes, but I could never do anything about it." I smile. "I was never very courageous. Robert would sleep with me, but he didn't like me to touch him. He wouldn't have sex. And after he married, I promised myself that I wouldn't go through it again. It was too difficult, too complicated, and I couldn't see any alternative."

Adrian looks quizzically up at me, unsure and hurt. "They want to take a blood test."

I look over my shoulder—the food trolley blocks our view out to the nurses' station—and lean forward to kiss him. Adrian turns his head, but he cannot avoid me. I softly kiss his cheek. There are white crumbs at the corners of his mouth. "I miss you," I whisper.

Adrian pushes his head hard back against the pillow and closes his eyes. "I don't want to be here. I don't want to take any more tests."

I rub my thumb across his smooth jaw. There is a slight stubble at his chin. "They won't take the tests if you don't want them to."

I spend the afternoon with Adrian, looking through books on Brazil and the Amazon, replotting our route. I have brought him some tacos. I help him to sit upright and place the food carefully on the bed between his legs.

"Close the curtain. I don't want anyone to see me with

this." He eats quickly, talking between bites. "You know, they said I can leave in two or three days," he pauses. "That tournament is in two days."

There is a small commotion in the hallway, and a nurse stealthily half-walks, half-runs past the door toward the nurses station, holding a flat stainless steel platter in her hands. I stand beside the door peeping around the curtain. There is a small group of doctors conferring in a huddle at the end of the corridor, away from the nurses' station. The commotion seems to be centered on Adrian's neighbor. The doctors move away as a group, nodding to each other, and I slide the door shut.

"He fell out of his bed," he shrugs, "last night, just after you left. His mother went crazy. One of the nurses said he did it on purpose. One time he tried to pull out all of his tubes and stuff. Made a big mess, but he didn't get very far. Nobody likes him."

"What's wrong with him?"

He shakes his head. "Cancer. I don't know. Most of them have cancer." He rolls the taco up tightly and folds it in half. "The doctors were asking for addresses." He takes one bite. "They want to contact all the people I've ever done it with."

"Did you tell them about your cousin?"

Adrian coughs into his hand. "What cousin?"

"You told me that your cousin was the first."

He shakes his head. "What would I say that for? I don't have any cousins."

I sit back down beside the bed and pick up an atlas opened at Brazil. "I was thinking," I place my finger on the map to keep my place and fold the book over my hand. "Perhaps we should fly there."

Adrian frowns over his taco and wipes his mouth with his sleeves. He swallows. "Fly straight to Brazil? Why?"

I shrug and hold up my hands, the book slides from the bed.

"I mean, the point isn't just to arrive there, is it?" He talks with his mouth full. "You still want to go, don't you?"

"Of course I want to go." I reply carefully, reaching for the book. "All I'm saying is that we'll not have as much money as before."

Adrian looks up from his taco and about the room, as if accounting for all of its expenses. "Don't worry about it."

The food is already gone. He rolls the foil into a ball and tosses it between his feet. "My sister can pay."

"What does this have to do with your sister?" I push my chair back, away from the bed.

Adrian holds his fist up to his ear, sticking out his thumb and little finger as a telephone. He nonchalantly blows out his cheeks. "It's already figured out. She pays for the insurance anyway, so what's the difference."

I push myself hard back into the chair, dissatisfied with his explanation.

"It's just how she does things," he explains with a shrug, and rests back against his pillow and closes his eyes. "And anyway, she's loaded."

As soon as I am out of his room and walking up the corridor, I realize, once again, that I am not sure which door leads to the exit. Perhaps the mistake is that I turned right out of Adrian's room and not left. I stand at the end of the corridor looking back, trying to avoid any further mistakes. I cannot walk past his room without him seeing me, and anyway, the hospital is square and sooner or later I should arrive back at the stairs or the lift.

I return to the motel to shower before dinner. The water pressure is down and I am standing under the trickle, trying to rinse off the soap when the dog jumps into the stall. I attempt to shove her away, but she winds herself between my legs, thinking that this is a game. As I step out of the shower the dog sits passive, directly under its stream, and barks in short sprite bursts until I turn off the water. I have no idea what I am supposed to feed her.

The dog pants as I dry her. She turns about, eager to be rubbed.

"All right. Sally? Lucky? Lucy? Sally?" I mistakenly wipe the towel across my lip. The towel and my hand smell peppery and musty. "How about Sally?"

The puppy, fluffier than usual, pushes her head into the towel. "Sally it is."

I sit in the diner looking at the car park. Sally stands up on the driver's seat her head peering just high enough above the dashboard to catch the green filtered light from the diner's windows. I'm smoking and my meal, strip steak, eggs over-easy, and hash browns, rests cold and untouched between my elbows. On the front page of the newspaper folded on the seat beside me is a photograph of Jon Koury, who died last night. Adrian will be disappointed when he hears. The waitress walks up to the table, tired and scuffing her heels, order book and pencil in hand. Her name GAIL is stitched in pink thread across a pocket on her blouse.

Gail's pen swings down between her fingers, and recognizing me she laughs into her hand. "I know you." She smiles warmly. "Did I just serve you without recognizing you? How is your son?"

I smile politely back. "Better. Much better, thank you. He had to go to hospital. But he's going to be all right."

The waitress shakes her head and looks down at the untouched meal. She is younger than I remember. Her face is heavily powdered, perhaps to hide a bad complexion, and her hair is pulled back, clasped in a pale yellow grip.

"I wanted to thank you, and I wanted to ask you if you know someone who wants a dog." I point out of the window at the car. "She walked into my motel room, and no one seems to know where she came from."

The woman squints through our reflections at the car. "Well, I don't think I know of anyone," she pauses, sucks in her lower lip, and looks back into the diner.

Aware that she has our attention, Sally jumps up and clumsily strikes her head against the windscreen.

"Kind of dumb," the waitress laughs, resting her hand on the window. "You just found her?"

"She walked into my motel room."

"Are you English?"

I nod.

Gail frowns into the glass, perhaps at her own reflection. She taps the window again and smiles. "Sweet baby. Why don't you keep her?"

I shrug. "We can't take her with us."

The waitress straightens up and running her hands through her hair she adjusts the clasp. "I tell you what. If you don't find someone in a couple of days, you go ahead and bring her back. I can't keep her," she rests her hand on the door, "but I might know someone who can."

I keep a pair of Adrian's underpants under my pillow. They are clean, and every now and then I put them on. They are of course too small for me, and a little worn in the seat. The puppy sits in front of the mirror as I turn about, watching myself, she sniffs gingerly at a beaker of Scotch on the floor beside my clothes.

There is a knock. Sally starts up and looks from me to the door. I muzzle the dog with my hand to stop her from barking and she growls into my palm. "Just a minute. Who is it?" I call.

"It's Travis from the office," comes the reply. There is a parcel for me if I would care to come and collect it.

I dress quickly in trousers and a buttoned-up overcoat. It is raining again. The parking lot is a large black muddy hole. The motel manager meets me halfway along the verandah with the parcel. I remind him that tomorrow will be my last night and that

I will settle with him in the morning. The parking lot is still flooded. The water is still, black and heavy, on the point of freezing.

The package is from Chicago, forwarded by the hotel. It is a new suit for Adrian. A dark charcoal-gray suit, with square-cut shoulders, wrapped in tissue, inside a simple monogrammed cardboard box. Two letters are enclosed; one in an official brown manila envelope marked U.S. Department of State, addressed to Adrian; the other, addressed to me, comes from England, from my sister.

The boxing shorts lay at the end of the bed. I pick up the telephone and call Adrian.

"I thought that you'd like to know that your passport arrived today," I tell him, stroking the shorts as I talk.

Adrian complains that he is bored, then falls silent. I have nothing to tell, and he hangs up disappointed. I should not have called. Less than a minute later the telephone rings. It is Adrian again.

"I was going to tell you tomorrow," he says, clearing his throat. "I don't know if you noticed, but there's a vacant lot across from the hospital." His voice is low, confidential. "There are some trucks parked on it. And anyway, last night there were these two guys hanging around the trailers looking like they were going to steal something. I watched them for a long time. It looked like they were up to something." He pauses. "I think they're, you know, I think it's for sex or something."

There is a click and a cough. Someone else has picked up the line. After a confusion of hellos, sorrys, and good-byes, we all hang up.

I drive to the hospital with two McDonalds' breakfasts packaged in lurid little boxes on the seat beside me. Because I ordered two breakfasts I had the choice of a free gift—a plastic yellow bird on what looks like a moped, or a plastic clown in a car, each just large enough to choke a child or a puppy. The clown reminded me of

Noddy. The hospital's car park is surrounded by a low plush wall of evergreens, and I am surprised to be stopped at the entrance by a policeman.

The pavement and road is thick with armed and helmeted policemen clad in heavily padded sleeveless jackets. Parked in front of the hospital's entrance is a whole fleet of gray and white police cars and two long black windowless buses, SAN ANTONIO POLICE DEPARTMENT stenciled in bold white letters along their sides.

The officer steps out of the gatehouse to the barrier. I roll down my window and the man asks me what I am doing, why have I come to the hospital. I hold up yesterday's pass and explain awkwardly who, where, and why. The officer appears not to listen, nods, steps back up off the road, and waves me through with his baton, looking into the car as I drive by.

The road, busy with police, runs about the building like a moat, wet and slick and black, and I am waved quickly through by a succession of policemen to a lot reserved for the hospital's doctors and staff.

Half of the car park has been cordoned off into an empty compound. A huge cross has been laid out in white plastic sheeting, weighted at each end with sand bags. At the far side of the enclosure are two television crews with pristine white antennaed vans. Across the car park, two policemen armed with batons patrol between the cars with muzzled and brutish dogs.

I walk, unchallenged, on the road back to the entrance, past an unbroken line of policemen. I count them as I pass, lose my place and count again. The men are silent and orderly, and although there is no outward sign, there is an anxious air about them.

The waiting room is empty. The receptionist writes my daily pass without comment, and I look back outside at the backs of the policemen, huddled protectively together.

Adrian is sitting upright listening to his headphones as I enter the room. When he sees me he switches off the tape and smiles broadly. He is wearing a white hospital apron and large yellow dishwashing gloves. The cradle has gone and his right arm is strapped in a sling to his chest. He has already eaten, his breakfast plate sits on the cabinet beside the bed, the foil cover rests askew, half on the plate and half on the table.

"You're sitting up now." I hand him his passport, the two breakfasts, and a bag with some magazines.

"Real food." Adrian gives a quick smile and claps his bound hand expectantly to his chest. "You better hide them."

"They won't be very good cold." I hide the breakfasts in the cabinet. "Did you know that there's about forty policemen outside?"

"Can you see them?"

I step over to the window and look outside. "They're round at the front. I've never seen so many. You don't have any idea why?"

"Uh-uh." Adrian pulls himself upright and about on the bed, dangling his feet over the side. "Is there anyone there?"

I look out. A student nurse sits at the desk. I give her a warm smile. "He's sleeping," I mouth to her, and she smiles back as I draw the curtain and pull the door closed.

Adrian tugs impatiently at the white paper hospital gown. In one wide sweep he pulls the gown over his head and drops it onto the floor. For the first time I can see the dressing. A wide white gauze square, about as large as my palm, wrapping under his right arm and reaching to his middle back.

"Do you want to see something?" he asks.

He flinches as I touch his shoulder, and I realize that he is talking about the view from the window. Standing naked in the daylight, he slides into the slender window socket. "You won't see them now, but down there, where the trailers are," he says, "that's what I was talking about last night."

I shake my head, worried that we will be caught.

"No, down there. The trucks." He points at several lorries parked in a fenced lot behind the hospital. The rubber glove squeaks as he draws his finger across the glass. Six trailer wagons, unhitched from their trucks, are parked together in a block. The containers are empty, their doors fastened open.

Adrian rubs his nose on his wrist, then taps his forefinger on the window. I stand nervously between him and the door, worried that someone might walk in on us.

"There are three guys, maybe four. They hide at the back so they can't be seen from the road." He turns so that his back rests against the glass. I rest my hand on his shoulder. "You know I can leave as soon as that doctor says so."

There is a noise outside in the corridor. Adrian sprints across the room, and is back in the bed before the door is open. He pulls the covers quickly up to his shoulder then reaches to the cabinet for the empty dinner plate. An orderly stands in the doorway and shoves back the curtain.

"Knock, knock." Adrian smiles, holding the plate out for the orderly.

The orderly stands obstinately away from the bed, his trolley in the corridor behind him. Adrian refuses to reach any farther forward. The man steps forward and takes hold of the plate, he looks down at the crumpled gown beside the bed and then looks up quickly, nervously, at me.

Adrian releases his grip, and we both look down at the gown.

"What's happening with the police?" Adrian asks.

The orderly takes the foil from the cabinet and looks warily at me. "One of the Koury brothers died last night," he replies. "So they're taking the body back to Huntsville."

"Why so many police for one dead man?" I ask.

"There have been threats to the family, I guess." The man shrugs. "I guess they don't want any mistakes this time. His brother is still in ICU. They've sealed off the whole floor. Only essential staff allowed."

I look to Adrian. "How does it feel to be in hospital with one of America's Most Wanted?"

He frowns and slowly wiggles his fingers on his chest. The orderly returns to his trolley and reaches up to close the curtain.

"No. That's all right." I say. The man looks back at the boy and then pushes his trolley on.

"What was his problem?" Adrian asks.

I am in the shower when the telephone rings. The puppy begins to bark in sharp little yaps as I have shut the door on her. I hurry across the dark bedroom, holding a towel close about my waist, and pick up the receiver on the fifth ring. It is Dr. Hollander.

"I'm afraid," his voice strangles and breaks into a bout of coughing. He apologizes and explains hoarsely that he has the flu. "I'm not getting very far," his voice strains and crackles, on the edge of coughing. "Without a full name there isn't much I can do."

I wave the towel over the dog's head as I listen. She sits upright and snaps at the corner, waiting for it to swing past her again. This is the second day that I have forgotten to buy dog food.

"Did you try his sister?"

Dr. Hollander is silent. I repeat my question and the man coughs and apologizes. "I wasn't aware of any sister." He sounds irritated.

I reach under the bed for Adrian's suitcase. Folded into his wallet is the card, the postcard of T. E. Lawrence. I squint at the card in the darkness and read off the number; the doctor repeats it back to me.

"She wouldn't talk to me, but perhaps you can persuade her. I don't know."

The doctor hangs up; immediately the telephone rings again. It is Adrian.

"What's the matter?" he asks. "Your voice sounds strange."

I tell him that I was coughing, that I should cut down on my smoking.

"Switch on your TV," he says, excited. "Hurry. Channel 5."

"What's happening?" I ask, stepping over the boy's suitcase to reach the television.

"St. Joseph's is on the news."

Adrian describes the scene as I search for the station. Sure enough, on Channel 5, there is a picture of the hospital. The shot cuts to a helicopter perched above a gray and empty car park. Impossibly huge, the machine slowly rotates behind the reporter as she delivers her report. The white cross ripples as the helicopter descends, one sand bag slips across the tarmac as easily as a puck on ice. The camera focuses on a gurney being wheeled across the blacktop between a barricade of policemen. Men brace themselves against the wind thrust down from the helicopter, their clothes flattened, their visors blown back as they load the gurney into the helicopter. Finally the helicopter ascends, tilting backward and skyward.

"That was the live one. The dead one is still here."

"But the orderly said that it was the other way around."

"He doesn't know the difference between his dick and his elbow. I asked one of the nurses. She said they've had bomb threats because of this." He pauses. "Anyway. Listen. They were here again," he begins to whisper as if someone else might hear him. "The same guys. Only this time I saw them get in. One of them has keys. It was exactly the same thing. It has to be one of the orderlies." There is a click on the line and he abruptly changes the subject. I sit at the end of the bed, happy that he is in such good spirits. "I was reading one of those books you left. About the Amazon. At one point these two rivers come together, and one is so thick with mud that it's red. The other is black from dead leaves.

And they run together, side by side, for miles, without mixing. Half of the Amazon is red, and the other half is black. What are you doing?" he asks.

I switch the television off as I explain that I had to run from the shower to pick up the telephone, and that I will shortly have to take Sally out.

His voice becomes hard. "You shouldn't have given her a name."

"Why don't you like dogs?" I ask.

"I like dogs. Dogs are fine." He protests. "I hate pets and the people who keep them. Dogs are supposed to be wild. People make them useless, and turn them into toys. Pets are pathetic. It's sick, really sick."

I hang up, eager for a drink, but before I have even crossed the room to turn on the light, the telephone rings for a third time. It is Dr. Hollander. "Mr. Harris? Success!" he announces. "Reyes was his last name. He went by his last name."

A car's headlights shine across the window. I step over the bed, stretching the telephone cord as far as it will go and draw back the curtain. Rain sparkles across the glass, each droplet trapping and reflecting the bright light, like beads of rosin.

"Hepatitis B."

The light sweeps again across the window, forcing me to squint, a shimmering bright square streaked with rain careens across the ceiling and the back wall; my shadow hovers in the corner, projected with exact detail beside the curtain's soft muslin edge.

"He tested negative for HIV."

The lights cut and the engine dies and the room falls dark. The image blinks and burns, soft and orange, shifting in the back of my eyes, as it slowly, slowly, fades.

Dr. Hollander begins to cough, he covers the receiver, and his muffled cough resounds like a dog's bark. "He was involved in an accident three weeks ago, a minor car accident after he was released from the hospital. Excuse me." He struggles between his coughs. "I don't know the extent of his injuries, but coupled with hepatitis and the likelihood that he was not taking sufficient care of himself . . ." The doctor pauses and coughs once. "I have the number of a clinic that I will contact tomorrow. And I'm hoping for a more complete history."

"What does this mean for Adrian?" I ask.

"I'd like to run some more tests. It's been over three months since he had sexual contact with him, so I'm fairly satisfied that we have nothing to worry about. But let's run those tests anyway."

Outside a car's doors slam. A woman's soft voice crosses the verandah. Keys crunch into a lock.

I thank the doctor and sit down, numb and exhilarated, clutching the telephone to my lap. The square of light still vague and ghostly hovers at the back of my eyes. I lie back on the bed laughing. It wasn't AIDS. Reyes died because of a car accident. I had never considered that it could have been an accident.

Sally jumps up on the bed and begins to lick at my mouth and face; from the room next door come the muted, tired, and testy voices of my new neighbors.

As I round the corner I almost walk headlong into a nurse pushing a trolley. The nurse breathes a quick "oops" and smiles. There is a perforated box on top of the trolley containing five suspended vials of blood. I walk quickly through the corridor to the elevator.

Adrian is lying on top of the bed in his underpants, the sheets and blankets kicked back. His right arm is still bound in a sling, a neat white linen pocket that covers his entire arm. A narrow splint of late afternoon sun reaches across the floor and mattress and cuts across his chest. I sit beside the bed. Adrian stares through me at the wall; he has been crying. His hand slides off the pillow as he turns onto his back. He rubs his eyes, and listlessly pushes the pillow up.

"What's wrong?" I ask.

Adrian swallows and his eyes narrow. "Reyes." He shakes his head. "Dr. Hollander came by this morning. He said it wasn't AIDS." He closes his eyes and stretches his neck, slowly tilting his head from side to side. "I keep dreaming of him."

I brush his forehead. "I'm sorry. I'm really sorry."

"He just got out of the hospital." Adrian stares up at the ceiling, compressing his lips tightly together, his eyes glassy and wet. He slowly sits up, as if sleepy, and points at the cabinet beside the bed. "He used to make tapes of himself singing. Things he made up. Songs." His voice wavers, barely louder than a whisper. "He taped everything. One time he set it under the bed and taped the whole thing." He nervously rubs his stomach and the light appears to soak into his skin. "There were these men he used to see. Sometimes he'd tell me about them. One of them used to buy stuff for him to wear. Mostly jockey shorts." He coughs and draws a line across his thigh. "And when they were dirty, he'd take them back, and exchange them for new ones. There was one guy he kept asking me to meet. Said it was good money, the guy just liked to watch, and I wouldn't have to do anything I hadn't already done. Usually he just wanted Reyes to undress, and then, you know, jack-off or something. I thought it would be too weird. But Reyes kept saying, he wants to meet you, he wants to meet you."

The strip of sunlight has narrowed to a fine red needle. "Then one day Reyes arranged this whole thing. He rented a room at a motel on Clybourne. I thought it was going to be just us, just Reyes and me. But when I got there there was this other guy. He just sat beside the bed and told us what to do."

"He didn't know that it was being taped?"

"No."

"Did you?"

"Reyes needed money to get to Florida. He thought this guy might pay a little extra for the tape, but instead he just freaked out. He thought that Reyes was trying to blackmail him." Adrian turns his head away and covers his face with his hand. He talks slowly as if measuring the sentence. "The thing is, I knew who this other guy was." His hand tightens over his eyes and he purses his mouth tightly shut, breathing heavily through his nose. "I couldn't leave. And Reyes had no idea."

"What happened to the tape?"

"I kept it at the gym. I don't think Reyes realized what he'd done." He turns fully over onto his side away from me. "That time with Reyes, when he recorded it, we hadn't really done it before, not really. He said I wouldn't have to do anything we hadn't already done. I thought it would just be a joke. But once he started, the other man kept asking him to do more." He winces. "It was the only time. He tried not to but it hurt, and I was bleeding for a while afterward. He said it was okay, but we hadn't used anything."

I reach across the bed, take his hand in mine, and lean close to him. Adrian coughs, and suddenly begins to cry, hard and heavy sobs. "It hurt so much." His voice sputters loud and angry. "I thought I was going to die. I didn't know what to do. I thought he'd fucking ripped something out of me. I thought I was going to die."

I cannot reach the dog. I was packing our cases when I stepped on her tail. She gave out a terrible, almost human yelp and hid beneath the bed.

"I didn't do it on purpose," I say angrily. I lie on the floor with my head jammed under the bed reaching for the dog. All the way back, against the wall, is a plastic bag. As soon as I touch it I can smell mildew. The bag contains the clothes that Adrian was wearing when he stabbed himself. I withdraw my hand. I had forgotten about the bag. Everything else I had carefully cleaned or thrown away.

My hair is caught in the box springs, the dog licks my outstretched hand, her eyes reflect a cold fluorescent light.

"I shouldn't have left him alone in the car," I say to myself. "I should have known."

From the room next door comes muffled shouts. They are arguing again.

The puppy pants through an open, gummy mouth; bright eyes and black mouth, like a little devil. She appears to be laughing.

The letter from my sister sits on the floor under the three-legged table, crumpled and soggy. It will be seven o'clock in the morning in England. I pick up the telephone and return to the chair, sitting quietly for some time before I decide to dial.

"Paul, where are you?"

"I'm in Texas."

"I've been trying to get hold of you everywhere. Michael's had a heart attack." She talks quickly, as if at any moment I might hang up. "Michael H." Michael H. is my brother, Michael B. is her husband. "They gave him a double by-pass. It's been awful, but he's going to be all right. He's already out of hospital. His doctors say that he was lucky, that it could have been much more serious." The line crackles and for a moment her voice is lost. "Hello. Hello?" she sounds anxious. "Paul, are you still there?"

Sally tumbles between the chair legs, and falling onto her back she begins to chew at the telephone cable.

"I think you should call him," she pauses, "at least for Christmas. He's back at home now feeling sorry for himself because he can't eat all the things he'd like to, and he can't smoke any more. He's depressed. They want him to go back to work as soon as possible in the new year, but I don't think his heart's in it anymore." She pauses again, embarrassed. "I didn't mean it like that."

Her voice sounds tiny, thin and ghostly, like a voice spoken on a toy telephone. "Paul, I think you should come back. It's a mess back here with Michael sick. I miss you. It's Christmas and we all miss you. The kids missed you on their birthdays. I was worried that you had forgotten us."

Adrian stands beside the hospital bed, black and serene in his suit jacket, silhouetted by the hospital window. One sleeve hangs empty, his arm is still in a sling. He stands erect and looks boldly up, his eyes seem hollow.

"How do I look?" He runs his hand down the side of his jacket. "Clean, nearly. No syphilis. No hepatitis." His voice drops. "I hear about the other one tomorrow. I didn't sleep last night. But I feel pretty good." He looks once around the room and sits back down on the bed. "Jesus. I wish I could go now."

The hospital will not release him without the admitting doctor's permission, and Dr. Hollander is not due in until tomorrow.

I help Adrian with the jacket. "The orderly I thought I saw," he points at the window, out to the trucks. "It wasn't the same man. But I asked him what was going on, and he said they used to have dogfights here, they used to bring dogs over from Mexico by train in freight containers. It was a big racket for a while, before the feds stopped it. He heard rumors about it starting up again. So maybe there is a dog in that trailer." He shrugs. "Whatever, I still think there was some sex going on."

I hand him an envelope.

"What's this?" he asks folding open the flap. There are two tickets enclosed, tickets for the boxing tournament tomorrow night.

"It starts at eight. Call me as soon as you are ready, and I'll come and get you. We can spend the day in San Antonio, and after the fight we'll drive to Brownsville. Christmas Day we should be in Mexico City."

Adrian looks up, eyes wide, surprised. "Mexico? What about the dog?"

"Sally? I think I've found her a home."

Adrian slides off the bed, steps forward and hugs me as hard as anyone can hug with one arm.

"You remember Robert?" Adrian nods into my shoulder, and I begin to stammer. "The one thing that I regret is that I never told him how much I cared for him. I assumed that he knew, but I was never able to tell him." The words dry up in my mouth.

Adrian steps back and looks down at his feet and shakes his head.

It is a cold morning, and there is a raw wind outside. As I hurry up the verandah my neighbor's door opens. A woman steps out, wrapped in a thick woolen marine-blue coat, and pulls the door to behind her. She lights a cigarette and draws hard, blowing the smoke forcefully away from the door, in case, by accident, any of it might blow back into the room.

"Cold." She smiles, scratching the back of her hand.

The door opens a fraction behind her, and as I pass I hear her husband's voice. "Look. Either step in or out. I really don't care. Just make up your mind." I turn about, surprised to hear an English accent, but I cannot see the man.

The woman takes a nervous second pull from the cigarette, drops it onto the verandah, stubs it out with her toe, and carefully picks it up before returning to the room.

The telephone rings as I am making my last trip out to the car. It can only be Adrian. I hurry to the car boot with my arms full, Sally jumps up in the seat as I try to open the door. The telephone stops ringing as I return to the room.

I park in front of the café and walk around the car to the passenger door. Sally sits in Adrian's seat. She will not move. I grip one hand forcefully about the animal's neck and slip the other under her belly; but she slithers limply from the seat into the foot space, and curls up tight, her tail hidden between her legs. She is shivering and whining, petrified by fear, and I realize that I do not want to part with her. I have to carry the dog up to the diner. Gail stands behind the glass door, arms folded, not entirely happy to be receiving the dog.

From across the road the hospital looks inhospitable and fortress-like. The entrance is overlooked by two long, vertical slits of windows.

A wheelchair is pushed up the ramp beside me. I smile at the woman, she does not smile back. The doors open automatically; there is some fuss, she has left her handbag in the ambulance. "Don't, please. Not in front of all these people," her husband whispers audibly, and after fidgeting with the breaks he returns to the ambulance with the attendant. For one brief moment I am left alone with the woman in the foyer. I am waiting for the lift.

The woman rubs her brow.

"Nice," she says loudly. "The flowers. Nice. Someone special?"

"Yes." I nod. "Very special."

"Nice. Roses. Has she been here long?"

I frown, hold up the flowers and smile at them, embarrassed that I do not know what she is talking about.

"Your wife? Has she been here long?"

I shake my head. "Not at all, actually, he's out today."

"Oh, he. That's nice."

"And you?" I point the flowers at her and quizzically raise my eyebrows.

"Me?" She points at herself. The woman appears exhausted. As she raises her arms her sweater sleeves fall back to reveal bandaged wrists.

I cock my head. The woman looks directly at me.

"They brought me to the wrong place," she says.

*

The bed in Adrian's room has been turned down, the mattress folded.

The staff nurse turns as she walks past, frowning. "I'm afraid," she says, walking backward to the door.

"Where's?" I point at the empty bed, but it's all too obvious to believe.

The staff nurse is standing by the automatic doors, unaware that because of her they will not close. "His sister came in from Chicago." She holds up Adrian's file.

"But what about Dr. Hollander? Did anyone check with Dr. Hollander? He was supposed to be released to me."

The nurse stands firm, and closes her eyes for a moment, summoning patience. "Dr. Hollander is ill. I spoke with him this morning, and he agreed that the patient could be released to his sister." There is a righteous edge to her voice, a faint smile on her lips. "It's Christmas. Everybody is going home. We try to place everyone with family during the holiday."

I stand in the hall shaking. "His sister," I shout directly into her face, "threw him out onto the streets when he was sixteen years old. She is absolutely the last person who should be responsible for him."

The nurse flinches and turns away from me toward the reception desk. The automatic doors shut softly behind her.

It is an absolute dead end. How could I have not anticipated this? He told me that his sister was paying the bills, how could I not have anticipated that she would come for him? I stand in front of the hospital doors, numb, sightless, unable for the moment to breathe.

15

By the time I return to the motel the sky has turned prematurely dark. A strong wind has picked up, and rain falls in fierce and heavy gusts. A low bank of sand bags has been built along the entire length of the verandah. The parking lot is now a large wet muddy field; the motel appears empty.

I sit in the car for a moment, looking out, wondering what I should do, trying to form some plan. But I cannot think clearly, and nothing occurs to me.

The manager is quarrelsome. I should have checked out before noon yesterday, he reminds me, pressing his thumb down hard on the counter. They are closing for Christmas, and having believed that they were rid of their customers, he is doubly annoyed to see me return, but aware perhaps that I am upset. "Everybody has to be out—out, out, out—by eleven tomorrow morning." He waves his hands grandly in the air. "Everybody" is only me and another couple whom he has allowed to stay one extra night. When I agree to pay more for the inconvenience, he is finally satisfied.

As I sign the traveler's check the manager watches a small portable television on the counter beside me. The room is cold and full of the stale stink of old cigars and a useless paraffin heater. "Did you hear that? Are you watching this?" he shouts over his shoulder into an empty office. "Everything is canceled until tomorrow morning. No flights. Nothing. You hear that?" There is no reply. He turns fully about to see that the room is empty, and tugs his shirt down over his stomach, his breath hissing through his teeth in frustration. "We're supposed to be out of here tomorrow."

The manager twists the television set about, and leans

across the counter, prodding a fat finger at the screen. He is watching the weather report. The color is vivid, out of whack, veering to purple. A huge pink swirl of cloud blocks out the entire Gulf of Mexico. There is a hurricane glancing along the shared coastline of Florida and Louisiana, leaning hard upon Texas.

"You see that there. That's my problem. We're supposed to be flying out of here tomorrow. But they canceled the flights."

The manager draws his finger along the edge of the clouds. "That's us. That's where we are." He brings his hands together. "We're right here between two fronts, which is why it was so nice yesterday. There's flooding in Houston and Corpus Christi. We're too far inland, but ten miles over." He waves his hand abstractly over his head. "Now that's a different story."

I look at the television. The cloud system slowly rotates and flickers as one image is superimposed over another. There were no flights. The cloud blinks and spins slowly. The manager said that there were no flights, no flights anywhere, not even to Chicago.

I slide the check across the counter, and the man picks out a key.

"Same room?" he asks.

I stand in the doorway without my cases and look in at the dark empty room. I do not have the heart to turn on the light. I had no intention of returning here. Closing the door behind me, I curl up on the bed and listen to the storm outside.

At nine o'clock a squabble breaks out in the parking lot. I turn onto my back and listen to the fight. A car's headlights shine directly across the ceiling and the back wall; the motor is still running.

I recognize the voice of the woman next door.

There is the hollow thump of a car door closing, and the woman shouts, "Stop it. Stop it," as she runs past my window.

A blurred shadow passes in front of the headlights,

momentarily darkening the room, and out of the darkness comes a harsh and brittle shout.

Hurrying to the window, I look out and am astonished to see Adrian standing in front of the headlights, hands raised high, fists clenching and unclenching, the sling hanging wet from his wrist. A man staggers blindly about in the rain, away from the car and the boy, stomping through the mud with his hands up to his face. Adrian strides a wide, confident circle around the man. There are two open suitcases tossed into the mud. The car's boot is open, and exhaust whips up into the air, red from the taillights.

The boy kicks at one of the cases, narrowing his circle; pebbles scatter across the verandah. He closes in on the man, his arms now tucked close to his body, fists raised like a boxer. He strikes at the man's head with his left fist, but does not hit him. The man jolts and cringes, stumbling sideways. Rain sparks in the headlights. The boy ducks and dodges and strikes again and again, never hitting but jabbing quick and close to the man's head. The man falls to his knees, his hands cover his head, and the boy continues to circle, throwing punches but not touching the man. Above the idle thrum of the car is a deep and guttural sobbing. The woman stands on the verandah hugging herself, begging for Adrian to stop.

The boy pauses and stands directly over the man, his left fist raised, his shirt untucked and stuck to his stomach, black with dirt and blood.

I turn on my lights and open the door.

Adrian's hand falls to his side and the man sits back on his haunches into the mud. Clearly frustrated Adrian clutches his arm to his side and shouts savagely at his sister. "You don't trust him with your fucking dog, do you?"

The woman cowers with her hands poised like her husband's about her head.

"So why did you trust him with me?"

*

Adrian sits in the manager's office, humming *Brazil* to himself. The woman, Allison, his sister, is in my room. The manager is driving the brother-in-law to the hospital.

Adrian picks at the skin on his knuckles. I ask him to stop humming; he examines his hands. I ask him if he is hurt. Adrian shakes his head; he is trembling. The blood on his shirt is his brother-in-law's.

"It was pretty stupid," he scowls. "Hitting him without a glove or anything. You can break your hand that way."

"Why did you do it, Adrian?" I kneel in front of him and talk in a calm and steady voice.

"He'll live." He looks away. "I hit him once. Once. I broke his nose." He sucks his knuckle, cleaning a graze with his tongue. "She came to the hospital this morning." He talks into his fist, still sucking on his knuckle. "She told me we were just going to talk, that she needed to talk. She said all she wanted was to do was talk it through." He wipes his nose. "She said I could go back to my parents. She said if we talked we could straighten everything out, but she needed to talk." Adrian sighs and frowns, possibly bored. "I tried calling but you weren't there."

"I must have been on my way to the hospital."

"I told her I'd talk, but that was all. I told her I wasn't going back with her. She insisted on finding a Denny's. So we drove all around San Antonio looking for a goddamned Denny's. I should have guessed that she was up to something. When we got to the Denny's, he was there." Adrian puckers his mouth and looks up. "She did most of the talking, and we were right back where we always were. He didn't say anything until we were in the car. And then he said that it was all my fault, pretty much. So I smacked him."

"What did he do to you?"

Adrian looks up and stares defiantly at me, momentarily lost for words, then slowly shakes his head.

*

Allison sits on the bed, shivering, looking out at the window. She is older than I had expected, much closer to my age than her brother's. The door is open and she leans forward hugging herself. Adrian stands outside with his suitcase in his hand.

"Do you understand what is going on?" I ask her.

She shakes her head slowly as if waking up. "I'm not sure what to do now," her voice is pure breath, almost without tone. "I don't know what to do."

"You can come with us to San Antonio, or you can stay here."

The woman stands up and brushes her skirt. "Tell him I only wanted to talk."

Adrian rolls his eyes and turns away from the door. I follow him outside and pick up the suitcase from the parking lot. I collect the soiled objects and place them side by side in a row on the sand bags. Nothing is broken; the clothes are dirty but not spoiled. I can only find one shoe.

"She's going back to the hospital, isn't she?" Adrian stands beside me and whispers, "Don't feel sorry for her," almost as a threat. "Tell him I only wanted to talk," he hisses, mocking his sister. He turns about to face the motel room and shouts. "Tell him I only wanted to punch his fucking brains out."

A large illuminated sign above the highway fills out in white lights, slowly spelling out the word Sheraton, letter by letter. The motorway swings wide around the hotel. Adrian shakes his head rhythmically, as if pacing, and checks his watch.

"What time did it start?" I ask.

He casually waves his hands as if it doesn't matter.

"Do you have everything from the hospital?" I ask.

Adrian nods.

"Did you hear about your last blood test? Did Dr. Hollander say anything to you?"

Adrian turns to look at the hotel. "Nobody said anything to me."

A valet signals me up to the entrance. He walks beside the car and opens the door for Adrian, holding an open umbrella over the door. Adrian laughs out loud and steps out, waiting for me under the awning. The valet walks about the car and I hand him the keys, telling him not to worry about the luggage.

The doors swing open automatically onto a wide, dark, and spacious foyer. The low lacquered ceiling opens out in the center of the hall to a shallow gilded dome; set beneath the dome on a small carpeted dais is a slick black grand piano, beside it is a huge Christmas tree. Christmas carols are piped throughout the lobby. Light reflects from the golden dome, illuminating every-thing with a rich red glow. Adrian walks purposefully beside me, his face and hair and clothes still caked with black dirt. The dark wooden counter is so highly polished that it reflects the lobby across its curve, pinching our figures into two tall and slatted lines. The receptionist sits upright as we approach. He is wearing a floppy red Santa hat; there is a bowl of red and white sweets on the counter. The man's expression remains fixed despite Adrian's appearance.

I book a room and request that we have someone come to collect Adrian's clothes.

As we step into the elevator Adrian begins to hum *Brazil* again. "You don't get it, do you?" he smiles. His eyes are full and black. "Do you know what just happened?"

"I think I do." I shake my head. "But I'm not sure."

Adrian steps naked out from the shower, pressing a white gauze dressing back under his arm.

"That's better." He smiles. "I feel much better."

I kneel in front of the television, changing the channels. A card on top of the bureau announces that the fight will be televised on closed-circuit and repeated throughout the night.

"I thought I'd lost you." I turn down through the channels and Adrian stands close to me, so close I can feel the warmth from his body against my face.

He opens and closes his fist, and rubs gently up against me, stroking his hand through my hair. "Sorry about the dog," he mutters, looking again at his left hand.

"We'll get her on the way back." I assure him, although I know that we won't.

He squints at his knuckles.

"You could have hit him, ten, twenty times." I turn back to the television. The boy's white body is reflected soft and glowing across the screen's smooth belly.

He sits down on the bed, scowling at the back of his hand. "I broke his nose. That was enough." He turns his hand and looks down between his legs. "He never fucked me, if that's what you're thinking."

I turn from the television and sit back against the bed. Adrian sits examining his hands as if absorbed, his knee close to my shoulder.

"I never liked him touching me." He looks quickly up for a moment. "It started slowly, really slowly, I must have been eleven. My parents liked how he took an interest in me. That's part of why they liked him in the first place. They didn't care for her other boyfriends." He coughs to clear his throat. "There was a time when I kind of liked him. He was the first person to take me seriously. And because he did, so did everyone else. But right from the start he was messing around." He gathers the bedspread around his waist and bunches it between his legs. "Hands all over me. Even before they were married. Whenever they'd visit he'd stay in my room. The most he did was just lie on top of me or mess around. But he never really did anything. Nothing really happened. I used to sleep in my clothes." Adrian's voice is calm, he coughs casually into his fist. "He came once. It was after they came back to live in Chicago. He'd been drinking. He crawled into my bed and came all over my sheets, and I had to sleep in it. I used to wish he'd gone ahead and fucked me or done something. I don't know. It was just too weird otherwise. Nothing happening. He'd lie on top of me for hours doing nothing." Adrian looks up at the television and rubs his stomach.

"She knew what was going on. She'll deny it, but sometimes she'd wait outside in the car if she thought it was just us in the house. He used her dog like an alarm. As soon as he heard the stupid thing yapping he knew she was home. I never liked it, but I never stopped him either. It's all just totally fucked up."

He stops and frowns half apologetically. "It's so fucking tedious," he shakes his head. "When she found out about me still seeing Reyes, she used it as an excuse to kick me out. He couldn't really stop her. And that should have been the end of it. I decided I wasn't going back. I don't know why I put up with it for so long. But what's really sick is that he was one of the people Reyes used to see. I had no idea who Reyes was talking about. It was Alan in the motel that time. He set it up with Reyes, and Reyes didn't even know who he was. As far as Reyes was concerned it was all just a laugh. I couldn't believe it. I don't know what I was thinking. Why I didn't leave, but after he was there in that room, it was like nothing had changed. Only this time he had Reyes to tell what to do. And Reyes really liked it.

"I never saw him after that. Reyes called him about the tape, and right after he went to Florida, and then he got sick. Just before we went to Wyoming Alan left me a note. I think he wanted to see me. I know he wanted the tape."

Adrian reaches across the bed for the remote, and clicks slowly through the channels.

"I never want to go back. I don't ever want to see them again."

There is a sudden roar from the television. He has found the station. The camera is far away from the ring, almost too far to clearly see what is happening. A flat white square hovers in the middle of the screen. Three men, their thin and flickering images rotate slowly, as if dancing. Voices ring and echo as spectators taunt the boxers. The fighters are young and black; a huge bank of lights illuminates the ring, burnishing the fighters' skin to a coppery blue. The three men are small, as small as toy soldiers. Adrian slips off the bed and kneels beside me and identifies the boxers.

The boxers circle each other, fists up, heads down, so concentrated, so intent on the fight that they appear to be mirroring each other. Suddenly they collapse together, gloves locked about each other's necks. Adrian throws up his hands and groans. "Oh Jesus. Come on. Fight. Fight." He shouts and slaps his knees. "Look, what are they doing? Where's the referee?"

I watch the two men, their faint and small bodies slowly turn and stumble, half naked, locked in each other's arms, almost as close as two men can be, and they cling to each other like children, unable to strike, and unable to let go.

16

Christmas Day. I sleep poorly and wake strangely sad. Adrian lies with his back toward me, one foot stuck out of the bed, the sheets pulled up about his shoulders. The dressing under his arm bulges beneath the sheet. The room is absolutely silent. The curtains are open, the morning light is cold and sooty, and although I cannot see out of the window, I am certain that it is raining. I turn to Adrian, ready to wake him, ready to ask, "What's the difference between us? What's the difference between him and me?"

Adrian turns the map upside down. The road is all but empty. We are heading back toward Bourne. I recognize the signs to Fort Stockton.

"We're going the wrong way." He folds the map up and throws it onto the backseat. "Never mind. Just head south, next exit."

As we near the Bourne exit Adrian taps on the window. "Get off here." He sits upright. "Let's see if Allison is still there. Let's check out the motel."

I turn onto the frontage road and stop at the lights. The cardboard sign for the diner has gone. There is an open-backed truck parked beside the lights, stacked with unsold Christmas trees. A Mexican in a cowboy hat sits huddled in the cab. He turns and nods at Adrian as we wait for the lights to change. The lights change, impossibly slowly, and I continue along the road skirting about the town, familiar now with where everything lies.

The motel is closed. The parking lot is empty: a flat black pool, with no sign of last night's fight. The windows along the verandah are also black and blank. Adrian sits suddenly upright and points across the road. "Slow down a second."

I stop the car and look to see what he is pointing at. A small tan dog sits in front of one of the motel's doors, her head just peeping up over the sandbags. I unwind my window and Adrian leans over me, squinting.

"Is that your dog?" he asks.

Sally sits patiently looking up at the door, her head quivering. A thin yap, a high-pitched wail hollows out across the parking lot as the puppy pleads for the door to be opened. I look back at Adrian and nod; Adrian leans farther forward, squinting, not so much at the dog, but at the door and the empty room behind it.

Adrian opens his door and resting his hand on my shoulder he asks me, "We're never coming back, are we? Promise me we'll never come back."

17

The drive from Inez to San Luis is perhaps four hours. For the past five nights we have stayed at a small retirement community west of the town, as none of the hotels in Inez would admit a dog. The proprietor, Premi, sits on a low stone wall beside the road, watching and smoking as we load the van, an old gray army Volkswagen dormer that Adrian has christened "the beast." Sally runs about the small gravel courtyard, curious at our activity, as Premi clicks his fingers trying to coax her into the shade. Finally, all packed, Adrian checks through his luggage and then sits gingerly beside Premi, complaining that this all seems stupid since we'll be back tomorrow night. Both Adrian and Premi are a little hung over; they sit side by side, their legs almost touching. Adrian rubs suntan lotion into his arms and chest and stomach as he looks drowsily down the side of the hill, over the red-roofed chalets, and the sparse but carefully tended gardens to a crisp blue ocean.

I stand beside the van, keys in my hand, ready to leave. Premi and Adrian are talking, and I jingle the keys several times to get the boy's attention. Premi rises reluctantly as if a little sad at our departure.

"I have drawn you a map," he says, handing me a ruled sheet of yellow foolscap. "And here is the address." He carefully closes the door.

Premi shakes Adrian's hand, and then pulls him closer to hug him. Adrian slinks into the van without a word and waves at Premi as we back out of the compound and turn onto the road. Looking over his shoulder as we drive away, he asks me if I am not curious about Premi. "Not even a little curious?" he asks.

"Why?" I shake my head. "Should I be?"

"You didn't seem to like him much, that's all."

We arrive late in San Luis. A dry stone aqueduct runs beside the road as we enter the town. The markets have already closed for the siesta, and most of the shops are closed for the holiday. I drive through the city center, down the Avenue Constituyentes toward the cathedral to locate the bank where I am to exchange American dollars for Colombian pesos, Peruvian inti, and Brazilian cruzados. Premi has negotiated a favorable though somewhat illegal deal for us through his cousin; we have already discovered the limits of carrying only American dollars and traveler's checks. I dislike doubling back on ourselves; San Luis is north of Inez, we have already traveled through it, and tomorrow we return again to Inez to leave Sally with Premi while we travel.

Adrian searches through the glove compartment for the traveler's checks, leaning forward and resting his arm on the dashboard. He is already quite tanned, and the sling has left a slender pale shadow over his shoulder. He says that he is hungry, and turning onto the promenade, I find a place to park.

Just as I park it begins to rain, sudden and heavy. A few pedestrians hurry off the promenade, shirts pulled over their heads, and cross the street to shelter under the brightly colored awnings in front of the bars and taquerias. Sally jumps down expectantly from her seat, excited by the noise and smell of the ocean and the rain. Adrian fishes the leash out from under his seat. "You know what you are?" he turns about and gently grabs her by the muzzle. "You're an illegal alien. Yes, you are." Sally places her paw on his wrist and begins to lick the salt from his hand. "Here. I'll take Sally. Do you know how long you'll be?"

"You're not coming?"

Adrian shakes his head and leaning between the seats, deftly attaches the leash with one hand to Sally's collar.

"Can we eat first?" he asks as he searches for his jacket.

Sally twists about in circles. He waves his hand over her head, then stops, suddenly self-conscious. The rain stops as quickly as it had started.

We choose a restaurant on the main boulevard close to the cathedral and sit outside. Four tables are occupied by soldiers in khaki uniforms and shiny black jackboots. Adrian grimaces as he wipes the rain from his seat. The air is hot and suddenly humid. Sally settles down into the shade under our table, her paws are dirty and wet. He ties the leash about the leg of his chair, then stretches out, smiling, eyes closed. "I could get used to this."

Planted down the center of the boulevard, separating the lanes of traffic, is a long thick cluster of hibiscus bushes, with big and full red blooms, trash caught between the branches.

I order two beers and a black coffee. The waiter smiles at my inept Spanish, which amounts to nothing more than a verbal pointing. The attempt embarrasses Adrian. "It sounds like you're reading it." There are peanuts on the table in a small hand-painted ceramic bowl, salt caked about their husks. I look at my watch. The siesta will be over soon, and the bank offices will reopen.

"Where do you want to stay tonight?" I ask.

Adrian shields his eyes. "We should stay in that place that Premi told us about. The salt lake with the flamingos."

Back inside the restaurant a band sets up. Loudspeakers hanging above the door crackle as the microphones are switched on. The music starts up with a vengeance, to what sounds like a strange and rambunctious polka. Adrian laughs at the implausible sound of it, and takes out a guidebook from his pocket. I look about at the other tables. The soldiers sit back brooding, hands in their pockets.

"Was there anything in there about the lake?"

Adrian shakes his head. "It's a lagoon, with two monasteries, one on either side. One's called San Filipe the Near, and the other's called San Filipe the Far." He closes the book. "Do you know what makes flamingos pink?"

I shake my head.

"Prawns. They eat prawns," he squints. "They're only here for the winter. They breed somewhere else."

A hot breeze cuts across the boulevard, stirring up a small curl of sand. At the far end of the square blue smoke billows up from an open grill, and the air is filled with the piquant aroma of brazed meat. Adrian counts out money in his hands, the coins seem too large, too thick. Sally sits up, disturbed by the music, then settles down, resting her head on the boy's foot.

I leave Adrian and Sally at the restaurant, and pointing out the bank, I agree to meet him in front of the cathedral in an hour and walk down toward the marina. Every wall, every available space not taken up by advertising or signage, is layered with political posters. Elections are in four weeks.

There are two credit unions on Avenue Constituyentes. One a bank, the other, closer to the plaza, is just offices. I wait in the lobby, sitting in the shade as I finish my cigarette, and sign and date the traveler's checks. The floor is checkered in black-and-white marble; and except for the large glass windows, it is a little like a bathroom.

The lift slowly descends in a cage set in the stairwell; cables, visible through the grating, arc down the open shaft. Inside is a young man in a blue cap and uniform; behind him is an older man, elegantly dressed in a fine black suit, with graying hair and a blunt clipped mustache. The man is very short, and I assume he is Jesus Aurelio Escalente, manager of the San Luis Credit Union. Premi had described his cousin as "not tall, not handsome, not married, and not fat." The attendant is wearing white gloves.

The banker hurries towards me, extending his hand in welcome. He smiles and introduces himself, and bows graciously as I shake his hand. In too much of a hurry I offer the banker the traveler's checks.

Turning to the lift, he indicates that I should follow him.

"Please, if you will come up to my office." He looks down as the attendant draws the grate in front of us, carefully folding his arms and slipping the checks into his jacket pocket. The staircase wraps about the elevator in one smooth curve. The ride is slow, and light floods into the elevator as we steadily rise to the top floor.

The banker sorts through his keys as the attendant slides the door open and steps aside. His office is spacious, perhaps empty; one entire wall is a series of large arching windows. The room is filled by the spectacular view of the boulevard, the square, and the cathedral. I look down at the wide cobbled street, at the covered arcades and the tramlines. The buildings are tall, built from a honey-colored sandstone and infinitely detailed with carved stonework and small iron balconies. Across the street are suspended banks of Christmas lights, grids of bulbs fashioned into stars and comets. The cathedral is also festooned with strings of naked white lights, feeble in comparison to the stark afternoon sun. Behind the cathedral's towers shine the brighter distant husks of the mountains.

The banker sits at his desk and inspects the traveler's checks to ensure that they are all valid and signed, then taking out his keys he unlocks a cabinet under his desk. With impeccable charm he asks if I would care for a cognac. Outside, the setting sun glances across the wet stone square in front of the cathedral, illuminating it as a solid plate of gold.

I look out of the window as the banker carefully lays out three short stacks of money. The notes in each pile are colorful and large and used. Below us, Adrian and Sally are walking across the empty square, black bodies and black slender shadows. The dog pulls at the leash, the boy lets go, and she immediately sits down.

Adrian slips off his jacket and twirls it above the dog's head. Sally ducks and twists, running about the boy, and the two of them hurry across a burnished square, beneath the bare bulbs of a flat star. I regret that we have to return to Inez tomorrow.

I watch until I am blinded by the reflection, until there is nothing to see—except the shadows of a slow and strange courtly dance of a boy and a dog.

The road from San Filipe follows the ocean along a steep gray pumice bank, then veers inland, following the perimeter of an immense salt lake. Either side of the road the salt has been bulldozed into huge powdery hills tall enough to hide the small village and the bright orange walls of the hotel. Adrian is still asleep, and I am taking Sally for a last walk before we return to Inez. The salt flats are astounding, white, crystalline, almost too bright to look at. Far in the distance the lake is rimmed with pink.

A long caravan of lorries takes up the road, heading back to Inez, laden with salt, spewing thick and black exhaust. Their tires make a steady, high-pitched bifurcated hum on the tarmac. Everything is white, encrusted with salt: the lorries, their wind-screens, even the road sparkles, tracked with the double white lines of the tire treads. The lorries shudder at each bump in the road, and Sally huffs as they pass.

I walk out onto the white flats, the salt crust crackles beneath my footsteps. The soil beneath is dark and damp. Sally sniffs cautiously at my hand as I loosen her collar. Once free, she charges ahead, kicking back small white tufts, divots of salt as she runs.

I am surprised by how familiar this seems. There are two similar salt lakes in Cyprus, at Akrotiri and Larnaca; and for the first time I feel the absence of not having a settled place, a home, but I cannot imagine what that might be—I have no picture of it. I walk across the salt flats calling to Sally. The dog's image shivers in the haze as she pauses. Her shadow, absurdly long and lanky, undulates in the heat. Before I can reach her, she scampers ahead, wild at the freedom open to her, and as I walk towards her she runs still farther ahead, widening the distance between us. A wind picks up, cutting across the flats from the sea, blowing salt into my eyes; and the dog crouches, surrounded by white swirls, wild funnels of salt, so bright, so luminous that the sky appears gray, darker than the land.